KNIGHT

A REED SECURITY ROMANCE

GIULIA LAGOMARSINO

Cover Design by Moonstruck Cover Design & Photography

moonstruckcoverdesign.com

❀ Created with Vellum

To my book reviewers who have been patiently waiting for this story. I hope I did it justice.

CAST OF CHARACTERS

Reed Security Employees

Sebastian "Cap" Reed- owner of Reed Security
  Maggie Reed
  Caitlin Reed

Team 1:
  Derek "Irish" Cortell- team leader and part owner of Reed Security
  Lola "Brave" Pruitt
  Hunter "Pappy" Papacosta

Team 2:
  Sam "Cazzo" Galmacci- part owner of Reed Security and team leader
  Vanessa Adams
  Mark "Sinner" Sinn
  Cara Donnelly
  Blake "Burg" Reasenburg

Team 3:
  John "Ice" Peters- team leader

Julius "Jules" Siegrist
Chris "Jack" McKay

Team 4:

Chance "Sniper" Newman- team leader
Gabe Moore
Jackson "Huey" Lewis

Team 5:

Alec "Wes" Wesley- team leader
Craig "Dev" Devereux
Florrie Younge

Training:

Garrick Knight
Kate Whittemore

IT Team:

Becky Harding
Robert "Rob" Markum

1

KATE

I HAD BEEN WATCHING over Garrick Knight since Sebastian's team brought him to the safe house for me to remove a bullet from his side. He was stable when he arrived, which I was grateful for. I didn't particularly want to do emergency surgery outside a hospital. Not to mention that I wasn't a surgeon to begin with. I had done my surgical rotation when I was an intern, but it wasn't for me. I liked to help people without all the craziness of the hospital. I wanted to help people with everyday problems.

Despite his pale complexion, he still had a dark aura to him. Not that I believed in mystical or spiritual things, but everything about him scared me for some reason. It could have been his black hair and black eyes. Maybe it was the fact that he had scars all over his hands, like he had been in one too many fights. Something about him screamed that he was not a man to be messed with, but I had taken a vow to help anyone I was able to and I wouldn't back away because he seemed to be dangerous.

By those standards, half the men in my life would be dead on the table. My cousin, Cole, though he promised never to hold a weapon again, was still just as deadly as he was during his military days. I had seen the reports of how he killed the man who strapped his wife, Alex,

1

to a pole and tried to bash her brain in. He had snapped the man's neck in one swift movement. I learned to live with the fact that some people saved lives in different ways than I did.

His color was better today, but he still hadn't woken. I checked his pulse and then removed the gauze pads to check his wound. I had the lights dimmed so I didn't wake him. I could only imagine how his body was suffering after having a bullet lodged in him for hours.

His steel grip latched onto my wrist, making me cry out in pain. I stumbled into the nightstand, rattling the lamp, and stared into the black eyes of the man on the bed in front of me. The light cast shadows across his face making him appear even deadlier than what I first imagined. My heart thumped wildly in my chest as his fingers bit into my skin.

"Who are you?" he asked through the gravel in his voice.

"Kate. Kate Whittemore. I'm a doctor. I was called in to remove the bullet from your side."

His eyes flashed before he lifted his head off the pillow, beckoning me closer. He leaned toward my ear and whispered, "Let me die. I'm not worth saving."

I pulled back sharply, never having heard a patient want to die before. He fell back to the pillow and passed out before I could ask him what he meant. Surely, everyone had a reason to live. If he was working with Reed Security, he was one of the good guys.

When he woke again later in the day, I made sure to keep my distance until he was fully aware of his surroundings. He glanced around the room and sank back into the bed. It was as if he was looking for a threat.

"Do you remember what happened?" I asked.

He closed his eyes and shook his head. "Last thing I remember was…" He opened his eyes and narrowed them in my direction.

"I'm a friend of Sebastian's. He called me in because you had a bullet lodged in your side. You were very lucky to have only minor damage. You should be up and moving around in no time."

"What's your name?"

"Kate Whittemore."

"Kate." His brows furrowed, and I wondered if he remembered that we had met the night before.

"Do you remember meeting me last night?"

"It's fuzzy."

"That's not unusual. I've been giving you morphine, so you may not remember a lot of things."

"No more drugs," he mumbled.

"You'll be in a lot of pain."

His eyes snapped open and he glared at me. "I can deal with pain. I can't deal with not knowing what's going on around me."

I knew what he was thinking. When Cole came back from his deployment, he was a wreck, and when he finally went out, he was always looking for the threat. I imagined Knight felt the same way.

"Sebastian's men are here to make sure you have everything you need. You don't have to watch your back right now."

"I always have to watch my back."

I wasn't about to argue with him. "I won't give you another dose, but if the pain gets to be too much, let me know. I can give you acetaminophen if you'd like. It may take the edge off."

"Nothing stronger than that."

I grabbed my bag and took out the pill bottle, shook a few into his hand, and grabbed a water bottle. I sat down on the edge of the bed and made sure he was able to take the medication. "I'll let you get some rest."

I started to get up, but he grabbed my wrist, and I had a flash of his deadly eyes from the night before. Shaking my head slightly, I pried my hand out of his grasp and took a step back. I could see his eyes searching mine for answers, but I had none to give. I didn't even know what the questions were. All I knew was that this man seemed to look right inside me and I wasn't sure I wanted to stick around to let him see.

I backed out of the room, not wanting to turn my back on him. I was equally scared and fascinated by him. Part of me wanted to see just how deadly this man was. Perhaps he was really a sweet guy who just looked like a killer, but I had a feeling that wasn't the case. His words from the night before echoed in my head.

Let me die. I'm not worth saving.

I just didn't understand what kind of person felt that way. And if what he was saying was true, what had happened to him or what had he done to feel he didn't deserve to live? I went down to the kitchen to get some food for him. He had to be hungry by now, and since he was refusing morphine, he wouldn't be as out of it anymore. I didn't see any of the guys around. Sebastian had left Chance, Gabe, and Jackson here with me. I had a feeling he didn't entirely trust Knight and didn't want to leave me alone with him. Most of the time, one of the guys accompanied me upstairs and stood outside the room as I attended to Garrick.

"Taking Knight something to eat?" Chance appeared in the kitchen behind me, making me jump since I thought I was alone.

"Yeah, he doesn't want morphine anymore, so he should be awake a little more now and getting hungry."

"Just be careful around him. If you want, one of us can go with you."

"Why? Do you not trust him?"

"Let's just say I trust him a whole lot more now than I did a week ago."

"What happened a week ago?"

"He held a knife to Maggie's throat."

I blinked and then shook my head, sure that I had heard him wrong. "He what?"

"Well, he was working under the assumption that someone had stolen something from his client. He was going to use Maggie to extract information from Cap."

I gasped and shook my head. "You're joking, right?"

"Afraid not. It all worked out in the end. Turns out that he was able to help us out and he ended up with a bullet for his trouble."

"But you still don't trust him."

"I don't know him. I know *about* him and that's enough to make me tell you that you should be careful."

"What would he have done to Maggie if he had gotten away with her?"

"I don't know. He's an assassin. Use your imagination."

I swallowed hard and tried to steady the plate that was now shaking in my hands. "Why didn't anyone tell me?"

"You're in safe hands, Kate. We'd never let anything happen to you."

I looked up sharply at him. "You weren't always there with me. An assassin could have killed me before you even knew I was in danger. You should have told me."

He had the good grace to at least look ashamed. "I'm sorry. I really didn't think you were in any danger. I'll be sure someone is with you at all times."

"I have to bring him this food." I headed for the stairs and was relieved when he followed behind me. Opening the door to Garrick's room, I walked in and avoided his gaze. I could feel his eyes watching me. When I set his plate down, I fumbled slightly and almost spilled the whole thing on the ground. My hands were shaking so badly that I could hardly keep the plate on the nightstand.

"What's wrong?" he asked. When I didn't answer, he reached out again and this time, I saw the tattoo on his wrist with more clarity. It was a cross with a snake wrapped around it. I felt sick at seeing it. I wasn't sure why, but it made me uneasy—like he was admitting that he was the devil. I saw his eyes flick down to where I was staring.

"It represents good and evil. We all have a little of both in us."

My eyes met his for the first time since I entered the room and what I saw was chilling. I could see it now. He had the face of a killer. What I had assumed before was a deadly man who had been trained to be a killer for the military, I could now see was an unrepenting assassin that took life as swiftly as I stepped in to save it. This was not a good man. This was a man who brought fear into the hearts of anyone in his path.

"I see someone told you who I am," he said, glancing over my shoulder at Chance. "Probably best that you know who you're dealing with."

I stumbled back from the bed and grabbed my medical bag. I had been here for two days. He was out of the woods and would be fine. There was no reason for me to stay any longer. As I rushed from the room, Chance grabbed my arm and swung me back around to look at him.

"Where are you going?"

"I'm not staying here with a killer. I did my job. He's recovering and he'll be fine. He's refusing morphine, so all he needs is some Tylenol. He should be up and moving around by tomorrow. Just make sure he takes it easy."

I started to pull away, but Chance stopped me. "Just wait. I have to have one of the guys bring you home."

"Fine, but hurry up. I don't need to stay around here taking care of a man who's probably killed more men than a Greek warrior."

Chance nodded and headed for the stairs. I took one final look back into the room at Garrick. He was staring at me and my heart started to beat out of control again. It was strange because as much as I didn't want to be around him, something about him drew me to him, too. I wanted to know more, but I also knew that a man like him was not someone you kept in your life. I turned and walked away, knowing this wouldn't be the last I saw of him.

"Kate, your last patient canceled. Do you want me to stick around?"

My receptionist, Kathy, was a woman my age that I had met in college. She had been going to nursing school, but had to drop out when she lost her scholarship and couldn't get enough money together for her tuition payments. Her parents weren't able to help her out and she didn't want large student loans hanging over her head. She decided to work for a few years and save up as much money as she could, but that hadn't worked out too well for her. When I was setting up my practice, she applied for the receptionist position, and we worked out a deal for her to work during the day and take classes at night. When she finished, she would have a job working in my clinic.

"No. I'll be heading out soon. Just make sure everything is filed and I'll see you tomorrow."

"Thanks. Wish me luck. I have a big test tonight."

"Break a leg."

"That's for the theater. With my luck, I'll break a leg on the way to class tonight."

"Sorry, hope I didn't jinx you."

She sighed dramatically and placed the back of her hand to her forehead. "Lord, whatever will I do?" she said in a southern twang.

"Alright, Scarlet. Enough of the dramatics. I'll see you tomorrow."

The office was quiet as I cleaned up the rooms, preparing them for the next day. I had two rooms in my small clinic and they were usually both filled. I had been doing this for close to six years now and I had built up quite the clientele list. I had one nurse, but she usually left when she brought in my last patient. She only worked a half day today because her son had gotten sick, so I was a little behind where I normally was at the end of the day.

I ended up working late and it was past eight when I finally locked up my clinic. I was pulling my keys out of my purse when I felt someone behind me.

"You got anything good in there?" the voice slurred behind me. I turned to see a man who was obviously coming down off something strong. His whole body was shaking and he was sweating like crazy.

"I don't give out drugs. You need a hospital before you collapse."

He gripped my arm with more strength than I had imagined and pushed me up against the brick building. "Lady, I ain't messin' around. I need something now and you're going to get it for me."

"No, I'm not." I tried to go for strong and unbending, but the shake of my body gave me away. He could probably see the fear in my eyes also. But if I gave in and gave him drugs, he would probably come back for more every night. I couldn't let druggies think they could come to me for their next high.

He slammed me back against the wall, causing my head to bounce painfully off the brick. I saw spots as he shook me harder and harder. I had to get away from this maniac, and chances were, if I could get away, I could probably outrun him. I brought up my knee and nailed him right in the groin. He doubled over and coughed as he held his hand over his pants. I ran toward my car, but spun around when I heard something sharp and then a thump on the ground. I turned back to see the man lying on the ground with blood oozing around his head in a wide circle that was growing by the second.

I eased toward him and didn't see anything that caused that much blood. Bending over, I turned his body so I could see his face, which he had landed on. I shrieked and jumped back when I saw that half his face was missing. He had been shot. Stepping back, my head swiveled wildly as I searched for who shot the man. There was nothing but silence. I pulled my phone out and quickly dialed 9-1-1. It took me several attempts because my hands shook so hard. I gave my location and was told to wait inside for the police. I quickly unlocked the clinic and slammed the door behind me, hiding in the shadows until I heard the sirens approaching outside.

When the police banged on the door, I slowly got up and opened the door for the police officer.

"Kate? Is that you?" I recognized the voice, but couldn't see his face. I hadn't turned on the lights yet, so we were still standing in the dark. He reached over and flipped the switch, filling the room with bright light.

"Sean. Oh, thank God it's you. I was so scared." I flung myself into Sean Donnelly's arms, thankful that someone I knew was here. He ran a hand up and down my back in a soothing gesture. He was my cousin's friend and helped to bring him out of his funk when he returned from war.

"You want to tell me what happened?"

"I was leaving the clinic and that man approached me. He wanted drugs. I told him no and he attacked me. He slammed me up against the wall. I kneed him and then ran, but before I could get far, I heard something and turned back to see him lying on the ground. I went to check on him and saw half his face missing."

"Did you see anyone? Or hear anything else?"

I shook my head. "No. I looked around after I saw him on the ground, but there was no one. I locked myself inside and waited for you to come."

"That's a pretty good shot. It looks like someone was looking out for you. Do you have any idea of who would be watching you?"

I shook my head, but I knew that was a lie as soon as I did it. I had

8

no idea why he would kill someone for me. Maybe it was payback for me saving his life. But he was out there. I didn't need any evidence to tell me that Knight had been here and had been looking out for me. I was just grateful that he was. I had no idea if I would have gotten away otherwise.

Sean looked at me assessingly, as if he could sense I wasn't telling him everything, but I couldn't. Anything I did for Sebastian was strictly between us. I would never do anything to get Sebastian in trouble. I would just have to talk to him and let him know what had happened.

"We'll have someone escort you home and check out your house, unless you want to go stay with Cole."

"No. I'm sure I'll be fine. It was probably a good samaritan that was worried about getting in trouble."

"I'm sure you're right." He didn't believe me, but he didn't say anything else. He led me over to a squad car and helped me inside. "I'll let you know when we find out something more. Why don't you come down to the station tomorrow to give your statement."

"I will, Sean. Thank you."

He shut the door and then an officer drove me home. When we got there, the officer walked through my house, making sure that everything was secure. Once he left, I locked the door and went to my bedroom, then sat on my bed. I couldn't get the image of the man's half-blown-off face out of my mind. I had seen some terrible things when I was an intern, but it was never related to me. This was a man who had attacked me and then paid the ultimate price because someone was watching.

The hairs on the back of my neck stood up and I stiffened. He was here. I stood and looked around the room, but I didn't see anything. Walking over to the window, I looked out into the dark, hoping that I could see something. I would rather know exactly where he was than wonder the whole night if he was going to come for me.

Hot air trickled across the back of my neck. My breath hitched as I felt a hand brush against the nape of my neck as my hair was shifted over my shoulder.

"You should be more careful when you're leaving work."

9

His voice washed over me in that rough, deep tone that sent shivers down my spine.

"Why did you do that?" I asked, my heart beating out of control.

"He was hurting you."

"I was running away. I would have gotten away."

His hand brushed down my arm and then back up to rest on my shoulder. "He might have come back another night. A man like that—someone who would attack a woman just to get a fix—he doesn't deserve to live."

"That's not your decision to make," I said shakily.

"I made it my decision the moment he put his hands on you, and I'd do it again."

I spun around and faced the man I had last seen just a week ago. "I don't need anyone killing to protect me. I heal people and that man could have been helped."

"That man was scum and if he went after you, he would go after someone else. He didn't deserve to live."

"Like you?"

He took a step back and his jaw tightened. "I repaid my debt. You won't see me again."

"I didn't want to see you again to begin with."

He backed out of my room and was gone. I had no idea how he got in or how he left. He moved so silently that I didn't hear even my noisy stairs creak. Even though the man had just killed someone in front of me, I couldn't help but still want to see him again, no matter what I said. He intrigued me and terrified me all at the same time. I turned back to the window and stared out into the night, wondering if I would see him again.

2

KNIGHT

I watched from the shadows just as I had every night for the past two weeks. I was still recovering from the gunshot wound that I received trying to take out an arms dealer and his crew. I was no stranger to bullets and knives, and being shot was not a first for me. It was just the first time that I woke up to an angel.

Kate Whittemore. I repeated her name over and over in my head as visions of her leaning over me came to mind. She was the most beautiful woman I'd ever seen. With long, chestnut hair and large blue eyes, I was instantly mesmerized by her. She was the light guiding me to the surface when I felt like I was drowning.

When I left my military life behind, I thought I had left behind everyone I knew also. But then Pappy showed up and my past collided with my present. I couldn't turn my back on the man who had saved my life because there was no way I would have survived prison. Killing my superiors guaranteed that I would be shivved or beaten to death within days of being locked up. The details of my actions had been covered up by those who didn't want the names of "good men" tarnished.

When I agreed to help out Reed Security, I felt for the first time in years that I had chosen the wrong path in life. I didn't regret killing the men that profited from soldier's deaths, but I started to wonder if my chosen profession was a bad decision. I only killed men that truly deserved it, but when that bullet hit me and I waited for hours, floating in and out of consciousness, I began to wonder if I even deserved to live.

When I woke to Kate taking care of me, I just knew that I would never be worthy of a woman like her. I didn't deserve to live because I had taken too many lives. My hands were stained with so much blood that there would never be any amount of repenting that could wash away my sins. When she practically ran from my room in fear, I hated myself just a little more than I already had. I vowed then and there that I would never kill another man as long as I lived. I would do everything I could to one day earn the right to call a woman like that mine.

Even though I told myself that I would stay away from her, I couldn't. I found myself following her and watching her every move. I worried about her when she worked late at night. It still got dark early and the nights that she left late had me constantly worrying for her safety. Then, two weeks ago, it happened. She left late at night and a man approached her. I didn't hesitate to grab my rifle from my car when I saw him approach. I knew he was up to no good. I barely had enough time to take him out before he went after her again. She had kneed him in the balls and run away, but he was going to chase her down. I just knew it. So, I broke my vow and pulled the trigger, ridding one more lost soul from the earth.

I had followed her home that night, needing to know she was okay. When the officer finished checking out her house, I made my move. I had gotten used to moving through the shadows without anyone noticing, but I knew she felt me. There was some kind of connection between us. I saw her stiffen when I entered her room, though I hadn't made a sound. I couldn't resist feeling her warm skin beneath my fingers. I wanted to know what it would be like to touch her, but she didn't want me there. I suspected she would feel that way. She was a healer, after all. She saved lives when I took them. I knew she could never appreciate what I had done for her.

She made it clear that I was not welcome, nor would I ever be. As much as it angered me to walk away, I made myself do it, and then I watched over her from outside until I was sure she was okay. Since then, I hadn't been able to walk away like I had planned. Every time I tried to leave, I convinced myself that she could be in danger and I needed to check on her again. So that's what I did with my time now. I waited for her to wake up every morning and I watched as she sat at her table with her first cup of coffee. I watched as she undressed every morning and put on a show for me with her beautiful curves. She didn't know I could see her, though part of me wondered if she suspected and purposely undressed where I could see her. It was ridiculous to think that she wanted me to see.

I followed her to work every day and then watched from a coffee shop across the street as she went about her day. I didn't see her very often because she was usually with patients, but every once in a while, she would come out to the reception area and I got to see her face light up as she greeted a patient or talked with her receptionist.

Today though, when she walked into reception, she looked out the window right toward the coffee shop. She knew I was here waiting. She seemed to always sense me, even if she never saw me. I was good at hiding, but I saw when she would tense up and start looking around for me. We had some kind of strange connection where I knew when she needed me and she knew when I was there. Like that night two weeks ago, I hadn't intended to kill anyone, but I had put my rifle in the car anyway, just feeling like I might need it.

When she left that night, she stopped outside the door after locking up and looked out into the darkness. She wasn't afraid. She was just looking for me. She shook her head and walked away. This was crazy. I had to stop this. I was basically stalking a woman night and day, just so I could see her and know she was alright. She didn't want me around, so why was I so obsessed with her?

I walked away and broke my routine for the first time in two weeks. I didn't follow her home that night. I went back to my motel room and picked up the phone, going through my dozen or so messages from people who needed me to do a job. I hadn't been taking any new jobs since the job with Reed Security. I figured my reputation was shot after turning on an arms dealer and killing him and most of his crew. I thought no one would want to hire me again, but it seemed that wasn't totally true. There were still people that wanted the best and I was that man.

I called the number that had the best offer and decided to take the job. I needed to get back out there and get my shit together. I would not follow Kate around anymore. I would not waste another minute of my life chasing a woman who hated me so much. I would get back to what I was good at and live my life the way it was intended.

I WALKED INTO MY RUNDOWN MOTEL ROOM AFTER FINISHING ANOTHER JOB. Another easy kill. The adrenaline rush was wearing off and I was ready to go to sleep. That wouldn't happen since Hunter "Pappy" Papacosta was hiding in the corner of my hotel room. Did he really think I didn't know he was there? I had spotted his truck as soon as I pulled into the parking lot. He thought he was so slick parking in the back of the lot.

"I thought you were out of that life." Pappy came out of the shadows and smirked at me.

"Why's that?" I peeled off my shirt and threw it in the corner.

"I guess I assumed that after you tarnished your reputation, you would be working under a different name or give up the profession altogether."

"Jobs are still coming in. Apparently, some people don't care if I turned on an arms dealer. They want the best and that's me. My reputation says enough. Besides, the asshole was lying to me. He had it coming."

"Aren't you tired of this life? Don't you want to settle down?"

"Settle down? You mean, like get a wife and kids with the white picket fence?"

"I mean, like have a normal job. One that doesn't make you live out of shitty motel rooms that are probably crawling with bed bugs." He sneered at the bed and moved a step away.

"You mean a life where I don't answer to anyone but myself? I kind of like that aspect of it. I think we both know that I don't work well under the authority of someone else."

"You could come work at Reed Security with me."

"Doing what exactly? Watching over princesses who want to go out and catch their ten minutes of fame? No thanks."

"That's not all the work we do. There are other jobs. You could work with training the guys. You're one of the best I know."

"I am the best, but what you're suggesting sounds like the most tedious work on the face of the planet." I pulled out my gun and placed it on the nightstand along with the other weapons I had on me. "I'd rather eat a bullet than do that shit."

"You didn't seem to have a problem helping us in the Dominican Republic."

"That was one job. Tell me how many of those you get. How many times do you get to pull out your weapon and use it?"

"A lot more lately than I care to admit."

"It's not enough. I put my gun down for a week. A whole fucking week and then I saw some scumbag walking around, attacking—" I had to stop and take a deep breath before I spilled my guts to Pappy about my obsession with Kate. "That was it for me. This is what I'm meant to do and I'm real fucking good at it."

"Attacking who?"

"Doesn't matter. He's gone and she's alive."

"Does this have to do with Kate?"

I didn't say anything. I had already given away too much. Pappy could always read me like a book, and I didn't need him giving me shit over a girl.

"I heard about what happened to her. His face was blown off by the bullet from a rifle. There aren't many people I know that walk around with a rifle in their car."

I shrugged. "Sounds like she got lucky. A random citizen, I'm sure."

"A random citizen would have gone to the police and told them what happened. Only someone who wouldn't want to get caught would have walked away."

"Why don't you ask Kate if you want to know?"

"We did. She says she doesn't know who it was, but she was lying. She wouldn't look at any of us when we asked her about it. She knows who did it and wouldn't tell us. Now, why do you think she would be protecting someone unless she was worried about them being caught?"

"I guess you'll have to ask her. Are we done here? I'm kind of tired and I'd like to get some shut-eye."

Pappy shook his head and walked to the door. "You don't have to do this anymore, Hud. You can have a different life. You just have to let me help you."

"When I want a different life, you'll be the first one I come to."

Pappy walked out the door, and I fell back onto the bed, closing my eyes and coming down from the aftereffects of my latest kill. The feeling of crawling on my skin had me jumping off the bed.

"Goddammit, Pappy."

Now, I was never going to be able to sleep as long as I was thinking about bed bugs. Grabbing my stuff, I left the motel, knowing I wouldn't be able to sleep in a motel ever again.

I TRIED. I REALLY FUCKING TRIED, BUT I COULDN'T STAY AWAY. SINCE I LEFT her a month ago, I had taken job after job, trying to erase her from my memory. I told myself that if I was bad enough—if I killed enough people—I wouldn't want her anymore. But no matter how much I tried, I just couldn't erase her from my mind.

Every time I took out my gun and used it, I told myself that I had way too much blood on my hands to ever be worthy of Kate. I picked my targets well, taking out the worst of the worst and when that didn't work, I went around different cities looking for someone to take out just to release the tension that had built up in my system. When I came across gang members gang-banging a teenage girl, I subdued all five of them and then made each one watch as I slit their throats.

When that still wasn't enough, I tracked down the other members of the gang and took them out one by one until I finally felt my body start to relax. But as soon as I went to bed the night I took out the last gang member, my thoughts drifted to Kate again and I just had to know how she was.

She was out with friends tonight, laughing and having a good time drinking. Men were buying her drinks and trying to get into her pants. The more I saw, the more I wanted to take each of them out, but not from far away, with my rifle. No, I wanted to strangle the life out of every one of those fuckers who thought they were good enough for a night in her bed. I wanted to watch the life drain from their eyes as I snuffed out their life. Thankfully, she turned every one of them down and I didn't have to kill anyone.

Again, she must have sensed I was there because as soon as I arrived, she started looking around for me. She rubbed the back of her neck a few times and rubbed the goosebumps that broke out on her arms. I had my binoculars with me tonight so I could get a good look at her. It made me feel like I was there with her. Maybe that's why she turned down those men. She must have sensed I wasn't happy about them hitting on her.

As the night wore on, I grew concerned about how much she was drinking. Even if she didn't go home with anyone, the amount of alcohol she had consumed would be enough to make her an easy target for any man with the wrong intentions. Enough was enough. Packing up my stuff, I put it back in my car and headed for the bar. It was time to get her out of there before she did something she regretted.

Walking into the bar, I quickly cataloged all the potential threats and headed over to her table. One of her friends shot me an appreciative look, but my focus was all on Kate. She stiffened as I approached, but relaxed slightly into me when I wrapped my arm around her waist, pulling her into me. I hadn't been expecting that.

"Kate." My voice came out in a deep gravel because of the effect she had on me. She turned and looked up at me with a mixture of want and repulsion.

"What are you doing here?"

"I think you know the answer to that," I whispered in her ear.

"Kate, who's your friend?" The blonde across the table was attractive enough, but she didn't hold a candle to Kate's beauty.

"Um..." Kate looked up at me, unsure of what to say. I gave a slight shake of my head, letting her know not to say a word.

"Just a guy I know through my cousin. Gar-Gary, this is Samantha. Samantha, Gary."

I gave a slight nod to her, but returned my gaze to Kate.

"You don't look like a Gary to me."

"Family name," I muttered, never taking my eyes off Kate. Her face flushed slightly as she felt my gaze burning into her. "I think it's time we took this someplace else, don't you think?"

She smiled up at me hesitantly, showing me that she still feared me. "I'm going to stay here a while. Maybe I'll catch up with you later." She turned back to her friend and I leaned down to whisper in her ear.

"I've got no problem taking out anyone who stands in my way. I've killed more than my fair share of men, and it's still not enough."

I saw her visibly swallow and she pushed back from the table. "I'm sorry, Samantha, but I'm going to have to leave. Let's do this another time."

Samantha looked stunned, but didn't say anything. I took Kate's coat and helped her into it, then wrapped my arm around her waist and led her out the door.

"You didn't have to threaten anyone."

"You weren't going to come with me."

"Why would I? You're a killer."

"You've been waiting for me to come back for you. Do you think I don't see you looking around for me? You always know when I'm around."

"You're right. I do know when you're around, but that doesn't mean I want you here. I'm just wondering when you're going to take out your gun and shoot another innocent person."

"Honey, no one I shoot is innocent. Every single one of them deserves the fate that's handed to them." I led her to my car and though I could tell she didn't want to go, she didn't fight me either.

"How can you be so callous with life? Everyone deserves a second chance, don't they?"

"Not the way I see it. Would you give a second chance to someone who kidnaps and molests a child?"

She stopped and looked at me in stunned silence. But then her nostrils flared and she took a step back.

"Should you get a second chance when you took a pregnant

woman hostage and were going to use her to get information on another innocent woman?"

"I would have never hurt her."

"Why don't I believe you? Somehow, I think you would do anything necessary to achieve your goals and it doesn't matter who gets in the way."

"That's true in some cases, but when I found out the man I was doing the job for wanted her killed to prove a point, I took him out."

"That's so noble of you."

"I don't do things to be noble. I do things that are necessary. Someone has to be the one to pull the trigger."

"And that's you."

We stepped up to my car and I unlocked the door and helped her inside. Spreading my arms between the car door and the roof, I leaned in. "That's me, and I'm damn good at my job. I could give you another demonstration if you need it."

"I think I've seen enough bloodshed to last a lifetime. In case you didn't realize this, I help people. I make sure they can live a long, healthy life so they can see their kids grow old. Maybe you should try that instead of living in the dark hole you call a life."

"I might consider it if I had the right person to share it with. Are you up for the job?" I smirked at the anger radiating off her.

"I wouldn't attach myself to you in any way, even if my life depended on it. You're a killer and nothing you do could ever make you a good man."

She crossed her arms over her chest and stared out the front window. I slammed the door and crossed to the driver's side. I wasn't sure why I was so upset at her words. I knew they were true and I also knew that she would feel that way, but hearing her say them sliced me wide open. I wanted her to know that a long time ago, there had been something good inside of me, something that a woman like her would want. That if I hadn't seen all the terrible things I had in this world, I might still be that man, worthy of a woman like her.

It wouldn't matter even if I told her. She had made up her mind about me and she was right. There was no coming back from the man I had become. I drove her home and took her inside, checking her house out.

"You don't need to do this. I don't live in your world where people are constantly lurking around every corner, waiting for the right moment to strike."

"You might not, but I'm paranoid and it's kept me alive this long."

"Well, you can go keep yourself alive somewhere else, and please don't come back. I don't know what made you think that I would want you in my life, but rest assured, I would be much happier if you weren't."

I stepped into her personal space and let my fingers skim the sides of her body. It was just a small touch, but one that had me aching for more. "Then tell me why you always know when I'm around. Tell me why I can be watching you from across the street and not two minutes later, you're aware that I'm there."

I was just a breath away from her lips and I wanted a taste so desperately. Her harsh breaths fanned across my face, leaving me aching for more.

"I don't know why," she said, shaking her head. "But that doesn't mean I want you." She put her hands on my chest and pushed herself back. I snaked a hand around her back before she could get too far and pulled her flush against me.

"One kiss. One kiss and then you can tell me to fuck off. I'll never bother you again. I just need to know."

I waited as she made her decision and when she gave a slight nod, I crashed my lips to hers, consuming her and filling a void inside me that had been missing for years now. One taste would never be enough. I plunged my tongue into her mouth and took what I sensed from the first moment was mine. As her fingers twisted in my hair, I knew I was meant to be with this woman. She was the one person who could save my wretched soul.

She broke the kiss quickly and pulled away from me. Her fingers went to her lips and she wiped them as if she was tainted by my kiss. I recognized the look of disgust on her face immediately. Disgust that she had let me kiss her and disgust that she was actually attracted to me.

"Satisfied? You can go now. I gave you one kiss. We're through."

"We're far from through, but I'll leave you alone. For now."

I walked out of her house and drove away, back to my new house that just happened to be two doors down and across the street where I could keep an eye on her. She didn't know I moved in on the same street, and I would keep it that way so that I could watch over her. She would be furious if she found out I was so close and always watching.

My new house was nothing like anything I would ever choose, but it was available and close to the woman I wanted. I had to have Pappy buy the house for me, but since I was paying in cash, the transaction went through quick and easy. All the bills went to Pappy, but I gave him access to an account that had enough money to take care of the property for a few lifetimes. He seemed so shocked that I was actually sticking around that he didn't even balk when I asked him to do this for me. I couldn't purchase the house under my given name since that would land me in prison and purchasing under my new name was a great way to have every enemy I ever made come after me.

Walking into my house, I bypassed the unfurnished rooms and headed straight for my bedroom, which was in the upstairs corner of the house with a perfect view of Kate's house. From my room I could see directly into hers with my telescope. I couldn't see all angles of her bedroom, but she had wide windows on her house that gave me a good enough idea of what she was doing at any given time.

It looked like she was getting ready for a bath right now and I was sorry that I hadn't bought the house directly across from her. Still, this view allowed me to keep an eye on her without invading her privacy too much. Not that it was really a concern at this point. I had pretty much crossed the boundary from stalker to psycho.

My phone rang and I answered, writing down the details of my next assignment. This would be a long one, and as I hung up the phone, I found myself worrying about how Kate would be while I was gone. Would she go home with the wrong man? Would anyone be looking out for her? It seemed unlikely, so I called Pappy over for a last-minute consultation of sorts. When he arrived, I had a whole plan in place.

"You want a beer?" I asked as he walked into my house.

"Gee, I really like what you've done with the place," he said, glancing around at the bare walls, bare carpet, and bare kitchen.

"Hey, I just moved in and I'm not here that often. I've got beer in the fridge and a bed. Not much more I need."

"Then why did you want a house this big? It's not like you're ever going to fill the space. And why this neighborhood? You know, I was so shocked when you asked me to buy it that I didn't even question where you would be living."

"About that, I have a favor to ask of you. Well, really, all of you at Reed Security."

"Shoot."

"I'm going out of town for a while on a job and I need some help with an installation."

"Security?" I nodded. "Uh, you don't have anything to steal," he said as he spread his arms as if to show the empty house.

"It's not for me. It's for a neighbor. I want to keep an eye on her while I'm gone."

"Does this neighbor know you're planning to do this?"

"Not exactly."

"Then, no. I'm not installing security on someone's house without their knowledge."

"I need this. I won't be able to concentrate if I'm thinking about her safety while I'm gone."

"Who is it?"

I sighed, knowing that he wouldn't do it unless I gave him all the information he wanted. "Kate."

"Kate? As in Kate Whittemore? The Kate that helps out Reed Security? The Kate that saved your life?"

"Yes. That Kate," I said in exasperation.

His eyes widened and he put his hands on top of his head. "Oh shit. You wanted this house so you could be close to her. So you could spy on her. Fuck. I can't believe I did this. Goddammit. I knew there was something strange about you wanting to live here. Cap is going to kill me."

"Cap doesn't need to know. As far as he's concerned, you bought this house."

"But you fucking live here. Next to a woman who works for us. And you didn't fucking say anything!"

"Would you calm the fuck down? It's not a big deal. I just want to make sure she's safe. You can tell Cap that you realized that she was living across from your rental property and you saw that she didn't have security. Tell him that since she's been working for him, you think that Reed Security should take extra precautions to ensure her safety."

"You just got that all worked out, didn't you?"

"Well, I had to have a plan for when you got here."

"Hud, I can't believe you put me in this position. Why are you even doing this? Are you planning on sleeping with her or something?"

I laughed and scratched the back of my head. "I'm the last person Kate would ever want to sleep with. Trust me. But that doesn't mean I don't want to keep her safe. She saved my life. The least I can do is keep an eye out for her."

I hoped that my little plea would work and when he took the beer from the counter, I relaxed a little, knowing I had gotten through to him. "Fine. I'll talk with Cap and see what I can do, but you don't access any of the video footage. That will all be monitored from Reed Security."

I held my hands up as a sign of surrender. "You have my word. I just want to make sure she's safe." It was a total fucking lie.

"I'm going to hell for this," he said as he took a swig of his beer.

MY NEXT JOB WAS IN PITTSBURGH, SO I DIDN'T HAVE TO BE GONE FROM Kate for more than a few hours. My target was a man in his thirties who liked to get young kids hooked on drugs. He had quite the business going for himself and the father that approached me only had a thousand dollars. I told him I'd do the job for free. The last thing Pittsburgh needed was more kids addicted to drugs.

I was scoping out his house when Pappy called me. "What's up? I'm kind of busy."

"Oh, well, I was calling about Kate, but I can check it out myself."

23

"Check what out?" I asked, suddenly not at all interested in the drug dealer.

"There was an alarm tripped at her house, but it could be anything. It was just the perimeter alarm, not the house alarm. I'll head over there and check it out."

"Alright. Let me know what it is. I'll be back in a few hours."

"You got it, man."

I hung up and went back to my recon, but I couldn't concentrate. My thoughts were on Kate and if she was alright. What if she was at home and someone was trying to break in? I wasn't there to protect her. I shook my head and tried to clear my mind. I just had to finish this job and then I could get back to her and make sure she was okay.

I snuck around the back of the house that was so run down, it made me wonder what the hell this guy did with his money. I made my way inside, being sure not to make any noise as I crept toward the back of the house where the man was working at his desk. I pulled my gun and held the gun to the back of the man's head. I had already confirmed his identity from outside.

"Selling drugs to teenagers is a good way to end up dead, jackass."

He raised his hands slowly, but I wasn't about to let him walk away, no matter how much he begged. This man didn't deserve to live. I usually liked to take my time with my kills, but right now, I just wanted to get back to Kate. Just as I fired, my body jerked forward as something pierced my left shoulder. I spun and quickly fired off a shot, hitting another man right between the eyes. The pain was excruciating and I had to take deep breaths to clear the spots from my eyes. How had I missed the second man? He must have entered when I got distracted by Pappy's phone call.

I stumbled through the house and back out to my car. I had an emergency medical kit that I kept in my car, so I pulled it out and grabbed as many gauze pads as possible and placed them on my shoulder under my jacket. I gritted my teeth and tried my hardest not to yell from the pain. I needed to get this taken care of ASAP. I was pretty sure the bullet hit bone, so I had a little time, but not much before the pain would make me pass out. There was only one place I could go right now. I just hoped I could survive the drive.

3

KATE

I COULD FEEL his eyes on me almost every night as I shut down my practice. I couldn't see him because he always dressed in black and he blended into the shadows, but my body was tuned into his. I could feel his eyes on me the same way I could still feel his touch.

He had left me alone for a few weeks now, but he was always lingering in the shadows. I didn't understand why he felt the need to watch over me, but on nights when he wasn't there, for some reason, I felt very alone. I always knew that as long as he was around, I would be safe. I never worried anymore about leaving my practice late at night, and even when I went home, I felt safer. It didn't make any sense. How could I feel better knowing that an assassin was watching out for me?

I was just closing up for the night, gathering up the lingering notes I had made and filing them when there was a loud bang on the front door. I rushed to the reception area and sighed when I saw Knight standing at the front door. I hesitated, not sure if I should let him in or not, but then he put his hand on the door and it left a red streak behind. Rushing forward, I pulled open the door and caught him just as he collapsed into me.

"Knight. What the hell happened?"

He was shaking and sweating, which was never a good thing. I did my best to pick him up, and luckily, he was still conscious. "Just a little gunshot wound," he slurred.

"Come on. I need you to help me. You have to walk or I'll leave your butt here on the floor to bleed out."

He staggered as he leaned heavily against me, just barely making it into my exam room. When I got him into a seated position on the exam table, he collapsed backward, luckily in the correct position. I could see blood staining his shirt and assumed that the wound was somewhere on his upper body. Running my hands over his chest, I felt the stickiness of blood, but couldn't feel a wound. That's when I saw the hole in the shoulder of his jacket. I rushed to the supply room and grabbed everything I would need to treat him as best I could. I didn't run a hospital, but I kept most of the necessary supplies on hand in case I had an emergency at the clinic. I was just on my way back to the room when Hunter came running into the clinic.

"Oh, thank God. I saw the blood on the door, and I thought something had happened to you."

"Not to me, but your friend showed up here with a gunshot wound."

I rushed off to the exam room and set everything on the desk, laying it out so I could easily grab what I needed. Hunter came in behind me and took off his jacket and rolled up his sleeves to help. He grabbed the scissors and started cutting away Knight's jacket and shirt. I had almost forgotten that he was a medic in the military.

"GSW to his left shoulder," he said as he examined the wound. Hunter helped me roll Knight so I could see the back of his shoulder. The entrance wound was lower than the exit wound, which meant the bullet might have ricocheted off bone.

"I need to get an x-ray of his shoulder. The bullet probably hit bone. I need to see what I have to work with."

"You wouldn't happen to have a portable X-ray machine, would you?"

"Down the hall. Last room."

Hunter ran off to get it and I took a moment to calm myself. My heart was beating out of control and I worried that it wasn't because of the emergency in front of me, but the fact that I cared what happened to him. Knight was pretty much out of it now and I took a moment to study him. He still looked deadly, but this time, I saw a man I was drawn to. A man I couldn't help but care about, even if he was a stalker and scared the shit out of me.

Hunter came back with the machine and I quickly assessed that the bullet had hit his Acromioclavicular joint. He was going to have at least a six-week recovery time and then physical therapy, but he would be okay. I took a deep breath and was surprised that I felt like crying. Since when had I developed feelings for my stalker? I wasn't even sure what kind of feelings they were at this point. I just knew that it felt wrong to feel them.

"It doesn't look like there's anything still in his shoulder, but I can't be sure. He should be treated in a hospital."

"You know that he can't go to a hospital. He would be sent to prison."

"That's where he belongs," I said, even though I wasn't sure anymore that I really wanted him there.

"You don't know everything about him. Don't be too quick to judge."

"He's an assassin. Last I checked, it's against the law to murder people."

Hunter's gaze turned to steel, but he kept his mouth shut, obviously not wanting to argue with me about it.

"If you can help me get him out to my truck, I can take him home with—" Hunter ran a hand over his head. "Shit. I have a job tomorrow. Any chance you could take him home with you?"

I let out a humorless laugh. "You've got to be joking. You want me to take him home? To my house?"

"You know he's not going to be able to do jack shit. He's going to be in a lot of pain and someone needs to keep an eye on him and tell him how to take care of himself. I have to leave at five in the morning. There's no way he'll be with it enough for me to explain everything to him."

"When do you get back from your job?"

"Three days. A week max."

I glared at him, but I didn't really see another option at this point. "Fine, but only a week and then he has to go stay with someone else."

"Thank you. I'll get a cleaning crew over here to clean up your clinic. They'll get it done by the morning. Do you have a spare set of keys?"

I grabbed my purse from up front and handed the keys off to Hunter. I looked around and hoped to God that Hunter would follow through and get this place cleaned up before the morning or my staff would be asking a lot of questions. Hunter hauled Knight up over his shoulder and carried him out to his truck. I looked around in the darkness, waiting for someone to jump out and call the police on us.

I quickly locked the door behind me and jumped into my car as Hunter got in the driver's side of his truck. Driving home, I kept thinking the police would pull me over, or pull Hunter over, and we would be hauled off to jail. What would I be arrested for? Aiding and abetting a criminal? Could I somehow be wrapped up in one of his murders?

I was sweating through my clothes by the time I got home. I didn't want Knight in my home and I certainly didn't want to be an accomplice to whatever the hell was going on. But Reed Security had been good for my business. By helping them, I was able to buy new equipment for my clinic that I otherwise wouldn't have been able to afford. On top of that, a small part of me actually liked the idea of Knight in my home, which was completely perverse. He was a killer and deadly to boot, but I couldn't help the way his smoldering gaze set my body on fire.

I lived in a neighborhood where it would look odd if someone was carried in over someone's shoulder. I couldn't risk any of my neighbors finding out that I had a house guest, so I opened the garage and pulled off to the side so Hunter could drive in. I ran in and closed the door behind him, then opened the house as he pulled a still-unconscious Knight out of the truck and upstairs to the spare room across from mine. I wasn't sure I was okay with him being that close to me at night, but he was pretty out of it, so I shrugged it off and decided I would lock my door tonight. Attraction or not, the man was still a killer and I couldn't trust him.

"What am I supposed to say to him tomorrow?" I asked Hunter as I watched Knight out of the corner of my eye. I was still nervous this was going to blow up in my face. He had broken into my house before, so what were the chances that I could keep him in this room?

"You're a doctor," he said, looking at me funny. "I'm pretty sure you know what you need to tell him."

"I mean, what am I supposed to say about everything that's going on? Am I supposed to keep my mouth shut? I don't want to end up on his kill list," I shot back.

Hunter chuckled, which really pissed me off. How dare he laugh at me. I was scared and he didn't even seem to care.

"He's just a guy. He's not going to kill you because you know he was shot. He came to you for help, remember?"

"That doesn't mean he wouldn't hurt me."

"Relax. I know Knight, and despite his profession, he's a good guy and he would never hurt you."

"Sure, until I overhear something I'm not supposed to. Then I'll end up at the bottom of the river."

"That's more the mafia's style. Knight would put one in your head and call it a night."

I blanched at his flippant attitude about the whole situation. Would he really put one in my head? Hunter must have noticed my discomfort because he sighed and pulled me out of the room.

"Look, I know that what he does scares you, but he came to you for help and he wouldn't have done that if he didn't trust you at least a little bit. He's not going to hurt you, and I wouldn't leave him alone with you if I thought there was a possibility he would."

I nodded and followed him down the stairs, not ready for him to leave yet.

"I gotta take off. I have to get my shit ready for tomorrow. If you need anything, call Sebastian. He'll help you with whatever you need."

"Are you really sure this is a good idea?" I asked, twisting my fingers in nervousness. "I mean, I'm sure that someone at Reed Security could watch him better than I could."

"You're probably right, but he came to you. If I took him somewhere else and he woke up to someone else, he'd probably pull out his gun and shoot them."

"So, take away his gun," I said incredulously.

He shook his head and laughed. "You're cute." He headed for the garage door and I quickly followed behind.

"What the hell is that supposed to mean?"

"It means that if Knight wanted to kill someone, he wouldn't necessarily need a gun to accomplish it. You don't become one of the best assassins by killing with only a gun. Hell, he learned how to kill a person a hundred different ways in the military."

"Gee, that's so comforting as you leave me here alone for the night with him."

"Look, I promise that he's not going to hurt you. There aren't many people that Knight trusts, but obviously, you're one of the few." He turned and opened the door, but then turned back to me. "Just…don't say anything to piss him off."

With that, he turned and walked out the door, leaving me staring after him and wondering what the hell I had gotten into. After the garage door closed, I shut the door and made sure to lock it up tight. I looked at the stairs and decided there was no point in cowering away from the man. Hunter was right. Knight had come to me, so I had nothing to worry about. Besides that, I knew he had been watching and following me, and he hadn't tried to kill me yet, so what were the chances that he would try something now?

I crept up the stairs, almost afraid that I would wake him, even though I knew he was out and would be for hours after the pain medication I'd given him. I looked in the doorway to his room and saw that he was still passed out on the bed. Hunter hadn't bothered to cover him with a blanket and I didn't like to sleep without one, so I walked hesitantly over to him and pulled a blanket from the foot of the bed and draped it over him.

Here in the darkness, he didn't look quite so threatening. Of course, he was passed out and I knew that he was injured, so maybe it was my brain trying to convince me that I didn't have a killer in my house. Not knowing why, I reached forward and ran a finger over one of the lines of his face. He looked so tired tonight. It must be exhausting to live a life always watching your back and never being able to really settle down.

What the hell was I doing? I shook my head at how ridiculous I was being. This man had been stalking me and here I was, letting him into my house and staring at him in the dark as he slept. I left his room and shut the door behind me. I didn't have a lock for his door, but I wished I did. I could lock him in there overnight and not worry about him roaming my house while I slept.

It turned out that I didn't need to worry about him roaming my house, just breaking into my room. I had locked the door to my bedroom before I came to bed, but when I woke up a few hours later, I knew he was there before I even opened my eyes. I could feel him, just like every time before. I sat up and looked at the chair across the room. Knight lounged in it as if he hadn't been shot just hours before. But what really made me sit up and take notice was the gun resting on his knee. My eyes were glued to it in the dark. Dawn was just breaking on the horizon and it gave off just enough light to see clearly that he was not only awake but was staring at me. I had a feeling he'd been there for a while. What I didn't know was why he had his gun out.

"Are you going to kill me?" I asked quietly.

He didn't answer, just continued to stare at me. I swallowed around the lump in my throat and felt my heart start pounding out of control. What was I supposed to do now? Hunter's parting words echoed in my head.

Just...don't say anything to piss him off.

Perhaps I should have had Hunter write me a list before he left, since I had no clue what might piss off an assassin. I was sure we should stay away from topics like: *How many people have you killed?* Or, *What's your weapon of choice?* Probably even, *Are you really as good as they say you are?* He would probably offer a demonstration.

"Do you remember showing up at my clinic?" I asked, trying to mask the fear in my voice. He gave a slight nod, so I continued. "The bullet hit some bone, but luckily, it didn't leave anything behind. Hunter helped me patch you up and brought you here. You'll have to wear a sling until your arm heals. I'd say you'll be out for six to eight weeks. Unless you can kill people with only one arm," my eyes widened and I quickly tried to cover my mistake. "Not that I would say anything. I'm not going to the police or anything. Hunter's sending over a crew to clean up my clinic, so there won't be any evidence," I babbled. The whole time, he just sat there and stared at me, his dark eyes boring into my very soul.

I stood up and pulled my shirt down further so it didn't show off my ass. "I'm just going to use the bathroom." I scurried off to my bathroom and breathed a sigh of relief when I was locked behind the door. While I was in there, I decided I would go ahead and take my shower. I didn't really want to go out and see him again anyway.

I finished washing up and shut off the water, pulling the curtain aside. I screamed and pulled the shower curtain back over me when I saw Knight leaning against the bathroom door.

"What the hell are you doing?" I yelled at him. "Have you ever heard of privacy or boundaries?"

He looked at me like he could see through the shower curtain. I felt so vulnerable standing here naked, yet a part of me wondered what he would do if I pushed the curtain away.

"Just making sure you were alright in here."

"Why would I not be alright? I'm taking a shower, not chopping someone into pieces."

The corner of his lip twitched, but he didn't say anything else.

"Would you mind?"

"Not at all. Please continue." His eyes burned hot and dark as he continued to stare at me. I grunted in frustration and pointed to the towel bar.

"Would you please hand me a towel?"

He picked up the hand towel and tossed it to me. I narrowed my eyes at him, but decided that two could play at this. I was a doctor, after all. I had seen more parts of the human body in my lifetime than any regular person. So, what did it matter if he saw me? I flung open the shower curtain and stepped onto the bath mat, ignoring how his eyes roamed over my body in appreciation. Pulling the towel from the bar, I made a point of bending over to dry my hair, so he got a nice view of my ass and maybe a little bit more. I swear, he growled behind me and I looked back at him in question.

"Something wrong?"

His jaw flexed hard and he turned around, whipping the door open and storming out of the room. I chuckled softly to myself and then reprimanded myself for being such an idiot. I was playing with fire. I had no idea how a man like him would respond to me poking him.

Wrapping the towel around my body, I was relieved to see that he had left the room. I quickly dressed and headed downstairs to see where Knight had run off to. I found him in the living room, staring out the front window. When he turned toward me, I could see pain etched across his face and realized that I hadn't given him the sling for his arm yet. I grabbed it off the kitchen counter where I had left it the night before and walked over to him.

I looked up into his stormy eyes as I slowly lifted the strap around his head. He was tall, and even though I was 5'7", I still had to stand on my tiptoes to get it over his head. I sucked in a breath as my breasts grazed against his chest. Pulling back quickly, I stepped back and secured the wrap around his wrist.

"This will help your shoulder drop into alignment so it will heal properly and help with the pain," I said, looking down as I adjusted it to the proper spot. I took another step back, but I could still feel his eyes burning into me. "I have to work today, but you can stay as long as you need to. I mean, Hunter will be back in a few days, so I agreed to let you stay here while he was gone. It's going to be hard for you to do things and you'll probably be in pain. I have medicine for you on the counter and I'll make some food for you before I leave for work. If you need me—"

I stopped as he placed his fingers under my chin and lifted my head to meet his gaze. My heart beat wildly out of control and it took all I had not to look away.

"Thank you for taking care of me."

"Why did you come to me?" I asked.

His eyebrows furrowed and he didn't answer right away. "Who else would I go to?"

"You could have gone to Hunter. He's a medic. He could have taken care of you."

He nodded, but didn't say anything else. I figured that was the only response I would get out of him and turned to leave the room. I had to finish getting ready for work. Hopefully, Hunter had come through and I wouldn't be walking into a mess.

HUNTER HAD COME THROUGH IN A BIG WAY FOR ME. NOT ONLY WAS THE front door and the room that I had put Knight in clean, but the entire place sparkled. He must have wanted to make sure that there was absolutely no trace of Knight left behind. Kathy was the first to show up for the day, after me, and I kept waiting for her to find something that let on to what occurred here last night, but instead, she only commented on how clean the place looked. I simply told her that I found a new cleaning service, and based on how good the place looked, I was definitely going to have to get the number from Hunter.

I was about halfway through my day when I felt his eyes on me. Sighing, I went to the office window and looked out across the street. I could see him from here, sitting in the coffee house, staring out the window at me. I gave a little wave, but he didn't do anything but stare back. It was infuriating. I could barely get him to speak this morning. Honestly, I didn't have a clue what he was doing here. He should be resting. It's not like I needed someone to look after me. It was more likely that he was the one that needed looking after, considering he had just been shot.

I did my best to ignore him the rest of the day and went about, taking care of my patients. This was Kathy's night to get off early for school, so I finished up with my nurse, Kay, and then sent her on her way as I finished up paperwork. I was sitting in the reception area when I felt him in the room. I looked up and gasped when I saw him standing in front of the desk. He looked pale and I could see that he was in pain. Stepping out from behind the desk, I quickly went around to the other side and linked my arm with his, dragging him to a chair.

"You shouldn't have been out all day. You were supposed to be at my house resting."

"Someone had to look after you," he grunted.

I pursed my lips at his comment. "I find it funny that I need to be looked after, but you're the one with a bullet hole in your body."

"I was distracted."

"By what?"

"You," he said bluntly. I got up, deciding that I really didn't want to know anything else he had to say. It was weird enough with him following me around, but then to hear him say something like that? "You know, I wouldn't worry so much if you would learn how to take care of yourself. You don't even have a bell on your door. You didn't hear me come in."

"Look, for some reason, you've decided to stalk me—"

"I'm not stalking you."

"Then what would you call following me around?"

"Protecting you."

I shook my head, unsure what to make of that. "I don't need protection. I need to not feel creeped out every time I leave the house, or when I'm at home for that matter."

"If I hadn't been following you, you would have been killed by a druggie."

"I would have gotten away."

He stood up from his chair and stalked over to me. I was sure he could see my heart beating wildly through my shirt. He just seemed to know these things. When he got into my space, my breath caught and I waited for what he would do next. "You're mine to protect," he said quietly.

"I'm nobody's. And I don't need protection," I said, pushing against his chest and scooting out from where he cornered me by the desk. He caught my wrist and pulled me back to him. The scowl on his face reminded me that I wasn't dealing with just any man and I would be wise to watch what I said to him. I swallowed hard and pried his fingers from around my wrist. "I'm going to get you something for the pain."

I stepped away quickly and hurried back to the room where I locked up the medicine I kept on hand. Locking the door behind me, I leaned against it and took a deep breath. "Don't piss off the assassin,

Kate," I muttered to myself. He pounded on the door behind me and I jumped in surprise. "Dammit, you scared me."

"Hurry up. We're leaving in two minutes."

I flung the door open in shock. "I still have work to do. I can't leave yet."

"Too bad. Let your receptionist deal with it in the morning."

"Knight, maybe you don't get it, but I have a job to do and I can't just leave because you want me to."

"If I have to throw you over my shoulder and carry you out of here, I will. I said we're leaving," he growled at me.

"You're such an asshole. I don't have to go anywhere with you," I said, feeling more brazen than I should. "You're just someone that stumbled in here with a gunshot wound. I don't owe you anything."

His jaw clenched in anger and for a second, I thought he might actually pull out his gun and shoot me for talking back to him, but he just turned and walked out the door, leaving me relieved and turned on at the same time.

I was scared at how much I desired this man. It wasn't right. I shouldn't want a man like him or feel like my heart was going to pound out of my chest when he was around. Still, there was something about him that got me wet whenever he touched me. It wasn't just his good looks. It was the way he protected me as if I was his. But I wasn't his and there was no way I ever would be.

I WALKED IN THE DOOR A LITTLE AFTER TEN. I HAD A TON OF PAPERWORK to catch up on and since Kathy had left early, I had to get her paperwork filed also. I really needed to hire another person who could deal with some of this extra stuff. Kathy was great at keeping reception running, but she didn't work with billing or anything to do with running the clinic. That's what was killing me day in and day out. It was the one thing I hadn't really considered when I started the clinic.

I threw my bag down on the kitchen table and walked over to the fridge for the bottle of white wine I had stashed there. I needed at least one glass so I could relax before I went to bed. Pouring myself a glass, I sat down on the couch and flipped through the channels. There wasn't really anything I was interested in watching, but I just wasn't ready to go to bed yet. Plus, I had no idea where Knight was. Would he creep into my bedroom again tonight?

I finally settled on reruns of *Seinfeld* and finished off my glass of wine. I had no idea what time it was when I woke up, but I was covered in a blanket and lying down on the couch. I didn't remember pulling the blanket off the back of the couch and I definitely didn't remember the warm body snuggling in behind me. I shifted and saw Knight lying behind me with his eyes closed. His bad arm was resting partially on me and it looked like he was uncomfortable. I tried to slide out, but the arm underneath me tightened around my shoulder.

"Stop." His voice was gravelly, like he had been sleeping and just woke up.

"That can't be comfortable with your shoulder."

"If it was a problem, I wouldn't be doing it."

"Why are you doing it?"

He shrugged. "You looked uncomfortable, so I laid you down, but then you asked me to stay."

"I did not."

"Think whatever you want, but you asked me to stay."

"Knight—"

"Call me Garrick."

"Garrick. Is that your real name?"

"It's the name I go by now."

"What did you used to go by?"

"If I told you that, I'd have to kill you."

"Why?" I asked, believing that he actually meant it.

"Because, if you knew who I really was, a whole lot of other shit would come up that you don't need to know about or deal with."

I didn't want to get involved, but part of me was very curious about this man. "You're an assassin. What could be worse than that?"

His face hardened and he sat up. "Right now, I have a few agencies that are mildly interested in me. They keep track of my kills, but don't care too much because the people I take out are scum. If they knew who I really was, I would have the entire weight of the government bearing down on me."

Now, I really didn't want to know who he was. Could who he used to be really be even worse than who he already was? That was terrifying to think about.

"I think I'm going to go to bed," I said, sitting up quickly. But I ended up sitting face to face with him, just a few inches from his lips and as much as I knew that he was not a good man and I shouldn't want him, his lips were just so damn inviting. I stared at them and remembered how good it felt the last time he kissed me, when he possessed my mouth. I wanted that again and before I had a chance to give it a second thought, I leaned forward and pressed my lips to his.

He didn't hesitate and shoved his tongue into my mouth. He wrapped his hand around my head and held me still, but fell off balance with only one good arm. I ended up underneath him and spread my legs so he could lay between them. I could feel his hard length pressing against my core, and I wanted so much more. I thrust my hips up, moaning as it hit me right where I needed it. I did it again and again, feeling the pressure build within me. He met each thrust with one of his own. I couldn't take it anymore. I gripped onto his arms as I ground my hips into him again, but then stopped when I heard his strangled groan.

Opening my eyes, I saw pain shoot across his face and realized that I was gripping his injured arm and probably pulling it out of alignment.

"Shit. I'm so sorry," I said, sitting up and trying to get him in a more comfortable position.

"Stop moving," he growled.

"I'm so sorry. I didn't mean to—"

"Just shut up," he barked, causing me to flinch back. "I don't give a shit about my arm. If you keep moving though, I'm gonna come in my pants and I'd rather be inside you."

That shut me up really fast, and it also hit me like a dose of cold water. What the hell was I doing? Where exactly did I think this was going to go? I'd have casual sex with a murderer, and then what? Ask him to pick up some bread on his way home from his latest kill? I was such an idiot.

I pulled my legs out from under him and stood quickly, straightening my clothes. "I have to go." I ran up the stairs as quickly as possible and slammed the door behind me, making sure to lock it. Not that it mattered. He had gotten in the other night and it was locked.

I woke in the morning with what felt like a hangover, but in reality was just lack of sleep. I hadn't been able to sleep after I came up here last night. I kept waiting for him to come in my room, but he never did. At least, he didn't while I was awake. I quickly got ready when I saw the time. I had slept in and I would be late to work if I didn't hurry up.

When I went downstairs, there was no sign of Knight anywhere. I did a quick search to be sure, but he was nowhere in sight. I couldn't worry about him right now. I had to get into work. Whatever was happening last night between us wouldn't be happening again.

4

KNIGHT

AFTER SHE RAN AWAY from me last night, I had a serious case of blue balls that I hadn't had in years. Since I was always moving around on different jobs, I had never tried to date a woman—not that I could. I couldn't ever have a future with someone because of who I was. Not just because I was an assassin, but because I had to keep the old version of me a secret. So, I slept with random women. Most were skanks I picked up at bars. They did the job, but were rarely satisfying.

I left this morning before she got up because if I saw Kate again this morning, I would shove her up against the wall and take her. I didn't follow her to work this morning. I went back to my house and hung out there for the day. If she had any clue that I lived just two houses down from her, she would kick my ass out. I couldn't let that happen. Being so close to her calmed all the shit in my head. I knew I couldn't actually be with her, but as long as she took pity on me and kept me in her home, I would enjoy what I had.

It was boring sitting around all day and I would be doing this for the next six to eight weeks, according to Kate. What the hell was I going to do? I certainly wasn't hurting for money, but since I was always working, I never really sat down and got bored. A few hours alone at my house and I was ready to slit my wrists. I called Hunter to help me out.

"Pappy, I need your help."

"I'm working. What do you need?"

"I need you to get me a TV."

"Seriously? You think I'm going to leave work to get you a fucking TV?"

"I'm bored. It's either you get me a TV or I go stalk Kate some more."

"Some more? You said you were just making sure she was safe."

"And how do you think I've been doing that?"

"Jesus, why can't I have normal friends?"

"So, is that a yes?"

"You're staying with her. Just watch her TV."

"It's weird being in the house without her."

"Do you realize how fucked up that is? You stalk her everywhere she goes, but you don't like being in her house by yourself?"

Well, when he put it like that. "I may stalk her, but I would never invade her privacy like that. I mean, besides the few times I was there with her when she didn't know it."

"That's so fucked up, I don't even know what to say about it."

"So, are you going to do it for me or not?" I asked in frustration.

"You'll have to wait until my lunch break. I only get an hour, so you better be fast."

"Yeah, I'm gonna need you to install it too."

"Not happening."

"How the hell am I going to do it with one arm?"

"That's not my problem. I have a job to do and I can't take that much time off."

"Fine. Be here in an hour."

I hung up before he could argue with me anymore. It was weird having Pappy back in my life. I wasn't sure what to think about it. It was nice to have the camaraderie again, but I just didn't know if it was a good idea. It was never smart for an assassin to have friends. Which begged the question, why the hell was I following Kate around? Eventually, knowing me would end up putting Kate in danger. Now, I had moved into a house down the road from her, and if anyone was following me, they would see me following her.

I was always very careful that no one could track me, but my last assignment had been sloppy. Had I screwed up on any other jobs because I was distracted? I didn't think so, but there was a first time for everything, and if there was a first time, there could be a second time.

I would have to leave once my shoulder was healed up. I couldn't risk sticking around and drawing attention to myself. I should leave now, but as long as I didn't wander out too much, it should be fine.

Hunter picked me up and took me shopping for a TV and an entertainment center. We argued about what I needed. He thought I needed the biggest screen with surround sound, but I didn't think that was necessary. I didn't usually sit around watching TV, so what was the point?

"You watch football, right?"

"Sometimes," I shrugged.

"Then you need the big screen. What if I want to come over for the game? I'm not watching on a twenty-four-inch."

"Fine," I groaned in frustration. "Just get whatever the hell you want. Anything to make you stop bitching at me."

"You two are so cute together," the sales lady said with a blush.

"Excuse me?" I said.

"The way you argue. My boyfriend and I are like that, too. That's how you know it's true love."

"What the fuck?" I said a little too loud, drawing the attention of everyone nearby.

"I'm sorry. I didn't mean to point it out. Are you not out of the closet yet?" she asked, pointing a finger between the two of us.

"Lady, I'm not gay." I puffed out my chest, showing off my muscles. *Like gay people couldn't have muscles*, I thought, rolling my eyes.

"Hey, I'm not judging. There's nothing to be ashamed of. I have a lot of friends who are gay."

"Pooky, it's about time, don't you think?" Hunter wrapped an arm around my waist and gave me a peck on the cheek. I flinched back and glared at him.

"Don't do that shit."

"She knows," he shrugged. "Why not let the cat out of the bag?"

"I'll just put your order in and give you two some privacy. You want the big screen, right?"

Hunter gave her a charming smile and a wink. "You got it, baby cakes. Should we go for the surround sound, too, Pooky?"

I was losing my patience really fast with him. "Pappy, don't—"

"Aww, that's so cute that you call him Pappy. Is that like calling him Big Daddy?"

I stepped forward, very willing to slap this bitch, but Hunter grabbed my arm and pulled me back. The lady, obviously sensing my anger, slunk away to quickly process the order.

"You need to learn to chill. Who gives a shit if she thinks you're gay?"

I shrugged him off and walked away. It wasn't about her thinking I was gay. In my world, I couldn't let anyone talk shit about me. It was a sign of weakness. I guess I wasn't so good at civilian life anymore.

Hunter caught up to me outside and pointed me toward the furniture store. "Might as well get something for you to sit on while you're here."

"Thought you had to get back to work?"

He shrugged as we headed down the sidewalk. "I told Cap that I had to help you out with something. He wasn't too happy, but he didn't bitch about it. You know, you could still come work at Reed Security. It doesn't have to be the type of stuff I do."

"We've been over this. I don't want to settle down or have a boss. I like my life the way it is."

"Then why are you looking out for Kate and buying a house down the street from her?"

"Call it an obsession. I'll get it out of my system and move on."

He flung his hand onto my chest to stop me. "What the hell do you mean, *you'll get it out of your system*? Kate's not a girl you fuck with."

"She's not a girl. She's one hundred percent woman."

"She also works for Reed Security, and Sebastian's not going to deal with you fucking her over. Not to mention that her cousin's a former sniper. You really want to go there?"

"You really think I'm scared of a sniper? Bunch of pansy asses. They kill from a distance. It takes a real man to go get the dirty work done up close and personal."

"You always were a cocky son of a bitch, Hud."

"It's part of my charm."

"You've got the charm of a rattlesnake."

"I bite like one, too."

I FINALLY GOT EVERYTHING SET UP THE WAY I WANTED. THE TV AND entertainment center had been delivered early afternoon and the furniture arrived right about dinner time. I sat down on the couch and looked around the house. What the hell was I doing? Buying a TV and furniture? It was like I was playing house. This wasn't my world and it never would be.

I couldn't decide if I was going to Kate's or if I would hang out here. I really should back off and leave her alone. It's not like she needed me or I needed her. But some part of me wanted her to need me. I decided I shouldn't go over there. After all, I was already getting in too deep with her.

I sat on the couch in the fading light and stared at the blank TV screen. I couldn't even bring myself to turn it on. My shoulder started to throb. I hadn't taken any pills in a while and the pain was starting to catch up to me. I went over to the counter and shook out a few Tylenol. I had left all the pain meds at Kate's house, and I was trying my damnedest not to go over there. I had refused to even go to the window and look outside for her car, but now that I was up, I decided I might as well take a look.

Not only was her car there, but there was a man standing in her driveway next to a truck. She leaned into him and gave him a kiss on the cheek, then hugged him. What the hell? I waited to see what would happen, and when he followed her inside, I about blew a gasket. She was mine. There was no way this asshole was going to touch my woman. I snuck out into the darkness and slipped around to the back

44

side of her house. He was sitting at her kitchen table and they were laughing together.

I waited them out and when she went upstairs, I slipped in the back door and snuck up behind him. Cocking my gun, I held it to the back of his head. He didn't even flinch.

"Garrick!" Kate's shocked voice threw me and I whipped my head around to see her pale face staring at me in horror. I hated the look on her face. It said that I was a monster, which I was, but I didn't want her to see this side of me. It was enough of a distraction that the man at her table spun around and grabbed the gun, kicking me in the stomach and sending me hurling back into the fridge. My shoulder slammed into it and I felt blood trickle from my wound. I was slower to react than usual and that wasn't a good sign, especially when he hauled me up and shoved his thumb into my wound.

I ground my teeth together, refusing to make any noise. In the distance, I vaguely heard Kate yelling at the man to stop, but I was fading fast and it wouldn't be long before I was down for the count. I used my good arm to knock away his hand and then ducked as he swung at me, hitting him twice in the kidneys. He grunted but didn't go down even the slightest. His knee came up and slammed into my ribs, making me double over. I knew I was fucked. I was never this slow, but this guy was good and knew where to strike.

With one final effort, I swept his legs out from under him and planted my fist in his face. It only temporarily delayed him, though. He grabbed my injured arm and pulled, sending blinding pain through my body. I wasn't sure how, but he was behind me and twisting my arm up behind my back. The pain was too intense and that was it for me. I hit the floor face first and the last thing I saw was Kate rushing over to me.

5

KATE

THEY WERE GOING to kill each other, but there was nothing I could do at this point. When two killers go after each other, you don't try to intervene. I could tell immediately that Knight was going to lose this battle. Cole was just as quick, but he was fighting uninjured. I winced when Cole dug his thumb into Knight's wound. That had to hurt like a bitch, but to his credit, Knight didn't make a sound.

"Cole, stop! Garrick is staying here while he heals."

Cole didn't respond, just kept going at Knight. When he twisted his arm behind his back, the first thing I thought was that Hunter was going to be pissed at me. He had asked me to look after Garrick and my cousin was attacking him. Though, in his defense, Garrick had pointed a gun at his head.

I ran toward Knight as he collapsed on the ground. His eyes drifted shut and he was done. I looked up at Cole, but I didn't see my cousin there. There was a darkness to him that scared me. Standing slowly, I put my hand on his arm and spoke softly.

"Cole." He didn't look at me. His chest was heaving as he stared down at Garrick's limp form. "Cole, it's Kate. Can you hear me?"

Slowly, Cole turned to look at me and his face softened. He shook his head and took a step back, running his hand over his face.

"Fuck, what the hell was that? Who is this guy?"

"This is a...friend. He was hurt and he's staying with me while he gets better."

There was no way that I could tell Cole who Garrick was. First, I couldn't betray Hunter like that, and second, Cole would go all big brother on me and haul me out of the house. I didn't know if he knew who Garrick was, but I didn't want to find out either.

"What kind of a friend pulls a gun on a man sitting at a table?"

"The kind of man that lives in paranoia," I muttered.

"He could have killed me. You shouldn't be keeping that kind of company."

I shot him an amused look. "Somehow, I really doubt he could have killed you. You didn't even seem scared when he pulled the gun on you."

"That's because I knew he was there."

"So, how exactly would he have killed you?"

"Kate, you're missing the point. You don't keep men around that pull guns on random people."

"He's injured. You saw for yourself."

"Yeah, I saw that he has a bullet hole in his shoulder. You can't just pick up every stray that you come across."

"Like you?"

He had taken Alex, his now-wife, in after he found her staggering out of the woods.

"Alex was different. She had been abducted by a serial killer."

"You don't know anything about Garrick. Why do you assume that he's the dangerous one?"

"Because, even injured, I saw how he moved and those weren't the moves of an amateur. He's trained to kill, just like I was. And if he has fresh bullet holes, that means he's still living out that life over here. He could put you in danger," he growled at me.

I didn't know why I was defending Garrick. Cole was right. He was dangerous and he had a sick fascination with me that even gave me the creeps. He had snuck into my home and held a gun to my cousin's head, yet I was trying to convince Cole that he wasn't dangerous.

"Look, I need to get him upstairs and take a look at his shoulder. If you're not going to help me, then you can leave."

His face hardened, but he bent over and hauled Garrick over his shoulder, none too gently. "I can't believe I'm doing this for you," he muttered. I grabbed my first aid kit and the scissors and followed Cole upstairs. He tossed Garrick on the bed I had made up for him the night before, and I started cutting away his shirt. Blood had soaked through already and was dribbling down his chest. I grabbed some towels and cleaned him up the best I could and then cleaned up his wound. It was a good thing he was passed out because this part would have been very painful.

When I was all finished, I put some gauze over the wound and walked out of the room, shutting the door behind me. Cole was standing in the hall with his arms crossed over his chest. His face radiated anger.

"Who the hell is he?"

"Cole—"

"No, Kate. I'm not leaving here until I know who the fuck he is. I don't want to find out that you were murdered in your sleep because I left you alone."

"He would never hurt me."

"Are you sure about that?"

Was I? Not really. I mean, I knew he had some sort of obsession with me, but I wasn't certain that he would never hurt me. He was an assassin. He killed people for a living. I must have waited too long to answer because Cole swore and ran a hand over his face.

"I'm calling Sean to come deal with this."

"No!" I shouted as he pulled out his phone. "You can't do that."

He narrowed his eyes at me. "What the fuck do you mean? This man is obviously dangerous. I'm not leaving you alone with him."

"Cole, please don't do this."

"Why are you so loyal to him?"

I didn't have a good answer for that. I wasn't sure if it was Hunter or the fact that no matter how hard I tried to deny it, I was attracted to Garrick.

"That's what I thought."

He started to search his contacts, and when he dialed, Sean would be on his way here. Not knowing what else to do, I blurted out, "Call Sebastian."

That stopped him in his tracks. "Why?"

"Just call him. Tell him Knight is here."

He pulled up Sebastian's number and let it ring. "Sebastian, I'm over at Kate's house. Knight is here."

I didn't hear any response from Sebastian, but Cole's eyes shot up to mine and turned deadly.

"What the fuck does that mean? Fine. I'll be here waiting. Get your ass over here before I put a bullet in his skull."

He hung up and sat at the table, staring at me as we waited for Sebastian to arrive. It didn't take long before my bell rang and Cole got up to answer it. There was no point in arguing that I could answer my own door. With the mood he was in, I would have better luck getting a tiger to dance with me.

Sebastian's eyes found me right away and he looked me over as if he was expecting me to be covered in blood. "What's going on?"

"That's what I'd like to know. The man snuck into the house and held a gun to my head."

"And you escaped?" Sebastian sounded baffled and Cole snorted.

"I'm not some pussy who can't take care of myself."

Sebastian cleared his throat and glanced over at me like he didn't want to say anything in front of me. "I already know," I said snarkily.

"Uh, Knight is Garrick Knight, as in the assassin," Sebastian said.

Cole's face turned to pure steel and he swiveled his head to meet my gaze. "You knew? Why the hell would you let him into your house?"

"Why don't you ask him?" I pointed at Sebastian. "Better yet, why don't you ask Hunter."

"Christ." Sebastian rubbed a hand over his face. "Hunter told me this morning that he needed to help him, but he didn't say anything about you. I had no idea you were involved."

"Wait. Hunter told me he was going out of town for a few days."

"His trip got canceled."

"And he left me with him?" I asked incredulously.

"Why did he?" Sebastian asked. "How are you involved in this?"

"Garrick showed up at my clinic with a gunshot wound. Hunter showed up also and we patched him up. He said he had to go out of town and asked me to keep an eye on him. I didn't want to, but I couldn't turn him away either."

"Why not? Knight knows how to take care of himself." Sebastian interjected.

"The bullet hit bone. It's not bad, but he's going to be hurting for a while. He can't really use his arm the way it is and the recovery time is longer. Hunter just wanted me to help out until he got back, but apparently he had a change of heart, seeing as how he never left."

"So, he left you alone with a killer?" Cole said, completely baffled by this revelation.

"I'm pretty sure he wouldn't hurt me."

"He held a gun to my head," Cole argued.

"That's because you were in my house. He probably thought you were here to hurt me."

"Why would someone assume I was here to hurt you while sitting at your kitchen table?"

"Because he's a killer and he stays alive by being paranoid." Sebastian had hit the nail on the head with that one.

"Why does he even know who she is?" Cole asked Sebastian.

Sebastian had the decency to look sheepish at his question. "You know Kate works for me when we need medical help."

"Is he working for you?"

"No, he helped us out on a job. Hunter knows him, used to serve with him. Anyway, he was shot on the job and Kate came over to take care of him."

"Are you fucking kidding me?" Cole exploded. There weren't many times that I saw Cole this upset, so it shocked me a little. "You brought my cousin to take care of a known killer?"

"We had men with her at all times. She was safe. He really came through for us. I couldn't just let him bleed out."

"So, drop him at a hospital and call it a day," Cole said in frustration.

"We couldn't. There's a lot more you don't know."

My ears perked up at that. I didn't know either and I really wanted to.

Sebastian sighed, "He's former military and he would end up in jail if we turned him over to the hospital."

"What is he supposed to be in jail for?" I asked.

"Murder," Sebastian said, his eyes never leaving Cole's.

"Kate, pack a bag. As long as he's here, you're not staying."

The tone of his voice said not to fuck with him, but I was still hung up on the murder part. I couldn't think. I needed to know more. Sebastian would never leave me with someone he felt would hurt me.

"Cole, it's not what it sounds like." Sebastian looked exhausted from the conversation.

"Then you'd better tell me what it is like right the fuck now."

"He killed his superiors because they were profiting from soldier's deaths. They didn't care that good men were dying, and Knight did what he had to do."

Understanding or something like it crossed Cole's face. "His name isn't Knight, is it?"

"That's what he goes by now."

Cole scoffed and shook his head. "McGuire, right?"

Sebastian gave a slight nod.

"He's supposed to be in Leavenworth. And you dragged my cousin into the middle of this shit storm. How much time did he spend with her?"

"Only a day," Sebastian said.

"Then why the hell would he trust her enough to go to her for help?"

Sebastian looked at me and then so did Cole. I felt my face heat and couldn't look away from their penetrating gazes. "He's been following me for months."

"Why didn't you say anything?" Sebastian asked.

I shrugged. "I don't know. I guess I wasn't afraid of him. I mean, I kind of was because he's an assassin and all, but he never tried to hurt me in any way and he even—" I stopped before I said anything else, but Sebastian already caught on.

"He was the sniper that took out the druggie outside your clinic."

I gave a slight nod. "He was just trying to protect me."

"Great, so a killer has an obsession with you. That's fucking perfect." Cole looked like he had a very short leash on his anger, so I didn't say anything else. "You're coming home with me. There's no way I'm leaving you here with him."

"Cole, I appreciate you looking after me, but he hasn't tried to hurt me, and now that you opened his wound and wrenched his arm, someone has to look after him."

"Let Hunter do it," he snapped. "It's his friend."

"I already sent him out of town a few hours ago. He got back from helping Knight with something and then he left."

"Call him back."

"I can't. He's already on a job. Knight can stay at Reed Security."

"No," I interrupted. "He's not going anywhere. He's in no position to be moved around tonight, and like I already told you, he has never tried to hurt me. I appreciate the concern, Cole, but I've got this."

"You don't know who you're dealing with. You do one fucking thing wrong and he won't think twice about taking you out," Cole said, stepping into my space to try to intimidate me.

"Imagine if people said the same about you."

"That's not fair. I only killed when I had to."

"You killed those men that were after Alex, and I saw you fighting tonight. You were just as deadly. Don't try to make it out like you're a saint."

"I know I'm not, but I don't kill random people either."

"Neither does he," Sebastian said. "All the people he kills are very bad people. I'm not saying it's right, but he does what needs to be done."

Cole shook his head and took a step back, gazing out the window at the darkness. "I can see I'm getting nowhere with you. Kate, just do me a favor and call me if you need me. I'll be here and I won't say a fucking word. Just don't wait until it's too late."

"I promise."

"I'll be by to check on you tomorrow." He gave me a kiss on the cheek and walked out the door. Sebastian just stood there assessing me and it was making me very uncomfortable.

"Now that your cousin's gone, how about you tell me about Knight following you."

"There's not much to tell. He's just been around. I only saw him the night the druggie attacked me and then when he came to my clinic."

"Then how do you know he's following you?"

"I can feel him," I said hesitantly. There was no other way to describe it. I wasn't sure Sebastian believed me, but he didn't say anything.

"You should have come to me. I put you in this position and I'm sorry. Do you want me to get him out of here?"

I shook my head. "He's going to be in a lot of pain. You should have seen the way Cole attacked him. It's not going to be pretty."

"He probably deserved it."

"I won't argue with that."

"Is there something more going on that I should know about?" he asked suspiciously.

"No, I'm just so conflicted. He's a murderer by all standards, but he also watches out for me. I guess I'm just confused right now."

"That makes two of us," he said cryptically. "I'm going to have someone come stay with you. I don't like the idea of you being alone here with him."

"That's not a good idea. If he sees someone hanging around, he's just going to get pissed off."

Sebastian smirked at me and headed for the door. "Good. He's not exactly one of my favorite people."

"Do you really think it's a good idea to poke the bear?"

"If he doesn't like it, he can leave. Don't get any illusions about him, Kate. He's not a good man. He could snap your neck before you knew it was happening."

I swallowed hard and nodded. "I'll remember that."

Sebastian walked out the door. I stood in the living room wondering what I had gotten myself into. Deep down, I really didn't think he would hurt me, but Sebastian was right. I couldn't start thinking that Garrick was something more to me. I didn't even know how long he would be sticking around.

6

KNIGHT

Everything on my body hurt, but at least I was alive. That big fucker from last night had nearly taken me out and I laid in Kate's guest room wondering why the hell he left me alive. I held a gun to his head and I wasn't dead. Which could only mean that someone had intervened. It must have been Kate, but I couldn't figure out why she had done it. I knew she thought I didn't deserve to live, but she kept helping me.

"How are you feeling this morning?" I turned my head to see her sitting in the chair by the window. I hadn't noticed she was there. I was really losing my touch. I couldn't fight back last night and a woman was sitting in the same room with me and I didn't notice. I needed to get my shit together.

"Shitty," I groaned as I tried to sit up.

"You really shouldn't do that. Cole beat the hell out of you last night and I'm pretty sure your shoulder is even more fucked up now than it was before. You probably have some bruised ribs too."

"Cracked. Heard it when he kneed me." I laid back against the pillows and fought the waves of nausea rolling through me.

Kate walked over to the bed and handed me a bottle of water and some pills. "Here. You need to take these or you're going to be hurting all day."

I shook my head. "They fuck with my head and make me slower."

"That's the point. You shouldn't be moving around too much to begin with."

"Who was that guy last night?"

She smirked at me and shoved the pills back at me. I took them and swallowed them with the water.

"That was my cousin. I would say he's not your biggest fan right now."

"*That* was your cousin? The sniper?"

"You were foolish to think you could beat him in your condition. Cole hasn't lost any of his training just because he's not active duty anymore."

I grunted, not really wanting to get into the topic of how he kicked my ass last night.

"Why aren't you at work?"

"It's Saturday. I don't usually go into the office unless I have paper-work to do. Which, I probably should be doing instead of babysitting you."

"I don't need a babysitter."

"Yeah, well, someone has to look out for you. You're being a little reckless. Here, I made you some oatmeal. You need to eat something so the medicine doesn't make you sick."

I took it even though I didn't feel like eating and swallowed down a few bites. It was surprisingly good, but my stomach just didn't want anything.

"I think you should know that Sebastian sent someone over here last night. He wanted to make sure I was protected."

I glared at her, pissed that she would think that she needed protec-tion from me. "And why the hell would you need someone here to watch you? I'm not going to hurt you."

"Well, Cole wasn't exactly happy when he found out who you were. I had to have him call Sebastian so he didn't kill you."

"Shit."

"Don't worry. Cole's not going to hand you over to the police, although he wanted to."

I didn't want to give away too much, but I also had to find out what Sebastian told Cole and if Kate heard it.

"What did Sebastian tell him?"

"He told him who you were, which was bad enough, but then he told him that you were wanted for murder. Cole seemed to know exactly who you were. He mentioned the name McGuire."

Fuck. This wasn't good. Nobody but the people at Reed Security were supposed to know who I really was. The more people that found out, the more dangerous it was for me and everyone around me.

"That wasn't his information to hand out."

"Would you rather have a bullet in your head?"

"If he doesn't keep his mouth shut, it won't be long before that happens."

She watched me and it made me squirm. I wasn't used to people studying me. Most people took the *don't fuck with me* look quite literally and stayed away. But Kate was getting more comfortable around me and wasn't as intimidated by me anymore. I didn't know if that was a good or bad thing.

"So, who are you really?"

"That's none of your goddamn business," I said with as much menace as I could muster. I couldn't let her think she could bat her eyelashes and get whatever she wanted from me. I still had to protect myself and even though she hadn't tried to fuck me over yet, that didn't mean she wouldn't in the future.

"Why don't you get some more sleep? Those pills will be kicking in pretty soon. I'll be downstairs if you need me." She stood and walked out of the room, leaving me cursing myself for being such an idiot. If I hadn't run over here last night because of my stupid jealousy, I wouldn't be in the position I was now, which was totally fucked. I not only couldn't protect her, I couldn't protect myself and that was a dangerous way to live.

When I woke again, it was late afternoon and I was starving. I didn't particularly want to get up, but I also had no way of asking Kate to bring me something. I sat up slowly, my ribs protesting the movement, and made my way over to the door. Just that little bit of movement was a little too much for me and I found myself leaning against the door frame to catch my breath. I couldn't remember the last time that I had been this out of it. Even when I was shot down in the Dominican Republic, the recovery had been fairly easy. Or maybe it just felt that way because I woke up to Kate's face. That had been the day that everything had changed for me. The day that I found myself wanting more than the pitiful existence I had.

Taking it slowly on the stairs, I found Kate sitting in the living room curled up on the couch. She looked over at me and I must have looked like hell because she rushed over to me and took my good arm, guiding me to the couch.

"We need to wrap your ribs. It'll make you feel better. Just sit here for a minute while I grab a wrap."

No problem there. Walking down the stairs had completely wiped me out. Kate came rushing back into the room with a wrap and her medical kit.

"Lift your arms as much as you can." I did as she asked, grimacing when my left arm protested just inches from my body. I felt myself hardening as her fingers ran along my pecs as she finished off the wrap. Her head tilted up slowly as she took in my face. Her eyes flicked from my eyes to my lips. I knew how much she wanted me. I could see it in her eyes. But I didn't know if she would act on it. I leaned forward, letting her know that I wanted her too, but leaving it up to her to make the first move. If she kissed me, I didn't know if I would be able to hold back with her, which would really suck considering that I was injured.

When her lips touched mine, I didn't hold back. I needed her. Her tongue slid against mine with a velvety softness that had me groaning as my cock hardened. Her plump lips sucked at my bottom lip, promising what things could be like if we ever took this further. After tasting her yesterday, I knew I would never have enough. Her kisses brought me back to the light, a place I never thought I would see again, and it made me wonder if I could have her for keeps. When she pulled back, her eyes were clouded with lust and her lips were plump and red. She was a fucking dream.

"That was probably a bad idea," she whispered.

"Nothing better than a bad idea," I said as I stared at her lips, wondering if she would allow me another taste.

"This won't go anywhere. We shouldn't do this."

"You're probably right, but that doesn't mean I don't want you. You're my angel. I think you might be the only person that could ever save me."

That must have been the wrong thing to say because her head snapped back and she narrowed her eyes at me. "I save people who are injured, but I can't save someone that so callously disregards human life. Your soul was lost the first time you pulled the trigger."

My face hardened and I looked away. I wasn't sure what the hell I was thinking, but obviously, this woman would never see me as anything other than a killer. And she would be right. I made my decision and I blackened my soul with little regard for the consequences.

"I'm going to make some dinner. You need to eat before you take any more pills."

I leaned back with a sigh and watched whatever the hell she had on the TV. It was some kind of medical show and I wasn't the least bit interested. Before I knew it, I had drifted off and she was shaking me awake.

"Hey, wake up. I've got some dinner for you."

My eyelids were heavy and I didn't want to wake up, but I knew I needed to eat something. Sitting up, Kate fussed over me, putting pillows behind my back to make me more comfortable, and damn if that didn't make my heart speed up. I tried to imagine what it would be like if I was a more permanent part of her life, but her earlier words came back to me and squashed any dreams I had that it would happen.

"What did you make?"

"Nothing fancy. Just some chicken and rice. I didn't think you would want anything too heavy, but you probably need the protein. I didn't think soup would fill you up."

I looked down at the plate that she set on my lap and saw that she even cut up the chicken for me in bite sized pieces. This woman was just amazing.

"Thank you," I murmured. I ate in companionable silence with her as she flicked through the channels.

"There's nothing on," she sighed. "Why don't you pick something."

"I haven't watched TV in years. I have no idea what's on. Whatever you choose is fine."

She put on some sort of action movie that had me laughing because of how ridiculous the scenes were. If only that was the way it worked in real life. When I finished dinner, she brought me my pills and some water.

"Why don't you put your feet up so you're more comfortable?"

I got comfortable on the couch and was surprised when she sat on the floor right in front of the couch. From where I was lying, I could just reach out and run my fingers through her hair. For some reason, it calmed me, so I continued even when she gave me a funny look. I fell asleep with my fingers in her silky strands, dreaming of what life would be like if I were a different man.

I PRETTY MUCH SLEPT ON THE COUCH ALL OF SUNDAY. THE PILLS WERE knocking me out and I could barely stay awake for a half hour after I took them. That was probably for the best, considering that I needed to let my body heal, and that wouldn't happen if I was awake and moving around. I was never very good at relaxing, so this was probably the only way that would happen.

In the afternoon, I got up to use the bathroom and paused in the doorway when I heard voices in the living room. It sounded like one male voice, but I couldn't be certain. I snuck to the corner of the living room and saw that it was the fucker from the other night.

"Cole, I'm fine here. I promise that he hasn't tried to kill me or take advantage of me. Not that he could, considering the beat down you gave him."

"I'll give him as many as he needs to remind him not to touch you."

"Relax, man." I walked into the living room, straight up to Cole. "You have nothing to worry about. I'm not going to hurt her."

His eyes narrowed in on me. "And I'm just supposed to take your word for it?"

"No. I'd be doing the same thing if I was her cousin. There would be no way I would let a guy like me near her."

His eyes assessed my body and he smirked. Yeah, I looked like shit. One arm in a sling and my ribs wrapped. Pretty sure I had some bruises on my face, too.

"Guess, I don't really have much to worry about. You don't look like you could pull one over on a kitten right now."

"Kittens have claws," I retorted.

"Boys, boys. Do we really have to do this right now?"

"Don't get any illusions here, Kate. He may be weak at the moment, but he's a trained killer."

I hated that he was right, about both parts. I was weak at the moment and I had no doubts that she could kick my ass. And I was a killer. She had pointed that out several times, saying there could never be anything between us because of my choices. I knew it was true, but damn, I didn't like hearing her say it.

"Thank you, Cole, but I've got this covered. Remember, I may be a doctor and save lives, but I also know a hundred different ways to end them."

"Just keep that in the back of your mind while he's here," Cole said firmly to her. He and I both knew that it didn't matter if she knew how to take a life. Kate didn't have a cruel or hateful bone in her body. It wasn't in her to take a life, no matter what. She would always try to find a way to help.

Cole left a few minutes later and I was already settled on the couch. It felt like no matter how much I rested, I was down for the count. Kate took a seat on the other end of the couch and pulled her knees up to her chest.

"Am I right about you? Would you ever hurt me?"

"Not willingly," I said fiercely.

"Not even if it was to get something you needed from someone else?"

I considered her question, but there wasn't much to think about. I already knew that I would protect Kate with my life. If she was the only way to get the answers I needed, I would sooner cut off my own arm than hurt her.

"Not even then. Kate, I know I'm not a good person and I also know you know that, too. I'm not suggesting that we'll fall in love and live happily ever after, because I already know you could never want that with someone like me. But there's something about you that makes me want to be better for you, even if my hands are already so bloody that no amount of washing would clean them."

"Why do you do what you do?"

"Why do you heal people?" I asked.

"Because people deserve a chance to live the best life they can. I like to know that I make a difference, even if it's just a small one."

"I do what I do for the same reasons." She looked at me funny. "There are people out there that are the scum of the earth and don't deserve to live. I've taken out drug dealers that sell to kids. I've taken out pedophiles and rapists. Those people don't deserve a second chance at life."

"How can you say that? I mean, it's not that I side with them, but you've made yourself judge, jury, and executioner. We have a legal system that deals with those people."

"And the system fails more times than not. There are so many ways for one of those people to get away with that shit and no one is there to stop them from raping a kid or getting them hooked on drugs. Do you know how many people are assaulted and never see justice? These people are smart. They know how to get away with the shit they pull because they know how to clean up after themselves or threaten a victim so they'll never talk. I do what I do because it prevents others from having to suffer the same fate as the person before them."

"But every time you kill someone, you're no better than they are. Don't you see that? That person is someone's child or father. You're taking their life like it means nothing to anyone else."

"I do what's necessary. I'm not making excuses or trying to say I'm a good person. I know what I'm doing is eating away at me every day, and that's something I have to live with."

She bit her lip as she considered what I had said. I could tell she wanted to ask me more, but she chose her words carefully.

"What happened when you were in the military? Cole made it sound like that's where this started."

"Are you going to run off to your friend Sean and tell him everything you know about me?" She looked shocked that I knew about him. "Yeah, I know all about your cop friend. Remember, I've been watching you for a while. There's not much that I don't know about you, including what kind of panties you like to wear." She blushed and squirmed under my gaze.

"I'm not going to say anything to anyone. I'm pretty sure I could get in trouble for aiding and abetting or something like that."

"Why do you want to know?"

"I'm just curious what made you start..." She waved her hand around like she didn't really want to say the words.

"Killing people?" She nodded. "I was in the military with Pappy for several years. I got called up for some special assignments, and over the course of a year, I began to realize that my superiors were feeding us bad intel and my brothers were dying. They were profiting from soldier's deaths. Every mission we went out on, we wondered who was going to end up dead."

"Did you try and tell someone else?"

I scoffed, "The people I worked for were at the top. They were untouchable. I knew that if I didn't do something, I would end up in one of those body bags, only there was no one at home to take the flag when I was put in the ground. I didn't have family, but a lot of my brothers did. I needed to end it before more of them died."

"There had to be something else you could do. Let them know you were on to them, or—"

"Let them know I was on to them? I'd be sent out on the next mission and I wouldn't return. Have you ever been to a military funeral?"

"No."

"I suggest you go sometime. Look at the widow as she's handed the flag that her husband earned with his life. You can watch his kids staring at the casket, not understanding why their father isn't coming home. Those families give up so much of their lives to support their loved ones and what do they get in the end?" I shook my head in disgust. "I wasn't going to sit back and watch that happen anymore. Those families deserve more than that."

"Don't you deserve more, too? I mean, you've basically given up your life. You've already said that if they find you, you would have the entire weight of the government coming after you. Don't you want more for yourself?"

"I made my decision a long time ago. There's no going back for me."

She looked away and I wondered if she had hoped for a different answer. If this was another life, would I have a shot with her? I hoped I would, but it was ridiculous to think that way. I couldn't change what I had done, so there was no point in dreaming of something more.

"What were you like before you became an assassin?"

"I'm not really sure. The only way I could describe it is having blinders on. I mean, in the military, you see how cruel the world can actually be, but when I came home and went on the run? The people I'm hired to take out are the stuff of nightmares. I guess it made me more untrusting of others."

"Do you ever miss that naivety?"

"What's the point in thinking about it? I can't go back. I can't forget what I know."

"I guess what I'm asking is, do you wish you could go back to being Hudson McGuire?"

I thought back to what it was like to be in the military with Pappy and the other members of our team. Those were good times and if I had never been requested for other missions, I would have continued to serve with Pappy and maybe even joined Reed Security with him. I could have had a family of my own and I never would have known all the shit that could happen in life. Yeah, part of me wished that I could be Hudson McGuire again.

"Sometimes. When I think back to what it was like being in the military, having that kind of brotherhood, I miss that. Being an assassin is a very lonely job to have. Friends can't be trusted and enemies are everywhere. Sleep never comes easily because I'm always watching my back. I never stay in one place too long because it makes me complacent. I guess if there was one thing I would want, it's to not always be on the move."

"What about regular life? Isn't it hard to know that you can't just decide to settle down one day and get a job somewhere?"

I didn't want her to know how much I craved that at the moment, so I lied.

"I don't think I'm cut out for a normal job. The military trained me to be a killer and they did a damn good job."

"But, you know what I mean. You could have gotten out and done something else with your life."

"Like I said before, I made my decision and I have to live with it. If I dwell on what could have been, I'd drive myself insane."

———

"HEY, YOU LOOK A LITTLE STIFF TODAY." KATE WAS SITTING AT THE kitchen table in lounge pants and a loose t-shirt. She looked damn sexy with her hair all ruffled from sleep and no makeup.

"Little bit. What are you still doing here? I thought you'd be at work already."

"The clinic's not open on holidays."

I shook my head, totally baffled that I had lost track of time so much. "So, what are you planning for the day?"

"Not sure yet. I was thinking about just hanging around, maybe reading a book. I have to run to the store and do some grocery shopping, but that's about it. This has been my first full weekend off in a long time."

"You work too hard."

"Says the man that doesn't even have time for TV."

"Just because I don't watch TV doesn't mean that I don't take time off."

"Where was the last place you went?"

"I was in Pittsburgh."

"I meant, someplace other than on a job."

"I went to Hawaii last year."

"And that was strictly pleasure?"

I thought about that trip and shook my head with a chuckle. "Well, I had intended it to be that way, but I ran into some business while I was down there."

"So, not a vacation then."

"No. I guess it has been a while. When was your last vacation?"

"Umm." She looked up, like she was trying to count out dates or something in her head. It was cute how her nose bunched up as she thought. "I guess it's been years. I haven't taken a vacation since before I started med school."

"You were a very serious student, weren't you?"

"How did you know?" she smiled.

"And I bet you never blew off class because you were hungover or just didn't feel like going."

"I almost did. I went to a party my freshman year and got really drunk. I woke up the next morning feeling terrible, but I went to class anyway. It cost my parents a lot of money to put me through school and there was no way I was going to disrespect that. What about you? Did you go to college?"

"I got my degree in computer engineering while I was in the military. It's come in quite handy."

"So, that's how you know how to bypass my alarm and sneak into my house."

"It's one of my many talents." I gave her a big smile and she rolled her eyes at me.

"You have quite the ego."

"I have the skills to back it up, so I don't see that as a weakness."

"Why do I get the feeling that you have the skills for a lot of things?"

And just like that, something changed in the air around us. Her skin flushed, meaning she hadn't realized how dirty that sounded.

"I'd be willing to show you my skills anytime you want."

She stood quickly and brought her cup over to the sink. "I think I'll go take a shower. I have a lot to do today."

"Want some company?"

"No, I don't think that's necessary."

"I meant it more for me. It's been a few days since I've showered.

I'm pretty sure that rancid odor is me, and since your cousin kicked my ass, I'm not really able to clean myself."

That wasn't true at all. It had been a while, but I'd been in worse condition and gotten along just fine. Still, if I could get her to offer, I'd take her up on it in a heartbeat. She looked like she wasn't sure if she wanted to go there with me, but the doctor part of her brain must have kicked in because she looked over my body and I saw the wheels turning in her head.

"If I help you, there's no touching on your part. This is just me helping you out because I know you must be in a lot of pain."

"Scout's honor," I grinned.

"I really don't believe that you were ever a scout. This is such a bad idea," she muttered under her breath.

"I told you I love bad ideas."

"Come on. Let's get this over with."

I planned to use this time with her wisely, and if I did it right, there would be no getting it over with. I followed her upstairs and was surprised when she stepped into the bathroom in a bra and panties. She shot me a look that said not to mess with her, so I held up my hand, letting her know I wouldn't try anything. Well, I wouldn't touch her. That didn't mean there weren't other ways to try to seduce her.

I pulled down my pants and caught the strangled noise she made when my cock bobbed free. She turned on the water to let it warm up and then wrapped my shoulder in saran wrap.

"That'll have to do for now. We'll just have to be careful not to get it wet. I'll clean and change your bandage after we get you showered." She undid the wrap from around my ribs and I hated that it hurt more now that there wasn't the pressure to stabilize them.

"Thanks," I said, gripping her chin so that she would look at me. "I'm sorry it took me so long to thank you. You've been taking care of me when you didn't have to."

"I would do it for anyone," she said quietly.

"I don't want you to do it for anyone. I want you to only do it for me. I know you feel it between us, too. We could have something explosive here."

She took a step back from me. "We would only ever have sex and you know it. Now, step in the shower and let's get you cleaned up."

I stepped under the water, letting the warm water relax my muscles. I wanted to put my whole body under, but instead, I stood off to the side so I didn't get my shoulder wet. She stepped in with me and reached up to remove the shower head. She rinsed my hair and then ran the water over my body. Dried blood trickled down my body, leaving light pink swirling down the drain. She grabbed the washcloth and squirted some girly-smelling shit onto it and then lathered it up. Starting with my good shoulder, she ran the washcloth over my skin and down to my pecs. I groaned when she lingered just a little too long over my nipples.

I was hardening and she was standing so close that I was sure if she moved even the slightest bit, I would be brushing against her. Nothing I could do about that. Her hands trailed over my abs and settled against the bruises on my ribs. When she bent over, I nearly lost it, thinking that she was about to suck my dick, but instead, she kissed my bruises. My chest heaved at her touch and I was confused as hell. This woman was repulsed by my actions, but she still wanted me. I didn't know if she was coming or going half the time.

Her hand slid down further and she looked up at me from under her lashes as she wrapped her hand around my raging erection. Damn, she was beautiful.

"I thought you didn't want that?"

"I thought I didn't, too. I guess my body was thinking something else."

"You need to be sure," I said, stepping into her space. "Once I have you, you're mine. I might not be able to give you the life you want, but I won't let anyone else have you either."

She jerked me harder, panting as her grip tightened around me. "Does that mean you're mine, too?"

"There hasn't been anyone but you since I first saw you. I promise, there never will be again."

"I think you're clean enough. I need to get you into my bed."

She shut off the water and threw a towel at me that I used to wipe off as much water as possible. I followed her into the bedroom and, for the first time, wondered how the hell I was going to do this with a shoulder that didn't work and busted up ribs. She led me over to the bed and pushed lightly on my chest, down into the mattress.

"Before we do this, I'm assuming you've been with a lot of random women. Do I have anything to worry about?"

"I've never been inside a woman without protection."

"Good. Then I want you bare inside me. Is that good for you?"

For once, I found myself completely tongue-tied and could only nod my head in agreement. She stepped over to me and straddled my waist, wrapping one arm around my good shoulder.

"I'm not much into foreplay. How about you?"

"I love foreplay, but if you want to sink down on my—holy shit," I groaned as she took me in with one swift move. My eyes crossed as I tried to control my body from erupting in the next few seconds. I hadn't thought it would be like this if I ever got inside her. I had imagined me being in control and having my way with her, but instead, she had me by the balls here.

"Tell me if I hurt you."

"Not a chance in hell. You could make me bleed and I wouldn't say a fucking thing."

She moved faster and faster, pushing down on my shoulder to give herself leverage. It pulled at my other side and caused some pain in my ribs, but I had never been harder in my life. She felt so good that I was finding it hard to really take in all that she was offering me. Her perky breasts were bouncing in front of me and I wanted to slip the cup of her bra down and take her nipple in my mouth, but I couldn't do that and keep myself balanced at the same time. If I ever got the chance to do this again, I was going to take my time with her and memorize every inch of her body.

"Ride me harder. I want to feel your pussy clench around my cock."

That must have done it for her, because she tightened around me, strangling my cock to the point of pain. I came hard inside her and then collapsed back onto the bed. Pain shot through me as I landed on the soft mattress. Shit, that probably wasn't the smartest thing to do. It had felt good at the moment, but now I was seeing spots. The last thought I had before I passed out was that I didn't really give a shit. It had been well worth it.

7

KATE

CRAP. I had fucked him into passing out. I giggled at the thought, and even though it was totally inappropriate, I couldn't help myself. Part of me couldn't believe I had actually had sex with him. I was a rule follower and I always tried to do the right thing, and Knight was the antithesis of everything I believed in. Yet, there was something so right in what he did, which made me question everything I thought I stood for.

Was it possible that he was right and I was wrong? Were there some people out there that couldn't be saved? I didn't want to believe that. I had always thought that if people got the treatment they needed, they could get better. Even a rapist could be reformed if he went through the proper therapy. But maybe Knight was right in that the victims never got justice.

I looked down at my dark knight sleeping on the bed and wondered if he would ever consider reforming for me. I wanted to believe there was still something good inside him, and I could even swear from time to time that I saw a glimmer of it. Even though I thought his form of doling out justice was wrong, I knew he was doing it for the right reasons. I couldn't sit here all day and think about it. The debate going on in my head was too much to deal with, so I got up, threw on a T-shirt, and went downstairs to make breakfast. When I brought it back up on a tray, Garrick was sitting up in bed with a smirk on his face.

"I think that was supposed to be my job."

"I'll forgive you. You have plenty of time to make it up to me."

His smile faded a little and I wondered what I had said that made it disappear. But before I could let my mind wander too much, he linked his hand with mine and pulled me closer.

"I have some different ideas about how I can make it up to you."

"Yeah?" He nodded. "Well, considering that you passed out after we had sex, I think you should take it easy."

"You're no fun."

"If you're a good boy, maybe I'll get out my stethoscope later and we can play naughty doctor."

"I like the way you think," he grinned.

"Eat up."

"Oh, I plan to."

"The food. God, you have such a dirty mind."

He shrugged and dug into his eggs. "One look at you and my cock gets hard. I can't help that you do that to me. If you think about it, it's really your fault."

We ate in silence and then Knight put the tray on the nightstand and pulled me closer, snuggling down into the bed. His hand trailed down my back, sliding over my skin and leaving tingles behind.

"What's your real name?" I asked after it had been quiet for way too long.

"Hudson McGuire."

"And you don't have any family?"

"None worth mentioning."

"What's that like?"

"Not having family?"

"Yeah. I don't know what that's like. I mean, I have a big family that supports me and loves me. I can't imagine not having that."

He sighed and continued to run his fingers up and down my back. "In a way it's nice. You live your life the way you want and no one is there to be disappointed in you or give you grief for your choices. I couldn't imagine doing what I do if I had a mother who would be worrying about me. The downside is I don't have anyone worrying about me. I have no one to see at holidays. I usually spend them getting drunk or working. There's literally no one in this world that gives a shit about me."

That sounded so sad and lonely. "What happened to your mother?"

"She died a long time ago. I don't have a single memory of her. My dad said she was a great woman, and I really hope that I'm not disappointing her, but I guess I never really think about it too much. She's not here to give a shit, so I live my life the way I want."

"Where's your dad?"

"He died right after I went to basic."

"Do you worry about what he would think?"

"Not really. He was in the military. I like to think he would be proud of me, but maybe that's just wishful thinking. The rest of my family are distant relatives that never gave a crap about us anyway."

"So, you live by your own rules and no one holds you accountable."

"Pretty much."

"What about me?"

He pulled away slightly so he could look at me. "Kate, whatever we have is something special, but I told you, I can't give you more than this. My life isn't made for settling down and raising a family. You know enough about my history to know that's not even possible. I can give you this and I can come to you when I'm not working, but it'll never be more."

"How do you know? Have you ever tried to have more?"

"What would you have me do? Sit at home and watch the kids all day while you go out and earn the money? I sure as fuck can't get a regular job. I go by a different name now, but that doesn't mean it would stand up to scrutiny. I have to be careful that I don't get my ass thrown in jail because if someone looks too closely at me, they would know I'm not Garrick Knight in any way other than name."

"So, you have to be careful so you don't get caught and you can go out and murder more people, but you can't be careful so that you can try for something with me?"

"Are you telling me you would seriously want that? Say we did it —stayed together and had kids someday. You realize that I could never marry you, right? What would you tell our kids? Would you tell them I'm a good person they could look up to?" He seemed to be getting angrier by the second and I wondered if he was upset because he knew he wasn't a good person or because he was pissed at me for even suggesting it. "What would you say about why we never got married? Would you trust that none of the people from my past would come looking for me and possibly take our kids to get to me? Because even I'm not sure about that."

Everything he was saying was so overwhelming, but even with all the information being crammed into my brain, I could see the logic in what he was saying. He was absolutely right about all of it. That wasn't the kind of life I wanted to live, but at the same time, I didn't want to let him go either, which was strange considering I barely knew the man, and what I did know didn't paint a pretty picture.

"You're right. I don't know why I even brought it up. We barely know each other. We live totally different lives. It would never work anyway."

He lifted my chin, forcing me to look at him. "We may not have a conventional relationship, but we could have something really fucking good. You just have to decide if that's what you want."

It was the same every time he looked at me. His black eyes held me captive and promised pain if I crossed him and immeasurable pleasure if I allowed it.

"So, what exactly would this unconventional relationship look like?"

"Well, I'm grounded for a few weeks while I heal up and then I'll get back to work. When I have a few days off, I'll come visit and we'll spend as much time together as possible while we can. I'm not saying it'll be perfect, but while I'm here, you'll have all of me, everything I can give you."

"And what about when you're not with me?"

"I'll be working."

"But, will there be other women?"

He blew out a harsh breath and looked away from me. "I'm not going to lie to you, there have been times that I've used women to get information I need. I've never wanted any of them, though. They were just sources for me. But I'll always be honest with you."

I sat up, suddenly pissed as hell. "Are you telling me you might fuck other women in the future to get the information you need? And I'm supposed to be okay with that?"

"Hey, this is my life. I do what I have to, not only to keep myself safe, but to get the job done. If I don't come through on a job, I end up with my ass on the line. And if these people are willing to pay for someone to be killed, they're willing to have me killed for not completing a job."

"I thought you said you were taking out rapists and drug dealers. Those are small-time jobs, right? Why would someone pay to have you killed?"

"Those are some of the jobs I do, but I have plenty of bigger ones, and most of them come from people who are just as evil as the ones I'm taking out."

"Then why do you do it? You're just taking out the garbage for someone else."

"It's one less piece of garbage to pollute the earth. And occasionally, I get to take out the big fish, too. But it takes lots of planning and time, something I don't always have. Besides, I work alone and the really bad people usually have an army protecting them. It's not like I can just slip in and take them out. But every time I get closer to these assholes, I make notes and plan for the time that I can get in and take them out."

"Your world is very complicated."

"It is. Is that something you can deal with?"

"I need to think about it."

Knight and I spent the rest of the day lounging around the house. I needed to get out, though, and have some time to myself, so I ran to the grocery store and picked up some food for the week. I was so confused by everything Garrick had told me, but deep down, I knew this would never work for me. How could I pass up a normal life with a family for someone who would only be around occasionally and couldn't fully give himself to me? Still, I had him for a few weeks more and I was determined to enjoy what little time I had left until he left me again for some other mission.

"WHAT DO YOU THINK YOU'RE DOING?" I ASKED GARRICK AS HE PULLED on a black leather jacket. "Where did you get those clothes?"

He was wearing all black as usual, but instead of a black T-shirt, he was wearing a black button-up. Probably because it was easier to get on. I don't know how the hell he got the jacket on, but he did, and he looked mouthwatering.

"I picked them up the other day."

"And why are you getting a jacket on?"

"Because I'm going with you to work."

"No, you're not. You can't follow me around all day."

"I think we both know that's not true. I've been doing it for months now."

"Fine. Do whatever you want, but you are not stepping foot in my clinic. You'd scare the shit out of anyone who went in there."

He stepped into my space and quickly grabbed me around the waist, hauling me against him. "Do I scare you?"

"Sometimes," I breathed out.

"Do you believe me when I said I'd never do anything to hurt you?"

I wanted to believe him more than anything, especially after our talk the other night. But he was an assassin by trade. It would be ridiculous to believe that he didn't have it in him to hurt me. When I didn't answer him right away, his eyes turned hard and he took a step back from me.

"Maybe you should be afraid," he said gruffly, then turned and walked out the door. What the hell did that mean? I followed where he had gone, but he wasn't there. I looked around outside, but I couldn't find him. I didn't have time for this. I had to get to work.

I was a little later than I liked, but I was mostly caught up on my work, so I tried not to let it bother me. I was just about to open the clinic doors when I saw Sean walking up. He wasn't one of my patients, which meant he was here in an official capacity. I broke out in a sweat at the thought of lying to him. He was probably wondering why Garrick was staying with me. I was sure Cole told him all about that. Except Sean was a detective and he would haul Garrick down to the police station if he showed his face. And if Garrick was serious about following me today, there would be no way he would stay away. I was going to have to have Sean follow me to my office so that hopefully Garrick wouldn't see him.

"Hey, Kate," Sean smiled as he entered the clinic.

"Hey, Sean." I gave a nervous smile and tried not to fidget, but I was a nervous wreck.

"Just thought I'd come check up on you. It's been a while since you were attacked. I thought I'd see if you were having any more trouble."

"Um, why don't we go back to my office? We're just about to open for the day."

"Sure."

He followed me back to my office and I prayed that Garrick hadn't seen him. Things could get ugly. I shut the door behind him and took a seat at my desk, hoping that having something between us would calm me down.

"So, have you had any more problems lately?"

"Nope. I think that must have been a one-time incident."

"Or the person who shot him is scaring people off. Have you seen anyone suspicious around lately?"

He was being friendly enough, but I had known Sean for years and he was in investigative mode right now. And he was intimidating as hell as he looked at me. I felt like he could see right through me, and to top it off, he probably already knew about Garrick. That could only mean that he was grilling me to see how far I would go to protect Garrick.

"Nobody suspicious. Like I said, there hasn't been anything unusual going on."

He grinned at me, which made the hairs stand on the back of my neck. Not because I was afraid of him, but because I knew he was ready to go in for the kill.

"That's good because if someone were to be hanging around and taking people out when he felt you were being threatened, that would be a serious problem for you."

"I didn't ask anyone to do anything," I said, swallowing hard.

"But if you knew who it was and you were protecting them, that would be aiding and abetting. Now, for murder, that's a pretty hefty sentence you would face. You would lose your clinic, your medical license, and your reputation would be shot."

My mind raced as I tried to think about what exactly Garrick said to me that night. Did he admit to killing the druggie? I didn't think so. He had alluded that he had done something about it, but he had never actually said the words.

"I don't know who shot that man. I didn't see it and it's not like anyone admitted to me they did it. I don't see how I could be implicated in anything."

Sean took a seat across from me and stared at me, waiting for me to say something.

"Sean, I've known you for a long time. Why don't you just say whatever it is you're here to say?"

"No bullshit. I can do that. I know you have a killer in your house. What I can't seem to get my head around is that you know exactly who he is and yet you aren't doing a damn thing to make him leave. From what I understand, you made Cole leave and insisted you could deal with it yourself. So, why don't you tell me what the hell is going on? This isn't like you, Kate."

"The man that's staying with me is injured. I'm helping him get better. End of story."

"That man is an assassin. He could—"

"Kill me?" I interjected. "Believe me, I've heard it all from Cole already. Did Cole tell you that he talked to Sebastian and that Sebastian put someone outside my house?"

"Do you really think that's good enough?"

"I don't feel threatened in any way."

The door swung open and banged against the wall. Garrick stood in the doorway with a scowl on his face, glaring at Sean. I stood quickly, hoping I could deflect the situation before it got out of control.

"This is my friend, Sean," I said, motioning to where Sean sat. To his credit, Sean sat lazily in his chair as if he didn't have a care in the world, but I could see how his hand inched closer to the weapon at his side.

So did Garrick.

He pulled a gun quickly from behind his back and pointed it at Sean. Kathy stood behind him, looking absolutely terrified. I gave her a quick shake of my head, hoping that she didn't decide to call the police. Luckily, she turned and headed back toward reception. I could hear her greeting patients up front.

"I wouldn't do that if I were you."

"I would point that somewhere else unless you want to go down for shooting a cop. I can guarantee if you shoot me, you'll have Cole, Sebastian, and the rest of Reed Security on your ass, not to mention the entire police force. I would imagine that would be pretty bad for business and probably not too good for you, *Hudson*."

"I don't want to shoot you. I just want you to back the fuck away from my woman."

Shit. Why did he have to say that? Sean turned to me, a slow grin spreading across his face.

"Your woman, huh?"

"Sean, it's not what you think."

"I would say that since I've been fucking you and sleeping in your bed for the past few nights, it's exactly what he thinks."

My face flushed bright red as Sean raised an eyebrow at me. "Never took you to sleep with a murderer."

"It's complicated," I said, clearing my throat.

"I'll bet." He slapped his hands on the armrests as he stood. "Either way, I just came to make sure you were okay. Cole is worried about you and wanted someone else to check on you."

"You're not going to say anything, are you?" I asked nervously.

"As much as I'd love to get this asshole off the streets, Cole asked me not to cause any trouble for you, and I have no fucking clue how I would explain your fucked up situation to my boss. As far as I'm concerned, he's an old boyfriend who showed up and I didn't catch his name." He turned to Garrick, who had lowered his weapon, but still had it at his side. "Don't bring your shit here. Whatever you do outside here stays outside or we're going to have problems."

Garrick nodded and stepped aside so Sean could pass. I heard him say hi to a few people in reception before I stepped around Garrick and quickly shut the door.

"What do you think you're doing? You can't pull a gun in my clinic!"

"I needed to make sure you were okay."

"How do you not see how messed up this is? You came into my place of business and threatened a cop. And not just any cop, a friend of mine."

"Didn't sound like he was being too friendly to me."

"He was concerned, and given what happened, I'm wondering why the hell I stood up for you. Just get out of here. I have work to do, and I can't do it if you're in here scaring my staff and patients."

When he didn't move, I pointed for the door. "I'm serious. Leave now. I don't want you here."

His dark eyes narrowed in on me and for a moment, I saw a flash of the killer inside. I had pissed him off big time by ordering him out, but I couldn't let him dictate what happened in my life. He slowly moved to the door and opened it, pausing and glancing over his shoulder. I could feel the anger radiating off him, but luckily, he kept moving. He left through the back door, which I was grateful for. Knowing how mad he was, I didn't want him around anyone in the building.

Kathy came hurrying into my office with a look of panic on her face. "I'm so sorry. I couldn't stop him from coming back and I didn't want to cause a scene. He was really scary. Who was he?"

"He's a friend of mine. Sort of." Her eyes widened in disbelief, but she didn't say anything. "I'm sorry he came in here. It won't happen again."

"Okay. If he does, should I let him back here?"

"I really don't think he will, but if he does, it's better to just let him in. Don't worry. He won't hurt me."

"What about everyone else?" she muttered, then slapped her hand over her mouth. "Sorry, it just came out. He just looks really dangerous."

I gave her my best reassuring smile. "Look, let's just get back to work. We're running behind now."

She nodded and quickly went back up to reception while I did my best to pull myself back together.

I GROANED AS I STEPPED OUT OF MY SHOES AND FLUNG MY KEYS ON THE counter. It had been an exhausting day and I was dead on my feet. Opening the fridge, I pulled out the white wine and poured myself a glass. I might just drink the whole bottle tonight. Walking into the living room, I wasn't shocked at all to see Garrick sitting in the dark in the corner armchair. What did surprise me was the gun resting on his knee.

"Planning a murder?" I asked as I lowered myself onto the couch.

"Just being prepared. It seems that people are running their mouths about me. Too many people know who I am and that's dangerous for me."

"Sean and Cole wouldn't say anything. If Sebastian vouches for you, that's good enough for them."

He huffed out a laugh. "Sure. I'll take your word for it."

"You don't have to take my word for it. If you don't believe me, call Sebastian. He'll tell you the same thing."

"Maybe you don't get it. I'm not friends with Sebastian. We did one job together. His word means jack shit to me."

"He saved your life."

"No, you saved my life. He brought you in, but that's as far as our brotherhood goes. Don't get any ideas that I'm going to work for him and everything will be great."

His voice was as hard as steel and I had to remind myself who I was dealing with.

"I wasn't suggesting you would."

"Well, now that my secret is out, it's time to move on."

"What?" I said, a little panicked. "I thought you were staying until you were healed?"

"Well, that plan's blown to shit now. I can't stick around with everyone watching me. It's bad for business and gives me the hives."

I stood and swallowed down the rest of my wine. "Well, I wouldn't want to stand in the way of your murdering, so by all means, please show yourself out."

I walked out of the room and headed for the stairs. I'd had enough of this day and a bubble bath sounded really good right now. Before I could hit the bottom step, Garrick grabbed my wrist and spun me around, pinning me to the wall.

"I'm not through with you. Just because I'm leaving doesn't mean this is over. I told you that you were mine if you let me in. You handed yourself over to me and now you belong to me. I'll kill any other man who tries to touch you."

"Is that supposed to make me swoon?" I snapped. "What a beautiful thing to say. It makes my poor, little heart go pitter-pat to hear such heartfelt words."

"I'm not fucking around, Kate. I meant what I said, and I'll know if you so much as say hi to another man." His grip tightened on my waist painfully and I swallowed down the fear I felt when he got this intense.

"I'm just supposed to wait around for you to come back? I don't work that way, Garrick. If you want me, you stick around. Otherwise, disappear and let me live my life."

"You might mean that now, but when you start getting lonely, it's going to be my cock you're thinking of."

He ground his hips against mine, eliciting a moan from me that I tried to hold back. His lips left a trail of kisses down my neck that had me thirsting for more. He was right. I craved his touch. It was only him I wanted, and no other man would ever make me feel a tenth of what I felt when I was with him. I hated that he had this power over me. I pushed him away and stared him down.

"I meant what I said. If you walk out that door, don't bother returning. You won't be welcome."

He clenched his jaw tight and turned, storming out the door and leaving me feeling completely rejected. I knew this was for the best. It would have never worked out, but I couldn't help the sadness that weighed heavy in my chest as I looked around my empty house.

I DON'T KNOW WHY, BUT PART OF ME EXPECTED HIM TO SHOW UP THE NEXT night or the night after that, but he never did. I kept looking outside my clinic for him, even though I couldn't feel him. I always knew when he was around and there hadn't been any sign of him for weeks. My nights grew lonelier and lonelier, and most nights, I just stared at the wall, wondering how I could be so devastated over a man I knew for only a short time. He had done something to me, though. I couldn't deny that what I felt for him was strong, and more than I had ever felt for anyone else.

After about a month, I fell back into my normal routine at the clinic. I had been moping around for too long and Kathy pulled me aside one day and asked if I was alright, that I hadn't been myself lately. That was the turning point for me. I couldn't allow my feelings for Garrick to rule my life. I was stronger than that and I needed to pull it together. But that all changed the day that Cole and Alex stopped by.

Cole claimed he wanted to check over the house, something he did for me because he didn't want me paying for a maintenance man when he could do small fixes. He went about checking out things while I sat at the kitchen table with Alex.

"So, what reason did Cole give you for coming over here today?" I asked.

She raised an eyebrow at me. "Like you don't already know? He wants to check on you. He said you haven't been the same recently and he was worried about you."

"Cole is always worried about everyone."

"Tell me about it. Don't get me wrong, I'm very grateful to him. He has helped me through some of the hardest times of my life, but he always wants to make everything better."

"Well, there's not much he can do to make this better for me."

"Cole hasn't told me much. He said you were involved with someone and he didn't think he was good for you."

"That about sums it up. Let's just say that this man is not necessarily a good man. I mean, he does bad things, but I think he does them for the right reasons. Does that make sense?"

"Sure."

"It doesn't matter anyway. He's gone now."

"Did you love him?"

"Can you really love someone you've only known for a short time?"

"I don't know. Cole and I had an instant attraction and I fell in love with him pretty fast. Of course, then I forgot him for a while, but when I remembered, all those feelings returned. He would do anything for me and he protects me the way no one else has. I'm not ashamed to admit that I need someone like that in my life."

"This guy takes protection to the extreme. He doesn't have any boundaries. He walked into my clinic and threatened Sean because he was in my office with me."

"He sounds intense."

"He's very intense. As much as I want him, I don't need that kind of drama in my life."

"So, why do you look so sad?"

I bit my lip, afraid to say the words out loud, but it was just us sitting here. "I miss him. As much as I don't agree with the way he lives his life and the things he does, I wish he was here with me. But he made it very clear that he could never be a full-time part of my life."

"Was he just planning to drop in when it was convenient for him?"

"Something like that."

"Well then, maybe you're better off. No matter how much you like someone, if they can't commit to you, how does that work?"

"I don't know, and the ridiculous part is that I was starting to not care. The past few weeks have been so lonely without him and I started thinking that maybe I could deal with only seeing him when he could come to me."

"I know I don't have any place to judge. I think we all live our lives the way we need to. That being said, I don't think that would be a very healthy relationship, but if it's what you want, then go for it. If he comes back and you decide you can live with that arrangement, then tell him. Don't waste time worrying about what other people think. Only you know what you can live with."

After they left, I really thought about what I had with Garrick and the truth was, we hadn't spent enough time together to really know what there was between us. I couldn't base the rest of my life on the promises of someone who would only be dropping into my life between jobs. And worse than that, would I even know if he wasn't coming back to me? What if he was killed doing a job? There would be no one to notify me he was gone. I couldn't deal with that, and if he ever came back, that's exactly what I would tell him. I hoped.

8

KNIGHT

I'D TAKEN Kate's advice and gone on a little vacation. She was right. It had been way too long since I just enjoyed myself, and since I was out of commission for a while, now seemed like a good time. The problem was, I hated it. When Kate mentioned vacation, I had this picture in my mind of going with her. We would lie on the beach, her in a skimpy bikini that showed off her beautiful breasts. Instead, I was on a beach all by myself with sexy women who didn't do a thing for me.

I ended up staying in my room more times than not because I was tired of random women hitting on me. God, I was really pussy-whipped. I cleaned my weapons daily while I watched medical shows. It made me feel closer to Kate. But after two weeks of doing absolutely nothing, I just couldn't stand the boredom anymore. I still couldn't take any jobs. I would end up getting myself killed if I tried. My shoulder was really fucked up at the moment, and I knew I needed some physical therapy, but there was only one woman I trusted to get me on the right track. That woman didn't want to see me.

I promised myself I would stay away from Kate. She had made it clear that she didn't want me in her life, but I was serious when I told her that she was mine. I had stayed away for as long as I could, but I needed to see her again. Even if I couldn't go to her yet. First, I had to call Pappy and get the lay of the land.

"Let me guess, you want to know how Kate is?" he answered with an exhausted sigh.

"Fuck you. I asked you to keep an eye on her. Just give me an update."

"Nothing new. Just like every other day you ask. She's just going to work and coming home. She runs to the store and she buys a lot of wine, but other than that, nothing else is going on."

"What about men?"

"Other than her cousin? No one. Jesus, why don't you just go see her?"

"I can't. She doesn't want me around."

"Well, yeah, if you're going to act like an asshole and threaten her friends."

"I was watching out for her."

"She doesn't need you to watch out for her when she's around her friends. She was with a cop, who happens to be a good friend of Sebastian's. What did you think she needed protection from?"

"She's mine," I growled into the phone. "She doesn't need to be alone with anyone else."

"But you're not there. You ran away and now you're still trying to dictate what she does by having me monitor her. Which I'm not too happy about by the way."

"What if it was your woman?"

"I don't have a woman, but if I did, I sure as shit wouldn't let her string me up by the balls the way Kate has with you."

I rubbed my head. This conversation was starting to give me a headache. "Look, I'll be heading back soon and then you won't have to watch her."

"Are you going to stick around this time?"

"Until I'm healed up, but then I have to get back to work."

"Don't do that. You're fucking with her head. If you're not planning on sticking around, then just stay the fuck away from her. It's not fair to her."

I was silent as I considered what he was saying. I was a selfish prick for doing this to her, but I just couldn't stay away. Would I end up hurting her more by coming and going from her life?

"Look, you could fix all this by taking a job at Reed Security. I don't know how many times I have to say this, but Sebastian could fix things for you. He could make you disappear."

"I need more than to disappear. I've made too many enemies over the years."

"Then let's kill you off. We can make that happen and you can live your life with Kate."

I snorted into the phone, "I'm not giving up my life, especially for a woman that's so fucking repulsed by me. I do things the way I want and I don't give a shit if Kate likes it or not."

"You're never gonna get her to want you to stick around with that attitude."

"News flash, Pappy. She doesn't want me to stick around no matter what my attitude is."

"Then why are you going back?"

"Because I can't fucking stay away. I can't explain it, but I crave her and being away from her is the worst fucking feeling in the world."

"Man, you are fucking clueless. Random fucks don't make you crave them. Women worth sticking around for do. If you hate staying away from her, then chances are you're in this deeper than you realize."

"Pappy, I don't think you're getting it. She doesn't approve of my lifestyle. She fucking told me not to come back."

"But you're going back anyway." I could hear the frustration in his voice. "Grow some fucking balls and tell her what you're telling me. Otherwise, leave her the hell alone."

He hung up. I must have really pissed him off. Throwing my phone onto the bed, I decided to give it a little more time before I headed home. I needed to get my head on straight before I went back to see her and decide what I really wanted from her. When I saw her again, I needed to feel her out and see if she was serious about not wanting me back. If she still didn't want me around, then I had my answer. But if I went back and she still wanted me, there was no way I would ever let her go again. We were just going to have to come to some sort of compromise about our situation.

———

I SANK DOWN ONTO THE BED BESIDE HER AND RAN A HAND DOWN HER smooth skin. I had stayed away for a few more weeks, but I was done now. This past month had been torture without her. Seeing her sleeping so peacefully lifted the ache that had formed in my chest over the past several weeks. Just being here with her made me feel at peace.

Leaving kisses down her neck and across her breasts, I slid my hand down until I reached her panties. Even in her sleep, she spread her legs for me, giving me access to her hot center. I slipped a finger inside her and was pleased when she moaned for me.

"Garrick," she whispered.

"I'm right here."

"Oh, God. I missed you."

"I missed you, too. But I'm here now."

I pushed her shirt up and placed little kisses across her stomach as I pumped my finger deeper inside. I circled her clit, fingering her faster as she groaned and squeezed around my finger.

"Ah!" She screamed as she came on me and I grinned as she opened her eyes as a slow smile spread across her face. But then she sat up quickly and pulled the sheet up to cover herself. "What the hell?"

"Honey, I'm home."

"What are you doing in my room? Were you touching me?"

I shrugged. "You didn't seem to be complaining a minute ago."

"I was asleep."

"See? Even in your sleep, you want me."

"That's beside the point. You can't just sneak into my house at night and start fondling me."

"I already went over this with you. You're mine and that's not changing anytime soon." I crawled up toward her, covering her body with mine and nudged my erection against her. "I told you I wouldn't be able to stay away from you."

"And I told you that if you left, you shouldn't come back."

There was no heat behind her words, and when she wrapped her arms around my neck and pulled me closer, I knew I had her. I undid my jeans and shoved them down, then slid inside her, groaning at how good she felt. She wrapped her legs around my waist, pulling me flush with her body.

"You shouldn't have walked away."

I thrust in and kissed her lips. "I had to make sure it was safe."

"Just don't leave me. Not yet."

"I won't," I whispered against her lips.

I made slow, lazy love to her, kissing down her body and giving her everything I had. I wasn't sure if it was love or just infatuation, but I knew this woman was all I would ever need. When her body shuttered against mine, I let go and collapsed in her arms.

After a few minutes, I rolled off her and pulled her against my chest. Her fingers ran over my shoulder where the bullet had entered, fingering the scar that was forming.

"How's your shoulder doing?"

"Stiff. I need to start doing something, but I don't know what."

"I can set you up with a friend of mine. She does in-home consultations."

"Thank you," I said, kissing her cheek.

"Where have you been?"

"I took your advice and took a vacation."

Her head popped up and she smiled. "Really? Where'd you go?"

"Hawaii. I hated it."

She laughed and shook her head, setting it back on my shoulder. "Why does that not surprise me?"

"I kept imagining what it would be like if you were there and I was bored out of my mind."

"Did you at least relax?"

"Yes."

"I mean, did business get in the way?"

"Are you trying to ask me if I've killed anyone while I was away?" She flushed and shook her head. "Don't ask questions you don't want the answers to."

She sat up, taking the sheet with her, and scooted to the edge of the

KNIGHT

bed, swinging her legs over the side. I slid in behind her and wrapped my arm around her waist, whispering in her ear.

"I didn't kill anyone. This time. But that doesn't mean every time I go away it'll be the same. You need to realize that I won't be able to talk to you about some things, and there are definitely things you don't want to know."

"I don't know how to deal with that."

"How about we just stick with *don't ask, don't tell*?"

"Does the same apply to my situation?"

"What do you mean?"

She turned to face me. "I mean, do you want to know what I'm doing while you're away? I could meet someone for all you know."

I shrugged. "That's not a problem. Like I told you before, I'll know if you talk to another man."

"Are you seriously spying on me?"

"Not spying. Watching out for you. If I can't be here with you, I still need to know that you're safe."

"You could just stay here with me and make sure I'm safe yourself," she snapped. "Or is going off and killing people more important than me?"

I sighed. It was like we were on a merry-go-round. We just kept rehashing the same arguments over and over. "Kate, I'm not going to keep arguing with you about this. I have a job to do. It would be different if we had a different future, but the way things are—"

"I know. You can't offer me more. I've heard it all before."

She stood and walked to the bathroom, slamming the door. I ran a hand over my face. I didn't know how to fix this. I couldn't go back in time and change what I had done. If my current job was the only problem, I could fix that. But murdering my superiors? That would forever put a target on my back.

When she came back to bed, she was a little more calm, so I laid back against the pillows and pulled her into me. She was quiet for a little bit and I knew that she was trying to figure out if she could deal with my life. So, I stayed quiet and let her figure shit out. Eventually, she would come around to my way of thinking.

I woke when the sun started streaming in through the windows. I hadn't slept the whole night in a long time. Being back with Kate eased me into a comfort I rarely felt. I looked over at her to see her staring at me.

"Good morning."

"Morning."

"Did you sleep well?" I asked.

"Better than I have in a long time."

"Me too. Usually I'm always watching my back. I slept like a log last night, though."

"Good thing I don't have anyone trying to kill me. You would have been useless," she grinned.

"I'll always protect you," I said seriously. "No matter where I am, I will always be there to make sure you're safe. I won't ever let anyone hurt you."

"Garrick, I love that you're so protective of me, but you have to be realistic. No one is coming after me. I'm safe and I would prefer that you concentrate on not getting yourself killed when you're away."

"Okay, first of all, does that mean you've accepted things for the way they are?"

"For now. I missed you too much and I know that whatever's going on with us isn't done yet. It doesn't make any sense to me that I want you so much, but I'm willing to go with it for now."

"That brings me to my second point. It's true that no one's after you now, but my job is dangerous. There are always going to be people trying to get to me and they'll use whatever means they can to accomplish their goal. That makes you a target, too. I'll do whatever is necessary to keep you safe and out of my world, but I need you to know the risks going in."

"Don't you think this is something you should have told me before you slept with me?"

"Probably, but I'm selfish and I wanted you. I've never needed anything or anyone the way I need you. It makes me act irrationally."

"You mean like stalking me?" I nodded. "Or holding a gun to my cousin's head when he was just sitting at the table?"

"Fine, that may have been a tad over the top."

"And pulling a gun on Sean when he was sitting in my office?"

"In my defense, I don't know those people. For all I knew, they could have been dangerous."

"See, that's the problem. You see danger wherever you go, while the rest of us just see regular people."

"Did you know you have a pedophile living in your neighborhood?"

"What? Where?"

"Down the road from you. It was a charge from twenty years ago. From what I can tell, he's reformed himself, but people are never who they seem to be. It's public information that he lives down the street from you, but so few people actually look into that stuff. You have someone that could be a potential threat living down the road and you didn't even know it. Seeing danger everywhere I go keeps me and the people I care about alive."

"Who do you care about?" she asked quietly.

"You and Pappy are the only people I trust enough to care about what happens to them. Everyone else is just collateral damage to me."

"That's kind of sad, Garrick."

"That's my life. Take it or leave it. I can't afford to have anyone attached to me in any way that matters. Loving someone is dangerous for me and the only way I'll agree to let this continue is if you understand what you're getting yourself into and you agree that you won't be linked to me in any way. When I come to you, it'll be here and I'll come when no one will see me. We won't go out on dates or have anything that resembles a normal relationship. I'll always take care of you and I'll always care about you, but that's as far as it can go. That's all I can offer you."

She looked sad, but nodded and leaned forward, kissing me lightly. "I understand and I can deal with that for now. I have to admit, I didn't really think this could go further than it was, anyway. I mean, we have very different morals, and while I understand why you do things, I don't think it's something I could live with long-term."

I was relieved that she had accepted things the way they were. I would have fought for her no matter what she said, but this just made it easier.

"Good. Let's go get some breakfast. I'm starving."

"I don't think I have any food in the house. I'll have to run to the store."

"Then hurry up, wench." I smacked her ass as she got up from the bed and she yelped as she rubbed it and headed into the bathroom.

I was finally back to work after Kate arranged for me to meet with a physical therapist and got me back in shape. It took longer than I would have liked, but I was finally feeling like myself again. I had come directly to her after my last job and had only been here for twenty-four hours, but they had been an amazing twenty-four hours.

"Garrick, stop. I need to run to the store. I'm never going to get out of here if you keep doing that."

"Maybe that's my plan, to tie you up and have my way with you whenever I want."

I saw heat flash in her eyes and her nipples pebbled under her shirt. I pushed her into the bed and took her nipple in my mouth through her shirt. She moaned and threaded her fingers through my hair, thrusting her breasts further into my mouth. I yanked her panties aside and pushed my fingers inside her, fucking her hard as she writhed beneath me. She screamed for me over and over until I couldn't take it anymore. I flipped her onto her stomach and hauled her up to all fours.

I pushed my pants down and took my raging erection, pushing into her tight heat. My eyes rolled back in my head as she milked my cock. I slammed into her over and over, but it wasn't enough for either of us. She started pushing back against me until she was slamming her ass into me. My fingers dug into her hips as I held on like my life depended on it.

"Garrick," she moaned and it lit something inside me I couldn't control. I pushed her down on the bed until she was flat on her stomach and I laid my body on top of hers, thrusting hard into her. I licked her ear, biting her earlobe with every movement until I had her clenching me hard. With her squeezing my dick, it didn't take long for me to spill myself inside her.

My breath fanned against her as I laid on top of her and let my body relax into hers. I moved her sweaty hair from her neck to cool her down and licked the tiny rivulets from her neck, loving the taste of her salty skin. I left wet trails down her spine as I let my tongue taste every inch of her body. She sighed contentedly as I came to lie next to her. The side of her beautiful breasts peeked out from where she was lying and I couldn't help but let my gaze trail over her curves.

"Can I ask you something?" she asked sleepily.

"Sure."

"What do you think you would have done with your life if Hudson McGuire hadn't done what he did?"

"I probably would have gone into security or some kind of intelligence work."

"Do you ever wish things had turned out differently for you?"

"Sometimes, but I also know that I wouldn't have been able to live with myself if I had let those men continue with what they were doing. There's not much point in regretting things you can't change."

"But you said yourself that you could never have a normal life. Doesn't it make you sad to know you'll never have a family of your own?"

I didn't know if she was trying to feel me out or if she was genuinely curious, but I wasn't comfortable with the way this conversation was going. I didn't like to think about things I would miss out on with my life the way it was. Sure, it was lonely, and I knew that my time on this earth would always be limited because of my job, but I was good at it, and that gave me a sense of satisfaction that I wasn't sure I would get anywhere else.

"Who needs a family when I have a woman in my bed that gives me everything I could ever want?" I said, deflecting from her question. She could tell that I was avoiding the question, but she didn't try to push. She just gave me a kiss and stood from the bed.

"I need to get to the store before they close. Anything special you want?"

"I have everything I need right here."

"I won't be long."

She got dressed and I decided to take a shower. I was just stepping out when my phone chimed with an incoming text. I had an account where people could contact me for jobs they needed done and then the account forwarded the messages to my phone. I didn't like anyone contacting me directly. I scrolled through the text, taking note of the job and where I would be traveling. The time frame was short, meaning I would have to leave right away to plan for the job. I got dressed and pulled on my leather jacket, making my way downstairs. Kate was just walking in with bags of groceries and stopped, her smile slipping as she saw me dressed and ready to go.

"I have a job. The time frame is short, so I have to leave right away. I don't know how long I'll be gone."

"Oh, okay. Well, I guess be safe and call me when you get wherever you're going."

I shook my head as I walked over to her. "I won't ever call you when I'm out on a job. I'm sorry, but it won't ever be like that with us."

"So, I won't know that you're okay or when you'll be coming back?"

"It's safer that way."

She smiled slightly, but I could tell it was forced. "Go do your job and I'll be here when you get back."

I kissed her hard and then slipped out the door. I had work to do and I couldn't allow her to affect me that much if I wanted to keep a level head. It would be impossible, but my two lives had to stay separate if I had any hope of keeping her safe.

I LOOKED INTO THE TERRIFIED EYES OF THE MAN ON HIS KNEES IN FRONT OF me. He had already pissed himself and now he had snot dripping from his nose as he cried in front of me. He disgusted me. This asshole had stolen $100,000 from his boss, Richard Patterson, essentially bankrupting the business and leaving the family out on the streets for months after they couldn't pay their bills. When Patterson finally got his business up and running again and was able to get his family back in stable condition, he contacted me to take care of his former employee who had put his family in danger.

"I'm sorry," the man whimpered. "I didn't mean to hurt anyone. I was desperate. My kid needed treatments and I didn't have the money for it. I just did what I had to so that my family could survive."

I almost felt sorry for the man. After all, if it was my kid, I would do the same, but that didn't change the fact that this man had taken from someone else and put that family in danger.

"Your boss's family was out on the streets for months after you stole from him. You took everything from him to save your kid and now you're going to pay the price," I snarled.

"Please," he whispered. "I'll do anything. I'll repay him every cent. I swear. I just want to go home to my family."

Kate's face flashed in my mind and I could hear her reprimanding me for taking a life that could have been saved. Did this man really deserve to die for his crimes? Not really. The more I saw of this man, the more I knew he didn't deserve me coming after him. He could easily have been forced to repay the money to his former boss. But that wasn't a decision for me to make. I wasn't a peacekeeper, and it wasn't my place to interfere. I had already been paid for taking this man out and I couldn't back out now. As much as I didn't want to do this, I knew I didn't have a choice. I took no pleasure from this kill.

"How's your kid?"

"He's doing better. They say he has a good chance of surviving," the man whimpered.

"I'll make sure he's taken care of," I said as I drew my knife across his throat and watched the life drain from him. I forced myself to watch, knowing this was one kill that would haunt me for the rest of my life. As soon as I disposed of his body, I made sure to transfer half a million dollars into his wife's bank account. It wouldn't do jack shit to bring her husband back, but at least she wouldn't have to worry about money for a while.

I didn't go back to Kate right after that job. I felt tainted for the first time and I didn't want that to touch her pure soul. Instead, I went to a hotel and hid out for a week, drinking myself to sleep every night, ashamed that I hadn't done more research into that job before I took it. Every night, I heard Kate's voice in my head, begging me not to blacken my soul any further. Every morning, I woke up and vowed to try and be a better man for her.

9

KATE

"How long has it been this time?" Cole asked as he put in the new light fixture. Since I never knew when Garrick would be coming back, I asked Cole to come over and help me with a few things around the house.

"Three weeks."

"And you're okay with that?"

"I don't understand how it's any different than if he were in the military. When you served, you were gone for months at a time."

"Yeah, but I could contact my family. I could let you know when I was coming back. When was the last time you heard from Knight?"

"He doesn't ever contact me when he's working."

"So, he just comes and goes as he pleases?"

"It's not like that. He doesn't want me involved in that part of his life."

"It seems to me like he doesn't want you involved in any part of his life except to warm his bed."

"That's none of your business. What we have is between us, and I don't believe I asked for your input."

"Kate, when are you going to see that this guy is just using you? I get that you like him, but you have no clue what he's doing while he's not here. He could be fucking women all across the country and you wouldn't have a clue."

My cheeks heated and I ducked my head so he wouldn't see the anger and embarrassment building. It was true. I really didn't know for sure that I was the only one he was with, but I also didn't want to know. If he was sleeping with other women, it would kill me to know I had been so stupid. I didn't need Cole to tell me Garrick could be out screwing other women. It had crossed my mind several times, but it didn't make sense that he would be. He had stalked me for months and had been sleeping in my bed even longer. I just couldn't imagine him wanting someone else.

"You don't understand, Cole. It's different between us. I know I don't always know where he is or what he's doing, but when he's here it's so different from anything I've ever had. We have a connection and I just can't picture him screwing around on me."

"Kate, you're acting like such a girl right now, going, on about your connection. This isn't like you. You're usually more level-headed than this."

"So, it's okay for you and Alex to have a connection that no one else understands, but with me and Garrick it's bullshit?"

"Alex and I were different. We stayed together. She didn't run out on me to do something else."

"Right, your connection was so strong that when she had amnesia, she practically ran away from you."

He sighed and ran a hand over his face. "Look, we could go back and forth with this all day. I just want you to be careful. The guy is a killer and I don't like the idea of you spending time with him. It's not just your heart I'm worried about, Kate."

"He would never hurt me."

"You say that now, but what happens when you say or do something he doesn't like? Are you so sure he won't ever lose his temper with you?"

"It's not like he just goes around shooting people for no reason. He always has a purpose for who he kills."

"Yeah, and it's called money. Do you honestly think he knows anything about the people he takes out? He needs a job and he was trained by the military to be a killer, and that's what he became. Don't romanticize this into something else."

"Maybe you should just leave. I didn't ask you here so you could berate me and make me feel stupid. I understand you don't like him, and I'm not asking you to. But you could at least have enough respect for me to not treat me like I'm a complete idiot."

He gathered up his stuff and headed for the door, turning to me with a serious look. "Kate, I care about you. I just don't want to see you get hurt. And that includes having a broken heart."

He walked out the door and I replayed our conversation over and over, wondering if he was right. There was a lot I didn't know about Garrick, so why was I so sure that this would end any way other than in devastation?

I MOANED AS STRONG ARMS WRAPPED AROUND ME, PULLING ME INTO THE familiar body I had come to know so well over the past few months. His long fingers knew my body well and played me like a piano. I couldn't get enough of him, and every time I thought maybe he wouldn't be coming back to me, he appeared in my bed. Sometimes, he stayed for a few days, but sometimes we would go a few weeks before he had to go out again.

He always woke me the same way, slipping his fingers inside me and giving me pleasure I only knew with him. Sometimes, it seemed like he was making love to me, while other times he took me hard like he was trying to get out his anger and frustration on my body. I liked him any way he gave me, and I didn't care if he couldn't give me more than his body. For now, that was all I could handle. If I thought too hard about what he was doing while he was gone, I might decide to break things off.

After hours of fucking, I finally drifted off in his arms, happy he was back for however long he could give me. When I woke in the morning, he wasn't in bed and I got up to go in search of him. Every room I looked in was empty and it became pretty clear that he had already left. There wasn't any sign he had been here. I began to wonder if I had dreamed the whole thing, but the soreness between my legs said otherwise. I wouldn't sit around and pout all day. I needed to be happy with the time he had given me and go about my life. Our time together was limited, and I needed to remember that before I let my heart get too involved.

I went into work the next day in a terrible mood. I had been bored all day yesterday or possibly just disappointed. When Garrick snuck into my bed, I had fallen asleep thinking about spending the day with him. Instead, I ran errands and did laundry, something I needed to do, but it wasn't nearly as satisfying as having sex with him all over my house.

I did my best to focus at work, but I kept hearing Cole's words over and over in my head, that Garrick was using me when he needed someone to warm his bed. It screwed with my head all day and I went back and forth between being okay with our situation to feeling like I was being used. I was so angry by the end of the day that I decided to go grab a drink instead of working late. I needed the distraction so I didn't totally lose my head. I called my friend, Samantha, and was excited when she said she could meet me.

I ordered a martini, needing to take the edge off and waved to Samantha when I saw her at a table. I plopped myself down on the bar stool and sighed heavily. "I'm so glad you came out tonight."

"I'm glad you called. You work so many hours, I didn't think I would get to see you again until you took a vacation."

"I don't take vacations," I said as I looked at her questioningly.

"Exactly. So, what called for this emergency night out?"

"Ugh, I need some perspective."

"I'm all ears," she said, wiggling her ears at me. I laughed and took a drink of my martini.

"Okay, basically I've been sleeping with this guy and he's amazing in bed. Like, so amazing that I'd be willing to overlook a lot to be with him."

"Please don't tell me he's married." She shot me a pained look and I waved her off.

"Nothing like that," but then I stopped and thought how strange it was that being a cheater was unacceptable to me, but apparently, killing people was okay. "Anyway, he doesn't have the kind of job that allows him to commit to me, and I thought I was okay with that, but then Cole basically told me that he's using me."

"Do you feel like you're being used?"

"Well, I didn't because he always spent at least a few days with me, but then he came by the other night and he was gone in the morning. There was no note, but then he never leaves one. I don't know. I don't know if I'm just letting Cole's words get to me or if I'm just too stupid to see the situation for what it really is."

"Well, what do you mean that his job doesn't allow him to commit to you?"

Shit. I didn't know how to explain that. I couldn't say, *well he kills people and his enemies could find me if I spend too much time with him.* "He travels a lot and he isn't in town very often. He really likes me and he's fine with being with just me, but he doesn't want me to expect more."

She grimaced. "I think I'd have to agree with Cole. He basically got you to commit to a fuck buddy relationship and he dictates when you get together. It sounds like he gets what he wants and you have to be okay with it."

"I know how it sounds, but when we're together, I don't feel like he's using me. Believe me, I get how bad this all sounds and I don't have any delusions that this is going to be something more in the future."

"Kate, I can tell you how it looks to me, but only you can decide if you're okay with your arrangement. I'm an outsider and I can't tell you what you feel when you're with him. I would just warn you to be careful. As long as you keep in mind that this can never be more than it is, then you'll be fine."

"I guess I just wanted someone to tell me it was okay."

"You don't have to justify your relationship to me. I don't have a boyfriend so I have no room to judge. Do you know of any good-looking men who are looking for a good time?"

"Uh, yeah. I know a whole bunch of good-looking men and I'm pretty sure that all they want is a good time."

"Do tell," she said as she scooted to the end of her chair.

I gave her all the dirt I could on the hot men of Reed Security and promised to hook her up the next time we got together. We drank and laughed for over two hours until my bladder was demanding I empty it.

"I hate to ditch you, Kate, but I just spotted someone I'm going to take home tonight."

I looked around the bar and didn't even need her to point him out. He was a handsome guy sitting alone at the bar. Tall with short, dark hair and clean shaven. He wore a business suit with the tie loosened. No visible ring on his left hand and just the type of man she usually went for.

"Don't let me stand in your way."

"Are you okay to get home?"

"Yeah, I'm just going to use the bathroom and head out. Call me later and let me know how he was."

"Only if it's good," she said with a smirk as she sauntered over to the man, immediately grabbing his attention. It made me a little sad that I would never be able to go out to a bar with Garrick. We would never grab a drink or hang out with friends. I shook my head and made my way to the bathroom. As I washed my hands, I looked at myself in the mirror and decided that it didn't really matter what Cole thought of my relationship with Garrick. I was happy for now and I was going to enjoy it.

I opened the bathroom door and stepped back in shock when Garrick stood in front of me, both hands resting against the door frame blocking my way. He looked pissed and his eyes skimmed over my body like he was checking to make sure I was okay.

"What are you doing here?" I asked in shock.

"I'm back in town and imagine my surprise when you weren't at work or at home."

"I wasn't aware I had to tell you where I was going," I said angrily. Now that he was here, I was pissed he had the nerve to be upset that I wasn't waiting around for him.

"I never said you had to, but the least you could do is be a little more careful. You came out to drink and you didn't even have anyone to look out for you."

"Why would you assume I need someone to look out for me? I'm a grown woman."

"You've been drinking." His dark eyes bored into me and the anger in his features left me shaking just a little. I could tell he was upset with me, but I didn't have the slightest clue why. It wasn't like I was his wife or even his girlfriend. I was just somebody he fucked around with.

"Why don't you tell me what you're really upset about? Because last I checked, we don't have to tell each other what we do when the other one isn't around." His gaze darkened and his face turned rigid. "Were you afraid I was going to find someone to take home and fuck? Because that could be arranged."

He pushed me back into the bathroom and spun me around to shove me up against the door. "You won't be fucking anyone but me." He ran a hand down to my waist and gripped me tight. "I'm the only man that will ever be inside that pussy again."

"Why would I agree to that when you come and go as you please? Usually, I get a few days with you. Last time I got a few hours. Tell me why I should hold out for you when you don't seem to care about me except when you're inside me."

"You agreed to this. What the hell happened that all of a sudden you're pissed with me? This can't just be because I wasn't around in the morning." I didn't say anything as I held his gaze. I didn't want him to know that Cole's reaction had made me question why I was with him. "Just tell me that you don't want this anymore and I'll walk away," he said, pushing up against me and spreading my legs with his thigh. His mouth skimmed across my neck and down my shoulder.

"No you won't," I whispered.

"No, I wouldn't. I already told you there's no way I'm walking away. So, stop overthinking this."

He pulled back suddenly and grabbed my hand, dragging me through the door of the bathroom. We didn't head for the front door, though. He pulled me down a dark hallway to an exit at the back and tugged me into an alley. I could barely keep up as he dragged me further into the darkness.

"Why are we going this way? My car is out front."

"I told you I wouldn't let anyone see us together."

The cock of a gun shot through the night and Garrick pulled me in close to him. A man stepped out of the shadows, and that normally would have scared the crap out of me, but with Garrick beside me, the man didn't look anything more than a puny kid.

"Give me your wallet," he snarled.

"If I were you, I'd put down the gun," Garrick growled at the man.

"I don't think you're in the position to make demands."

I watched as the man stepped closer and I tugged on Garrick's sleeve. "Don't do it. Please, let's just leave."

"Shut your bitch up." The man's hand waved in the air as he yelled. He obviously wasn't as good with a gun as he thought.

One second, the man was talking and the next, he was on the ground in a bloody heap. He had a hole in the middle of his forehead where Garrick had shot him, and I hadn't even seen him pull his gun.

"Oh my, God. You shot him."

"Let's go." Garrick started to pull me away, but I couldn't move. I was still staring at the man who was just threatening us moments ago.

"I can't believe you did that," I said, my voice shaking. I knew there was nothing I could do to help the man, but my instincts told me to go to him.

"He threatened you," Garrick said as if that was the only reason necessary to take another person's life. My head snapped up to meet his gaze and I stared at him in shock.

"You didn't have to kill him. You know you could have stopped him easily without killing him."

"I may not have had to kill him, but I sure as hell wanted to. I won't let anyone threaten me, and I definitely won't allow anyone to call you a bitch."

I stared at him in amazement. "You killed him because he called me a name?"

He pulled me roughly against me and wrapped his hand around the back of my neck possessively. "I told you I wouldn't let anyone hurt you."

"But he wouldn't have." My voice rose as my adrenaline surged. I was close to hysterics. "Don't you see that there are other ways to deal with people than to kill them?"

"If he did that to us, he would have done it to someone else, and they wouldn't have been so lucky. Imagine if it was your friend Samantha out here. Do you think she would have been able to get away from him?"

When I didn't say anything, he stepped back. "That's what I thought. You may not like what I do, but you're safer for it. Someone has to be the one to take out the garbage."

He dragged me out of the alley as we heard sirens in the distance. My body was trembling and I was finding it difficult to walk in my high heels. I wanted to sit down and wait for the tremors to pass, but Garrick wouldn't slow down enough or let go of my hand. He took me through a maze of streets before we came out a few blocks away where we could see the police lights surrounding the alley. I was crying and I wasn't sure if it was because I had seen someone shot for the second time in my life or if it was just my body reacting. Garrick gave me a strange look I couldn't begin to decipher and shook his head slightly before pulling me further into the night.

After the first few minutes, I tried to block out what had happened and just let my mind go blank. I didn't want to keep seeing that man being shot in front of me or see his lifeless eyes staring back at me. It was just too much for me to deal with tonight. I didn't know how long we walked, but eventually, he pulled me across a street where a truck was waiting. I was a little shocked to see Hunter sitting in the driver's seat. How had he known to come get us?

"Back in town one night and you're already causing a mess," Hunter said as Garrick lifted me into the truck when he saw I wasn't able to do it on my own.

"Just make sure we weren't seen. I don't want any of this coming back on Kate."

"I've already got Becky on it, but she thinks you're good. She doesn't think there are any cameras in the area that would have caught you. Cap sent someone to get her car."

Their casual conversation pulled me out of the murkiness I was feeling and brought me back to reality.

"Wait. Please don't tell me you're okay with what he did?" I asked incredulously. I couldn't believe how nonchalant they were being about Garrick murdering someone.

"I could lie to you, but what's the point? Knight doesn't just pull a gun on random people. If he shot the guy, he had a reason."

"How can you say what he did was alright? He murdered a man. Right in front of me. He could have easily taken him down some other way, but he chose to kill him instead."

"You're right. He could have taken him down uninjured, but you were there."

"What the hell does that mean?"

"It means that men who pull guns on people are desperate and you can't trust their decision-making abilities. If Garrick had tried to disarm him, which he could have done easily, the guy could have had a happy trigger finger and accidentally shot you. Sometimes the risks aren't worth it."

I looked at Garrick, who was staring out the window. "So, if I wasn't there you would have just taken his gun away?"

"Most likely. But then again, if you weren't there, I wouldn't have been in that alley and it might have happened to someone else."

I sat back in my seat, a little stunned by this revelation. I hadn't really thought of anything other than the fact that Garrick could have done things differently. Garrick had thought about all the things that could have happened in about five seconds and made a decision. In hindsight, I never would have been able to judge the situation and all the outcomes, and then make the decision to end someone's life. Now, I wasn't so sure how I felt about what happened. A huge part of me didn't want to be okay with what Garrick had done because I knew that killing someone was wrong. But the other part of me understood that Garrick did what he thought he had to protect me. My confusion left me with a guilty feeling because I was starting to sway more toward Garrick's side than sticking with my own morals.

I HADN'T SEEN GARRICK IN OVER A MONTH. I WAS CRANKY AND IRRITABLE because I was getting horny. I needed some kind of signal to let him know I needed his touch. Not only that, but I was constantly worrying about him. I had no way to know if he was okay out there. What would happen if he was killed? Would his body be disposed of and nobody would ever know? Would Hunter have some way of knowing? And if so, would he tell me? I came to the conclusion over the past two weeks that I was starting to feel way more for Garrick than I should, given the circumstances. I desperately wanted him to fuck me, but I was really starting to miss just lying in bed with him or the feel of his arms wrapped around me when I made coffee in the morning.

I was in serious danger of becoming way too attached to him and I didn't know what to do about it. He had made it clear to me that this would never be more than it was and I understood why he put those limitations on us. I made a point over the past few weeks to focus on work and try to stop daydreaming about Garrick. When whatever we had was over, I still had a life to live, and I couldn't let my business suffer because I was falling for a killer.

"Kate, your next appointment is in room two," Kathy said as she picked up the ringing phone.

I gave her a little wave and headed back to room two. The chart was in the box hanging on the wall outside the door and I quickly scanned the notes, noting that Mr. Dick Cummings was here for a blood pressure check. Dick Cummings, what an unfortunate name.

"Mr. Cummings, it's nice to meet you. I'm Kate—" I paused as I looked up and saw my dark killer sitting on the table with a smirk on his face. I quickly shut the door behind me and walked over to him.

"Dr. Whittemore. I'm glad you could fit me in to your..." his eyes skimmed over my body, "tight schedule. I think I need you to check my blood pressure."

"Garrick, what are you doing here? I thought we couldn't be seen together outside of my house?"

"It's Dick Cummings and believe me, I fully intend to do just that. Like I said, I'm here for a blood pressure check. If we could proceed, I would appreciate it. I'm on a tight schedule and I only have time for a quick check before I have to get back to work."

My lips threatened to break out into a huge smile. I had never really seen a playful side to Garrick before. He was always so serious and dangerous that I walked back to the door and locked it, fully intending to take advantage of my man.

"I think the first thing we need to do, Mr. Cummings, is check to make sure you're getting proper blood flow to all your…assets. Why don't you stand up for me?" He did as I asked and I pulled the zipper down on his pants, noting the bulge growing beneath. "Drop your pants, Mr. Cummings."

He pushed down his pants and boxers and I gripped his erection tightly in my hand. His eyes flashed and his gaze darkened as he stared at me. I stroked him hard, feeling the tip of his erection moisten in my hand. A rumble rolled through his chest and he pushed me down to my knees. His playful side was gone, and back was scary Garrick that wet my panties with just one look.

"Suck," he hissed.

I took him in my mouth, keeping my eyes on him the whole time. He rocked his hips, pushing himself further into my mouth. I could feel wetness seeping into my panties, and I desperately wanted for him to touch me. I slid my fingers down and hiked up my skirt, rubbing my fingers over my clit. I moaned at the electricity running through my body and his eyes narrowed in on my hand. He pulled me up and laid me out on the table, pushing my skirt up around my hips.

"Do you need me to eat you?"

"Yes," I breathed heavily.

He grabbed my stethoscope from my white coat and put the eartips in his ears. He popped the buttons on my blouse and placed the diaphragm of the stethoscope on my chest over my heart. His gaze darkened as he slid a finger down into my panties and my heart went off like a rocket. Pulling my panties aside, he bent down and thrust his tongue inside my heat, lapping at my juices until my body was so out of control I thought I would break apart. The paper on the table under me was making so much noise from my writhing that I was sure that even if I wasn't making any noise, everyone would hear the paper and know what we were up to.

When I came, Garrick stood suddenly and shoved his cock into my pussy while I was still coming down from my orgasm. He kept the diaphragm pressed to my chest as he pumped harshly in and out of my body. I bit my fist to keep from screaming out, but the table gave us away as it screeched across the floor with every thrust until it slammed against the wall.

My heart was beating so wildly as I started to come that I was sure I was going to have a heart attack. It seemed to spur Garrick on to hear my heart going crazy because his face turned dark and lethal. He tore the stethoscope from his ears and flung it across the room as he gripped me by the hips and pulled my ass off the table, ramming his hips into me over and over until he crashed into me one last time and stilled inside me.

My hips were sore from his grip as I lowered my legs down, trying to touch my toes to the ground. Garrick was still pressed against me, and I was suddenly very aware of the time and other appointments that were waiting. I was ready to push him away when he leaned forward and pressed a kiss right over my heart, melting me instantly. If I was hoping to come out of this without a broken heart, I was well and truly fucked.

I avoided Garrick's gaze as I quickly stood and straightened my clothes. My skirt was wrinkled beyond belief and there was nothing I could do to make myself look presentable again for patients. I quickly looked in the mirror, seeing that my hair looked like a good case of bedhead. Shit, I was a mess. I needed a quick cleanup before I saw anyone else.

Checking to make sure Garrick was put back together, I hurried to the door and unlocked it, opening it to look into the hallway. Garrick stepped up behind me and pushed the door shut harshly, pressing me against the door. His breath trickled down my neck as he left kisses along the nape of my neck.

"I have to go out of town for a few days. I won't be long this time."

He spun me around and kissed me breathless, then pulled me back and opened the door. He was gone in a flash and I took a deep breath, steeling myself for whatever awaited me. Kathy walked back to me while a slight blush tinged her cheeks.

"You have that spare outfit in your office and I put a hairbrush and hair tie on your desk," she winked. "Your 4:00 cancelled, so you still have some time before your next appointment."

She turned and walked away, not saying another word the rest of the night about what happened or anything she heard. I finished my night and went home alone, anxious for the next few days to finish so I could see Garrick again.

10

KNIGHT

I HELD my gun in my hand as I opened the door, but dropped it to my side when I saw Pappy standing there. "Is there some reason you're showing up at my woman's house?"

"Funny, I thought you were out on a job, but then I saw on the footage you were here again."

I shrugged and stepped aside for him to enter. "It's really none of your fucking business."

"You made it my business when you asked me to watch out for her. You're lucky I recognized the way you moved when you showed up at her house in the middle of the night. I could have blown your fucking head off."

"Not likely. Remember who you're dealing with."

"Yeah, the almighty Garrick Knight. Just don't forget who saved your ass."

"Believe me, I haven't forgotten. So, what are you doing here?"

"Just came to check in. Since you're back, I figured I'd better find out if it was for good or just a quick fuck."

I didn't like anyone referring to Kate as a quick fuck, and if it weren't for the fact that Pappy was already well aware of my obsession

111

with Kate, I might have knocked him out for it. "What I have with Kate isn't really any of your concern."

"It is when it starts showing up on our doorstep."

"What the hell are you talking about?"

He shoved a folder at me that I quickly flipped through, whipping my head up and narrowing my eyes. "What the fuck did you do?"

"I didn't do jack shit. You've been fucking the woman for months. Did you really think no one would notice?"

The folder was filled with information on Kate and pictures of her going to her clinic and coming home. There were also photos of her around town. In another section, there were pictures of me from when I was in the military and pages of information documenting my time while serving. There were also photos of me from the past few months. Pictures of me sneaking into Kate's house in the middle of the night. Someone had been following me and they had done a damn good job of making sure I didn't know they were there.

"No one could have gotten this information from just anywhere. There has to be a leak."

"Right," he snorted. "You just can't admit that you fucked up, can you?"

"I've been careful."

"Is that what you call showing up at her clinic and pointing a gun at a cop? How is that being careful?"

He was right. I had gotten sloppy because of my infatuation with Kate. Not being able to stay away from her had drawn more attention to both her and me.

"I don't get how they found me, though. I'm always careful that shit doesn't follow me when I leave a job. How did they track me?"

"I don't have a fucking clue, but someone knows who you really are and they know you're linked to Reed Security. And since you won't leave Kate alone, they know about her, too. So, what the hell are we going to do about this?"

Fuck, this was such a mess. I had to take care of this right away. If I didn't see this person coming, that meant someone good was on the job and it was going to take a lot of time to get to the bottom of this. I was going to have to draw the attention away from Kate. If I could get somewhere isolated, I could make my move and get all the information I needed.

"I'll take care of it. I'll have to go out of town for a while, so I'll need you to watch Kate again."

"Like I ever stopped."

"I'm serious, Pappy. You're the only one I trust to keep her safe. Don't let me down."

"Do you want me to take her somewhere else until this is sorted out?"

I shook my head as I looked around. "Let me talk to her about this first. I can't just drag her away from here without an explanation."

"You know, there's one thing you need to consider."

"What's that?"

"This may not be about who you are now."

"Why do you say that?"

"Look at all this information." He grabbed the folder from my hands and pointed to the page with my military record. "Only someone with a lot of pull would have this much intel on your military history. You have to consider that this is someone from your past tracking you. And if that's the case, what do they want with you?"

"Money to keep quiet?"

"I have no clue, but whoever it is, they know too much, and whatever they want, you have to find out before they come after Kate. Judging by these photos, you aren't the only one stalking her."

I threw the folder down on the table and walked to the window, staring out at the street and wondering where the hell this fucker was hiding. I hadn't seen a thing.

"Shit. I can't believe I didn't see this coming."

"As much as you'd like to believe otherwise, you're only human."

"I don't get involved with people for a reason. I ran into you, and suddenly I'm seeing your ass on a regular basis, and now I have a woman I can't get out of my head."

"You know, you could bring this to Sebastian. He would help you. Whoever this is knows you worked with us or they wouldn't have dropped this on our doorstep."

"No, I'm not bringing anyone else in on this."

"You may not have a choice. If they know about you, they might know about my part in your escape, and that puts everyone who helped you in danger, too."

Pappy had helped me at a time when I didn't think anyone would be on my side, and he probably shouldn't have been. But he was there for me and there was no way I would let this shit fall down on his head. He had already risked too much for me.

"Give me some time. If I can't figure this out, I'll let you know. For now, let's keep this low-key. If we go at this too hard, too fast, we could have a shit storm raining down on us."

"Fine, but just remember there are more people involved than just you. I don't want to see any more people caught up in this than necessary."

I nodded and walked him to the door. "I'll talk with Kate as soon as she gets back."

"Looks like now's your chance." He nodded toward Kate, who was getting out of her car. "Want me to stick around?"

"No. I have a feeling she's not going to be too happy with me when I tell her what's going on."

Pappy gave me a chin lift and headed for his truck, smiling at Kate as he left. I wanted to punch him for even looking at her, but I needed him to help me when I left. Kate walked in and gave me a kiss. I grabbed the bags and took them to the kitchen, unloading the food on the counter. I didn't want to say anything and burst the bubble we had been living in. While it wasn't the most ideal situation, Kate and I had come to have something I never thought we could have. I would kill to have more with her, but I had a feeling that after I told her this, she would want nothing to do with me.

"Kate, there's something we need to talk about."

Kate crossed her arms over her chest and leaned against the counter. "Let me guess, someone's after you."

When I looked up at her, seriousness written on my face, she paled a little. "Seriously? I didn't think…what happened?"

I handed her the folder and watched as she leafed through the pages. "Someone has been watching me. They know about you."

The anger on her face told me that she was not going to take this like I hoped, which would be for her to just let me handle this without getting her upset. With every flip of the page, her face hardened a little more. "Why would anyone care about me?"

"I already told you, Kate. Having you in my life is dangerous. I have to find out who sent this."

"Well, if you go away, won't they leave me alone?"

I tried not to take offense that she jumped to me leaving so quickly. I had kind of hoped that she would want me to fight for us. "If they've been watching me, they know I've been watching you for a while, which means they know you're important to me. I want to take you away from here for a little bit. At least until I can figure out what's going on."

She shook her head vigorously at me. "No. I am not giving up my life. When I agreed to this arrangement, you promised me you would protect me."

"It's not as simple as pretending this isn't happening. I don't know what these people want from me. It could be as simple as money or it could be a lot worse. I don't like that you would be here alone while I'm off figuring shit out."

"Well, while you figure it out, I'll be here going about my life. I didn't sign up for this. We talked about this and we agreed to keep me out of this side of your life." She threw the folder on the table and walked over to the fridge, grabbing a bottle of water.

"You're already involved. Whoever sent this has connected us."

"Garrick, I like you a lot and what we have is…amazing, but this is beyond all that. I won't give up what I worked years for so you can go off and play mercenary. I never wanted this part of you to be anywhere near me, and that hasn't changed because someone sent pictures of me. You go figure out what's going on, but I'm staying here and living my life."

I took a deep breath to calm myself. She didn't get how quickly this could turn bad. "I can't protect you if I'm not here."

"And how would I be safer if I was with you?"

"Are you comfortable with someone following you around? Because that's what has to happen if you stay here."

"And if I go with you, anywhere we go, people would see me with you. *A killer.* Tell me how that's safer for me."

I wasn't sure that it was, but I didn't want to leave her behind either. I wasn't ready to give her up just yet. Kate had shown me what it could be like to be with someone and truly care about them. Even though I knew this would come to an end someday, I really hoped I had more time with her.

"Kate, I'm just trying to do what I can to make sure this doesn't touch you."

"It already has. The minute someone put me in a file folder with you, I was involved. But I don't want to give up everything I worked my ass off for because you decided to stalk me."

That fucking hurt more than I wanted to admit. Here I was, getting all broken up about this shit coming down on us and how it could tear us apart, and she was already throwing my ass out the door. I normally didn't take shit from anyone, but this woman had me wrapped around her finger and I'd do anything she asked of me. Even if she did want me to walk away.

"You're right. You shouldn't have to give up anything for me. I'll get this sorted out and make sure nothing ever comes back on you."

"I would appreciate that."

"I'll let Pappy know to look out for you. That's non-negotiable. I won't be able to do this if I'm worrying about you."

"Fine."

The woman I had been infatuated with had turned to steel in front of me. She really didn't want me in her life, and I had to accept that I wasn't good for her, no matter how much I wanted her. I went to the front door and grabbed my black leather jacket and pulled it on.

"I promise, I'll make this right."

She nodded but didn't make any move to kiss me goodbye, and I took that as my cue to leave. Walking away from her, I knew I had fucked up in a major way, but I would make this right for her and make sure she would never have to worry about my actions touching her. I called Pappy within two minutes of leaving Kate's house.

"How did it go?"

"A kick to the balls would have hurt less. I'm going to get out of here and figure out who's behind this so she can live the life she deserves."

He didn't say anything for a minute and I checked to make sure the call hadn't dropped. "I don't get it. You're obsessed with her. Now you're walking away?"

"Pappy, you know my job is dangerous. I'm not some suburban house husband and my job is definitely not anything she needs in her life."

"Look, I know that I told you we should never see each other again after I helped you bust out, but I was wrong. It's been good to have you around again."

"I'm not the same man I was then. I can't just pretend that I haven't done all the shit I have the past couple of years. That'll only come back on me tenfold. If I stick around, she's just going to get dragged further into this shit storm. I need to make this right for her and the only way I know to do that is to walk away."

Pappy sighed into the phone. "If that's the way you want it, I won't try to stop you."

"Like you could. Just watch out for her. She's not exactly aware of the dangers around her. Or maybe she's just too stubborn."

"Yeah, I'll watch out for her. Do you want me to give her a message?"

"Nah. There's nothing that she wants to hear from me. She made it pretty clear that she would prefer I get out of her life."

"You have to give her time to adjust. This is all pretty new to her. She may still change her mind."

"Well, while she's thinking about it, I have work to do. I don't have the slightest fucking clue where to even start."

"Call me if you need anything. You know I'll help in any way I can."

"Just keep her safe so I don't have to worry about her."

"You know I will."

11

KATE

WHEN HE WALKED out the door, I almost broke down in tears. I didn't want to say goodbye to him and I didn't want to have to pretend like he didn't mean anything to me, but I had a decision to make and I chose myself. It was one thing to sacrifice for someone that I would have a future with. It was an entirely different thing to put my life on hold and risk everything for a man who told me he would never give up who he was for me.

Those photos of me had freaked me out. I had known for months that Garrick was watching me, and as scary as he was, it was nothing compared to the fear of knowing someone who wanted something from him was watching me. I knew I would have to be extra careful. With Garrick out looking for whoever this was, I wouldn't have him to watch my back. As much as I trusted Hunter, he wasn't Garrick.

I got back into my routine just as I had the last time he left. I was just as sad, but I forced myself to put on a happy face and pretend like my heart wasn't breaking. How could it be anyway? I liked to think I understood him, but that didn't mean I really knew him.

The weeks passed and I didn't hear anything from him, but I also didn't feel in danger in any way. I saw Hunter around from time to time, and he would call and check up on me, but that was the extent of it. Maybe he wasn't really watching me that closely after all.

I was closing up the clinic for the night when Cole came jogging up to me. "Hey, Kate. How's it going?"

"Good. I'm just done with work and I'm headed home."

"I don't suppose you want some company?"

"I take it Alex is having a girls' night?"

He smiled sheepishly and nodded. "Yeah. She left me on my own for dinner. I was just about to head down to the Mexican restaurant when I thought I'd stop in and see if you wanted to grab something to eat."

"Sure. I don't feel like cooking anyway."

While eating, I mentioned that my faucet was leaking and Cole insisted he could fix it for me. He followed me home and went to the kitchen sink, inspecting the leak that had developed.

"I just need to grab some tools out of my truck. I'll be right back."

While he got his tools, I grabbed a quick shower. When I came back down, Cole was finishing up and putting his tools away.

"Wow, that was fast."

"I told you it wasn't a big deal."

"So, what's Alex been up to lately?"

"Not much. She likes to stay home and take care of the house. I don't think she's really ready for more."

"It's been years. Maybe it would be good for her to get out more."

"I'm not pushing her. I know you're a doctor, but you didn't experience it the way I did. I saw every struggle she had to overcome. If she wants to hide out in the house for the rest of her life, there's no way I'm pushing her out of her comfort zone."

"And what if no one had pushed you?"

"I'd probably be rotting in my bed, but Alex isn't me. She's not refusing to get out of bed or do things around the house. She goes outside and does gardening, takes care of the house, and she's been taking cooking lessons online. To me, that's more than could be expected of most people that have been what she's been through."

"I'm not trying to push the issue, Cole, but she hasn't even been to a counselor. It might really help her to get past her issues and improve her quality of life. I'm just suggesting you take baby steps."

"I'll keep that in mind," he said, but I had a feeling he was just trying to get me to stop talking about Alex. "So, have you heard from Knight?"

"No." I tried not to sound disappointed as I answered. I didn't want Cole to know how upset I was by his absence. "He said he would be gone taking care of things. I don't know where he went and I don't care," I lied.

He raised an eyebrow at me. "Why do I not believe you? You really don't care that he just left?"

"Why would I? He brought his world colliding into mine and that's not something I'm okay with. He made his choice to live his life the way he does, and I made my choice to not be a part of it."

"Well, I think that's a good idea. It'll be good for you to move on with someone who can devote himself to you."

"Oh, come on, Cole. You never liked him and you didn't want me with him. Don't pretend like you're happy because you want me happy."

"You can't really think that—"

He stopped talking when his phone started beeping like crazy. He whipped it out and pressed something on his screen and his face went hard. When he looked at me, I knew something was wrong. Time moved in slow motion as he pushed to his feet and reached forward, yanking me from my chair and flinging me to the ground. I slid across the kitchen floor and slammed into the lower kitchen cabinets. Cole flew across the room as the windows shattered, spraying glass all around us. Cole covered my body with his, pushing me up against the cabinets. There was a loud popping sound and I heard Cole cursing, but I refused to look. My eyes were squeezed tight in terror.

"Kate. Kate!" I pried my eyes open to see Cole staring at me in urgency. "Here." He thrust a gun into my hands and I cringed at the heavy weight. "You get into that corner and hide behind the door. If anyone comes near you, point and shoot."

"Are you fucking kidding me?" I screeched. "I can't shoot someone."

"Kate, This isn't a joke. These people aren't here for tea and scones. If they come, you shoot to kill."

"Are you leaving me?"

"I have to take them out and clear a path to get us the fuck out of here. You stay low."

He was gone before I could beg him to stay. I couldn't believe he left me. I didn't know how to use a gun. Why would he assume I would have it in me to kill someone? The gun shook in my hands as I stared down at it, but I finally brought myself out of my daze and moved to the corner where he told me to hide, pulling the door open to hide me.

My legs started to go numb as I sat in silence. I heard the occasional pop and grunt and I flinched every time, but no one came for me. After what felt like an hour, I finally heard boots across the floor and was relieved that Cole had come back for me. Pushing open the door, I was stunned to see that it wasn't Cole standing in front of me. In fact, I had never seen this man before in my life. He had a thick, greying beard and his teeth were crooked and yellowing. I laughed in my head, thinking this man couldn't be more cliche if I had seen him in a slasher movie.

But then he advanced on me and my heart seized. He was just steps away when he pulled the knife from his pants, and that was the moment my brain came back online. Lifting the gun, I squeezed the trigger and jolted when the gun kicked back against my hand. I watched in horror as he flinched back as the bullet struck him and then continued toward me. Shaking my head in fear, I fired again, but it still didn't stop him. I scrambled to push myself further back, but I was already at the wall.

"It's going to take more than that to stop me," he grunted and swung his knife at me. I held up my arm to block it and screamed when it slashed into my arm. He pulled back the knife, swinging toward me again, but I raised the gun quickly and fired as he swung the knife, just barely missing as his body jerked and blood sprayed me. The shot rang out loudly in my mind as the man collapsed against me. Bile rose in my throat as his dead weight covered me. I couldn't move and I felt blood trickling over my body.

"Kate! Answer me!"

But I couldn't. As much as I wanted to, I couldn't make the words leave my mouth. The body was removed from me seconds later and Cole stared down at me along with Hunter. When had he gotten here?

"Where are you hurt? Is this your blood?" Hunter shoved Cole aside and knelt down beside me, running his hands over my body. When he saw that I was still clutching the gun, he gently removed it from my hands and handed it to Cole. "She's good. I don't see anything other than this cut on her arm. It's deep. We'll need to stitch it up, but I'm not seeing anything life-threatening."

I couldn't move. I couldn't speak. My chest was tight and it didn't feel like I was getting enough air, but there was nothing I could do about it. I just laid there as Hunter looked me over and Cole stared at me worriedly. I was in shock. I had seen it before with other people, but I had never experienced it myself.

"Kate, hang on. Just breathe."

His words were distant and muffled to me and when the darkness started to creep in, I didn't fight it. I didn't want to know what happened from here. I didn't want to think about what I had done. I just wanted to let go and forget any of this had ever happened.

"How are you feeling?"

"Terrible," I mumbled as I held my head. It felt like I had the worst hangover of my life, but then, when the memories came crashing back, I just felt numb. I sank back into the luxurious bed and closed my eyes, hoping I could go back to sleep and forget everything, but when I closed my eyes, all I saw were images of the man coming at me with the knife and the sound of my gun firing over and over again.

"Hey, you need to talk to me," Cole said as he sat on the side of the bed.

"I don't want to talk."

"Too bad. I can tell you're freaking out a little. You need to tell me what's going on in your head."

"What's going on in my head," I repeated. "Okay, here's what's going on in my head. I can see a man stalking toward me with a knife and I know that if I want to live, I have to kill him. I lift the gun that I held in my hands for the first time just a few minutes before, and I am forced to shoot the man. Only he doesn't stop. He just keeps running at me, ready to kill me, and I don't even know him. So, I shoot him again, but he still keeps coming and I have to stop his knife by holding up my arm and blocking his swing." I looked down at my arm to see a bandage covering the wound I knew I had underneath. "He lunges at me again and I have to shoot him for a third time. Not only do I kill him, but his bloody remains land on top of me, and I'm now covered in someone else's blood, and I'm not even in the ER."

I looked up at Cole with tears in my eyes. I felt totally numb inside, but that didn't stop my emotions from taking over and draining me. "I've never shot someone before, let alone held a gun. I don't even know how guns work, other than the one you handed to me. And all I keep thinking is that I'm supposed to be the one who saves lives, and I killed a man. I know that he was coming after me and I know that he would have killed me, but I wouldn't even be in this situation if it weren't for Knight. So, now I'm thinking that I want to be as far away from him and anyone that's going to help him because while I can handle a lot, I can't handle whatever happened in my house."

"I get that, but whatever's happening here, you can't just walk away. We have to get ahold of Knight and find out what brought this fight to your doorstep. We can only make a plan once we know more information."

"So, what happens in the meantime?"

"We keep you hidden. Hunter went out to grab some supplies and then we'll move on, find a new hiding spot."

"Wait, what about my clinic?"

"It was attacked. No one was there, but they didn't care. They were sending a message to you that they would get you no matter where you go."

I swallowed down the vomit threatening to rise. They wouldn't leave me alone until they got to me. What the hell had Knight gotten me into? I shook my head, trying to focus on what needed to happen.

"What do I even tell people—my patients and employees?"

"We'll fashion a good cover story to go with what happened. Sebastian has offered to pay your employees' wages until the clinic is up and running again."

"Why would he do that?"

"Because he feels responsible. He brought Knight into your life, and since you work for him, he takes it on as his personal responsibility to make sure you're okay."

"Well, that's very nice of him, but I can't just walk away from my clinic."

"It won't be forever, but we can't let you just walk around like this is no big deal. If they went after you at your clinic and your home, they're not going to stop until they get what they want."

I didn't want to think about it anymore. I would give anything to go back to sleep right now and pretend none of this ever happened, including Knight coming into my life.

"How's your arm feel?" Hunter was standing in the doorway, looking much more lethal than the last time I saw him.

"It hurts, but it's not too bad."

"I gave you some morphine so I could do the stitches without waking you up. It's probably wearing off now."

"That's fine. I'll just take Tylenol."

I started pulling at the wrapping, but Hunter rushed over and placed his hand over the gauze. "Whoa, what are you doing?"

"I just want to see how bad it is."

"We can look at it later. Right now, you need to get cleaned up and wash the blood off you."

I looked down and saw that my shirt had been removed and replaced with a much larger one. I could still see smears of dried blood on my arms and I could feel it on my skin in other places.

"I tried to clean you up a little, but Knight wouldn't like it if I spent too much time touching you in any way that he would see as intimate."

"Knight lost his rights to me a long time ago," I snapped.

"Look, I'm not going to get in the middle of whatever's going on between you two. If I think Knight wouldn't like me doing something, I'm not stupid enough to do it anyway just to piss him off."

"You were getting me cleaned up after people shot at me. I think he can adjust his scale on what's appropriate."

"Why don't you go take a shower," Cole interrupted. "We'll get some breakfast and head out."

"Where are we going?"

"Someplace no one will think to look for us," Hunter said cryptically.

STOPPING FOR BREAKFAST, I ORDERED A TON OF FOOD THAT WAS REALLY bad for me and I wouldn't normally get. But since I had seen my life flash before my eyes, I had decided I would order whatever the hell I wanted and eat as much as I wanted since I wasn't sure if this would be my last meal or not.

"What can I get for you?" The waitress, a young woman with teased hair and way too much makeup, asked as she popped her gum.

"I'll have the french toast with strawberries, the Denver omelet, bacon, sausage, hash browns, and orange juice. Oh, and a Belgian waffle."

Cole's jaw hung to the table as he heard all the food I just ordered. I shrugged him off and doctored up my coffee exactly how I liked it as the waitress took his and Hunter's orders.

"So, where is Alex since you're here with me?"

"I called her and told her to go stay with Sean and Lillian. I don't want her alone while we deal with this situation."

"And what exactly is this situation?"

"Still don't know," Hunter replied as he took a drink of his coffee. "I haven't heard from Hud for at least a week. The last time he called, all he said was that he was onto something big that could be a game changer."

"You should thank him for that wealth of information the next time you talk to him," I snarked.

"He doesn't give away anything until he's sure. He's always been that way."

"Yeah, well, this involves more than just him, and I would really like to know why someone is trying to kill me."

"Pull back the claws, kitty. We'll figure this out," Hunter replied.

"Sorry, but I'm not used to having people riddle my house with bullets or come at me with giant knives. You'll have to pardon my bad attitude."

"Look," Cole interrupted. "Let's just cool down and put together a plan. Once we know something, Hunter will contact Knight and get any intel we can. Kate's right, now that this has come to us, we need more information so we can be prepared."

We sat in silence while we waited for our food when something occurred to me. "Cole, have you been watching me?"

"What?"

"You were at my house with a gun. You never carry a gun, not since you got home from the war. In fact, you swore off ever holding a weapon again."

"That changed when Alex was attacked."

"Yeah, I know, but then you stopped carrying when all that stuff was over with. So, why did you decide to bring a gun to my house?"

Hunter and Cole exchanged a look that let me know all I needed.

"You've been in on this little security detail, haven't you?"

"Kate, I was just trying to protect you. Hunter couldn't watch you twenty-four/seven, and I needed to know that you were safe."

"Why didn't you tell me?"

"You didn't need to know that more people were watching you. It was better if you just went about your day like everything was normal."

"And what about Alex? Did you consider that by watching me, you could pull her into this?"

"Alex is safe," he said fiercely.

"That's what you think, but I've experienced how people get dragged into something they were never a part of."

"Playing the blame game isn't going to help anyone right now," Hunter said calmly. "We need to find out what's going on and make a plan. Anything else is pointless."

Our food arrived and I devoured all of it, needing the comfort of good food to get me through this disaster. I was stressed to the max and food always helped to calm me down. I had done my best to block out the images from yesterday, knowing that if I dwelled on it too much, I would send myself into a catatonic state. I couldn't afford that.

We finished breakfast and got back on the road. Hunter was driving and Cole sat up front with him, while I sat in the back seat. As the miles wore on, I found myself drifting off to sleep. The stress of the past twelve hours was proving too much for me to deal with. So, I let myself slip off to sleep where I could pretend this wasn't my life.

Hunter shook me awake when we arrived at a run-down motel that advertised color TV. Apparently, around here, that was the equivalent of other hotels offering a pool or cable. At this point, I didn't care. I wanted a hot shower and a warm bed. Neither of which I would have at this place. The shower looked like it hadn't been cleaned in years. There was soap scum all over the tub and shower walls. There was no way I was stepping foot in there. The bed had a cheap, floral bedspread that reminded me of something out of the eighties. When I pulled it back, the sheets were yellowing. There was no way I was lying down in that bed.

"No. I'm sorry, but I'm not staying here. I can tolerate a lot, but this place is a roach motel. There's no way I'm sleeping here."

"Don't be such a priss," Hunter reprimanded me.

"I'm not being a priss. I just draw the line at complete and utter filth. If I step in that shower, I'll probably get some kind of disease."

"Well, this is the only place to stop for the next fifty miles."

"I'd rather drive another two hundred miles than stay in this dump."

"Look, I get that this is all a little much for you and—"

The door swung inward, snapping sharply against the wall. A man stood in the doorway, gun drawn, and an evil smile on his face. A sharp crack tore through the air as Cole shoved me to the floor. I looked at Cole, who had his gun pointed at the man, who slowly sank to his knees and then fell to the floor. I tried to stand, but Cole placed his hand on my shoulder and shoved me back down. Hunter made his way to the door and peeked around the corner, then swung his gun out in front of him as he looked for any threats.

Cole hauled me up by my arm and dragged me into the bathroom, shoving me into the tub and placing a gun in my hands for the second time in just a day. I shook my head vigorously, but he just placed a finger over his mouth to shush me. Then he pulled the shower curtain and was gone.

I was terrified, so I took a few calming breaths and tried to slow my rapidly beating heart. Freaking out right now would not help. I tried to focus on other things, but the more I focused on other things, the more disgusted I became. Looking around the tub, I could see tiny hairs from whoever shaved in here last. There was also what appeared to be little pieces of dried vomit stuck to the tub. I looked up to avoid any more nasty discoveries and saw a giant spider hanging above me. It was getting closer and closer, and I really started to panic. I could see the tiny hairs on the body of the spider and almost threw up. I hated spiders more than anything else. I wasn't really scared of dying, but put a spider in front of me and I was sure my life was ending.

I scooted to the other end as the spider lowered itself to the floor of the tub and started crawling closer. Sweat broke out on my forehead and my palms got so damp that I was sure I would drop the gun. Flinging the shower curtain to the side, I leapt out of the tub and stared down the giant creature. I looked around, but other than toilet paper, there was nothing to kill it with, and there was no way I was getting that close to the spider. It could attack me. I looked at the gun in my hand and decided there was only one way to deal with this. Pointing the gun in the general direction of the spider, I fired, but I missed. I unloaded the entire magazine until I was sure there was no way the spider survived.

When I heard the door slam open behind me, I swung around, gun aimed, and started shooting, but there were no bullets left. That was a relief since Cole was standing in the doorway and I had almost shot him.

"What the hell? I heard gunfire."

I was momentarily stunned, but quickly recovered. "There was a spider," I said, pointing to the tub.

"What?"

"There was a spider!" I said hysterically. "It was trying to attack me."

"A spider. You unloaded your gun in close quarters to kill a spider," he said slowly.

"You didn't see the size of it. It would have killed me."

"Have you lost your fucking mind? Never mind. Don't answer that. Obviously, you have if you used all your bullets on a spider instead of saving them for someone who could actually kill you. Give me the gun. You're done."

I handed the gun over, but looked back at the tub to see if I had gotten it. I didn't see any spider remnants, which meant it had probably gotten away. Cole grabbed my arm and dragged me into the other room and out the door. I was shocked to see Knight standing and talking to Hunter, and there were at least seven bodies lying on the ground, all bleeding out. The doctor inside me wanted to go to them and check on them, but Cole continued to drag me to the truck.

"We have to leave. Let's get on the road before someone decides to call the police."

"In this dump? No one's going to call," Hunter said with a huff. "But we should move on before they have a chance to come at us again."

I couldn't take my eyes off Knight as Cole hoisted me up into the truck. He was watching me, but his eyes were dark and unforgiving. There wasn't an ounce of the man I used to see when I looked at him. All I saw was a killer. As Cole shut the door, I continued to watch Knight, but he didn't make any move to come to me or see if I was okay. It seemed it was way too easy for him to walk away from me. I wished I could say the same for myself.

We were back on the road minutes later and I looked behind us, seeing that another truck was following us.

"That's Knight. We're going to find someplace to hide out for a while and come up with a plan of attack," Hunter said as he stared out the window.

"Wouldn't I be safer if I wasn't in the middle of this?"

"No. You're safer if you're with us."

"How did he find us?"

"He has his ways."

"Why does everything have to be so cryptic? Why can't you just say what the fuck is going on?"

Cole turned around in his seat, his eyes fierce. "He's been tracking your phone. He dragged you into this mess and he's been doing everything possible to make sure you stay safe. When we got you out of the house and went on the road, he knew there was a problem and he came for you."

"What? Why would he come for me? He left. He chose his profession over me."

"He chose to find out what was going on so he could keep you safe. As much as I don't like the fucker, he would do anything to protect you," Cole said.

"He has a shitty way of showing it," I grumbled, watching the scenery fly by. I couldn't make up my mind and that really pissed me off. I didn't want to want Garrick the way I did, but I also couldn't stand the fact that he had walked away from me. I had pretty much told him to go, but that was only because I didn't want to be dragged into this mess he had created. I was scared and I pushed him away. I had already asked him to leave it all behind for me and he couldn't do it. Deep down, I wondered if he couldn't leave it behind or if he didn't want to. A man like him probably got some kind of thrill from the power he held when he took a life. I knew because I got a rush from saving a life.

We drove for hours, winding more and more through the mountains, coming upon what looked like a run-down hotel. We pulled into the parking garage and wound our way up about halfway. Hunter stepped out, and after looking around, opened the back door and helped me down. Looking around, I wondered where we were. The place looked completely abandoned and I wondered if there was even any place to sleep. Knight's truck pulled into the spot beside us and I couldn't help but look over to see if he was looking at me. He wasn't.

"What is this place?" I asked Hunter as we approached an elevator.

"A new base of operations. Sebastian bought it after Knight broke into Reed Security."

"I thought we were past all that shit?" Garrick said from behind us.

"This place is set up to run as a secondary location. It's not intended as a safe house, but it's the only one that isn't connected to Reed Security."

"I don't understand. If Sebastian bought it, how is it not connected to Reed Security?"

Hunter punched in a series of keys once the elevator opened and then went through a series of scans. "He didn't use his name."

The elevator doors opened and a bright, freshly painted interior lit the open space. It was very modern and very masculine.

"There are rooms upstairs, enough for everyone at Reed Security and a few guests. This floor is designed as an operations floor. Cap would probably kick my ass if he knew I allowed you in here, Knight."

"I'll send him a thank you card. Let's get to work. We have a lot of shit to sort out."

Garrick walked past me like I didn't even exist. How did this man go from stalking me to pretending like I didn't exist? I just didn't understand what was going on in his head. I followed Cole, Hunter, and Garrick back to a room that looked like a conference room. Garrick pulled out a folder and started spreading papers across the table.

"I've read up all I could on what happened after I took out the three men responsible for the deaths of all those soldiers. I'm guessing the government didn't want it known that I had escaped because they kept the whole thing pretty quiet. So, I went to see an old friend of mine who's still serving. According to him, everyone thinks I'm in Leavenworth. I don't know how the hell they did it, but according to the documents he gave me, I am currently residing at the United States Disciplinary Barracks in Leavenworth."

"That would mean a lot of people are being paid to keep your escape a secret," Cole said.

"Why would they go to all that trouble? Why wouldn't they want people out looking for you?" Hunter asked.

"That's what I want to know. What makes me so special that they wouldn't have had the whole fucking military out looking for me after I murdered those men? They were distinguished officers."

"Someone didn't want you talking. Maybe they figured if they

131

didn't chase you, you wouldn't tell anyone what was really going on out there. You'd go live your life, and you did," Hunter said.

"But in order for that to happen, whoever gave the order not to look for me already knew what was happening. They would be complicit in those soldier's deaths. We need to find out who was in charge of the investigation and sending me away. That's probably who's after me. I must have fallen on their radar and now they're worried," Garrick said.

"I'll get ahold of Cap. He can have Becky dig up anything we need," Hunter said as he pulled out his phone.

"No," Garrick cut him off. "I don't want to pull anyone else in on this. Especially Reed Security."

"Why? You know we can help. Hell, I'm already involved."

"This is my business. Reed Security doesn't deal with this kind of shit."

"I think you should call Sebastian," I said, turning to Hunter.

"No one asked your opinion," Garrick snarled.

"I have just as much right to say what we should do as anyone else. I didn't want to be involved in your shit, but you dragged me into it when you started stalking me. I shot a man today," I almost shouted. My voice sounded slightly hysterical, but based on everything that had happened, I was pretty sure a little hysteria was okay. "I held a gun for the first time and killed a man. That's not who I am. I don't live in your world. I shouldn't have to deal with men coming after me just because I'm unfortunate enough to know you. So, you do whatever the hell you have to do to make sure that I can get back to my life, and that includes letting other people help you."

His dark eyes narrowed in on me and I could feel the anger rolling off him. If I didn't know how infatuated with me he could be, I would swear he was seconds away from ripping my head off. Of course, maybe that had all changed since the last time I saw him.

"Fine. For now, we'll ask Becky for help, but let's keep things low-key. I don't want all of Reed Security getting involved until we know more."

"I'll call her now," Hunter said, walking from the room.

"I need to check in with Alex." Cole walked out of the room, shooting me a look that had me glaring at him. He was leaving me to clear the air with Garrick and I wasn't too happy about that.

"Let's get one thing clear right the fuck now. You don't have any say in my business, and if you ever try to dictate what I do again, you'll regret it."

"You dragged me into it when you started stalking me. I didn't ask for this."

"Just because I had an obsession with you doesn't give you free rein. If you get in my way, don't think I'll hesitate to remove you."

"You said you would never hurt me," I said, trying to hide the quiver in my voice. He stalked toward me, and suddenly, I didn't like the fact that I was alone in the room with him. Right now, he was downright terrifying.

"That was when you were mine. You made it very clear that you don't want me in any way. That means you no longer deserve anything from me. Including my protection."

I hadn't realized that he was backing me up until I hit the wall and it became clear I had nowhere to run. He raised his hand and placed it around my neck, squeezing just enough to scare me.

"Then why am I here?"

"Because Cole and Hunter brought you. Don't get any ideas that I'd be so stupid to involve you in anything in my life again."

He released me and walked out of the room. My knees shook as I realized I had taken too many liberties with a killer.

12

KNIGHT

"Is it done?" Cole asked.

"It's done. She doesn't have any illusions anymore that we could ever have something. I'm pretty sure she thinks I want to kill her now."

"Good. If it were a different time, you might have been perfect for her, but I'm not willing to take that chance right now with all this shit raining down on us."

I nodded, knowing he was right. I was the last thing Kate needed. When she told me she killed a man, I was shocked. Cole and Hunter had left out that little piece of information. I didn't want that for her. Kate was no killer and she would have only done it if her life was in serious danger. That made it even worse because I had told her she wasn't safe at the clinic because of druggies, but she was in way more danger now.

"I'm not sure that's true. I don't know that I was ever worthy of a woman like Kate. She's something special."

Cole looked at me assessingly and nodded. "She is, and she deserves someone who will fight for her. I see that in you. Hell, you stalked her. I'm not sure I'm okay with that, but I can see how much you love her. Like I said, if it was another time.."

"Whoa. I never said anything about love. I'm sorry to break it to you, but obsession and love are totally different things."

"Are they? Huh. Guess I was reading you all wrong."

He walked away, leaving me very confused. I couldn't tell if he wanted me with Kate and he was testing me, or if he was just trying to get a read on where I stood. Hunter found me a few minutes later while I was still trying to figure out what the hell Cole was getting at.

"Alright, I talked to Becky. She said she has to run everything past Cap. It's protocol, but she agreed to talk him into letting us handle things until we know more. She said that she should have something by morning. I say we get some shut-eye. This place is locked up tight."

"That's what you thought of the Reed Security building. Anything can be penetrated if you know what you're doing."

"Relax, man. No one even knows we own this building. I have alerts set to go off on all our phones if even a squirrel crosses the sensors."

"Still, I think I'll stay up and keep watch."

"You're just as stubborn as you were ten years ago." He sighed and headed back toward the conference room. "Wake me up in four hours. I'll take over watch."

I nodded even though he couldn't see me. I looked out the window, not seeing anything that even pointed to danger, but I couldn't let go of the feeling that if I dropped my guard for even a few hours, I would end up dead. I looked over my shoulder as I heard Kate's voice behind me. Cole and Hunter were guiding her to the elevator to take her upstairs.

I stared out the window and thought about what Cole had said. If it was a different time, maybe I could have something with Kate. But perhaps the reason I craved Kate so much was because she was the good to my evil. She balanced me out and made me feel like a little bit of my soul was still salvageable. I knew there was no redemption for someone like me. I was beyond any kind of salvation. I had killed so many men throughout the years that a woman like Kate shouldn't even want to be in the same room as me.

I still couldn't figure out what drew her to me. Was it the whole danger thing? She didn't seem like the type of woman that was attracted to danger. In fact, she pretty much seemed like she just wanted to live a calm, normal life. Something I could never give her. Cole had been right. I needed to keep her at a distance and make sure she never wanted to be with me again. I would only end up hurting her or getting her killed.

"Alright, Becky did some digging and she found the name of the officer pushing through your trial. His name is Daniel Marks. He was the commanding officer to Walters, Smith, and Jensen—the men Knight killed while in the military," Hunter said to all of us. Kate was upstairs, and we didn't think she needed to be in on this, no matter how much she insisted.

"Correction, Hudson killed." I looked at everyone, wanting them to keep it straight who they were talking about. Garrick and Hudson were two totally different men in my mind. "Just trying to keep it all straight for everyone."

"Right. So, anyway, Marks pushed for Hudson," Hunter paused for effect, "to receive the highest sentencing possible and it seems he also had some pull with the prosecutor, which is why no one ever wanted to hear your arguments."

"That doesn't matter. I deserved the sentence I got. Anyone else would have received the same. All this proves is that Marks wanted justice for his men," I said.

"And I would agree, but that's not all Becky found. She dug into the accounts of your superior officers and noted the amounts were the same in all accounts. They were never large sums, but they were deposited on the same dates with all three men and they were always for the same amount. Then, she looked into Marks' accounts and noticed he was receiving payments on the same dates, but for twice the amount. That means he was in on it and probably the mastermind."

"So, this is all him. He's the one that's coming after me. Revenge for screwing up his business."

"Not necessarily," Hunter said cryptically. "After the men died, he started receiving payments that were double what he had previously been receiving."

"What's odd about that? It makes sense if the men are dead, he receives their cut," Cole said.

"Right, but then he would have received all the money, but he wasn't. So, where is the last cut of the money going?"

"He had to have someone take over for the men that died. Whoever took over is his new ally," I deduced.

"Nope. Becky looked into them. They're all clean. If they're in on it, they're not getting paid."

Cole looked through the papers and ran a thumb along his lip. "Maybe Marks got tired of paying people off and decided to use threats instead."

"Becky looked into that also. If he has something on them, we're not seeing it," Hunter said. "So, what do you want to do from here, Garrick?"

I was silent as I considered my options. No matter what way I looked at it, we weren't going to get the answers we wanted unless we went to the source. "I need to get to Marks and find out what's going on."

"If you're caught, there's no way you'll get away this time," Hunter said.

"I know, but if I don't find out what's going on, nobody is safe. He's coming after me even though I've been gone for years now. He wants something from me and I need to know what. I need to do some recon and find out his habits. I'll make a plan and go with it."

"Do you want some help?"

I shook my head. "No, I'll handle this on my own. Why don't the two of you head back? I can't keep you here when you have other responsibilities."

"And what about Kate?" Cole asked.

"Kate stays with me," I answered before I had a chance to think about it.

"Do you think that's smart?" Cole asked. "She's not going to like staying away from her work while you handle your shit."

"The fact is that she's safest with me."

"I'm not sure that's true. You're the target," Cole grumbled.

"I'll stay behind and sort this out with you. Cap would have my ass if I left Kate alone with you."

"What? He still doesn't trust me?" I said with a smirk.

"Well, you did hold his pregnant wife hostage and try to destroy his company," Hunter said.

"There is that. I suppose a vase of flowers wouldn't go very far to smooth things over."

"Not unless you want them shoved up your ass."

"Cole, I need you to go back and find someone to take over running Kate's practice. Make sure that everything is running like a well-oiled machine. When this is over, I want Kate to still have a life to go back to. And keep Sean from asking too many questions. That guy could cause a lot of problems for me."

Cole huffed and shook his head. "You don't know Sean that well. I already asked him to back off you. He's not going to do anything to cause problems unless you bring shit into his town."

"I'll try and keep it out as much as possible. Don't want to piss off the local LEOs."

"I'll see what I can do, but you're going to have one pissed-off woman on your hands. I'm not entirely sure that leaving her with you is the best decision."

"Don't worry. I'm not going to hurt her. I swore to you that I would do everything possible to keep her safe, and I meant it."

Cole slapped me on the back and laughed. "I was more worried about you. Kate's not a violent person, but I think in your case, you might want to hide your weapons."

I COULDN'T HELP MYSELF. IT HAD BEEN TOO LONG SINCE I HAD WATCHED her and I couldn't stop the urges that flowed inside me. I couldn't have her anymore, but that didn't mean I couldn't pretend she was mine while I had her with me. I snuck into her room and sat down in the corner chair, watching her chest rise and fall as she slept. This was one of the things I loved to do, but she didn't know it. For months, I snuck into her house and sat in her room as she slept. It was a little creepy, I'll admit, but there was something about her that had me mesmerized.

I had pretty much blown any chance of ever keeping her in my life, and while I knew it was for the best, I couldn't help but wish things were different. She was the type of person who was genuinely good. She wanted to help others and believed that anyone could be given a second chance. I wanted that from her. I wanted her to look at me like I was worthy of redemption, but I knew it was too late for that. She knew too much about me and knew there was no going back.

There was still a lot I had to do before she would be safe, and chances were that she would witness some of my work. It would all be over after that. She would see me for the killer I was and she would decide that she truly needed to move on from me. I would have to watch from a distance as she found some schmuck to date and eventually marry. She would have kids and probably never think of me again, but at least she would be alive. If I had to give her up so she never had to worry about the dangers of my world, I would do it in a heartbeat. But I would always be watching and I would always have my gun handy in case whoever she chose got out of line.

She stirred in bed and I knew that was my cue to leave. I couldn't have her wake up to me in her bedroom. She would know that my earlier performance was bullshit and it would ruin everything. I snuck out of her room and glared at Hunter as he leaned against the opposite wall and grinned at me.

"Come on. We've got work to do."

"I CAN'T BELIEVE WE BROUGHT HER ALONG," HUNTER GRUMBLED FROM THE passenger seat. "You realize that if she gets caught, she would be an accomplice?"

"We won't get caught. We've been watching and I know what I'm doing. Believe it or not, I've done this before."

"Why couldn't I just stay back at the safe house?"

"Because we're driving hours from there. If something happened, we wouldn't be able to get to you to save that pretty, little neck," I told her with as much menace as possible.

"You could have let me go back with Cole. He would have protected me."

"You're my responsibility. Besides, I don't trust anyone but me to make sure you're safe."

It was true. I knew her cousin was well trained, but I would have seen the attack on her house coming a lot sooner, and she would have never had to pull the trigger. He kept her safe, but I could prevent her from ever doing anything like that again.

"That's so noble of you, considering you're the one that got me in this mess," she grumbled from the backseat.

"Alright, boys and girls. Here's the plan. Hud and I will go in and get our boy. There's minimal security at his house, so it should be easy in and easy out. Kate, you wait in the driver's seat for us to come out. If you see anything suspicious, you take off. Don't wait for us. We'll meet up with you back at the safe house."

"I can't believe I'm going along with this," Kate said.

"Do you want us to end this?" I snapped. "Sorry to burst your bubble on reality, but if you ever want to live a normal life again, this shit has to happen. And don't give me any more shit about how I dragged you into this. You didn't exactly push me away when I climbed into your bed."

I could see her turn beet red in the mirror and decided I had sufficiently embarrassed her enough that she would keep her mouth shut. I hated that I did that to her, but I had to concentrate. There was no room for fucking this up.

We pulled up to Marks' home a half hour later and parked on the street. Kate climbed into the driver's seat as Pappy and I made our way inside. It was easy enough to break in. Apparently, Marks thought he was untouchable because he had hardly any security. After clearing the rest of the house, we made our way up to his room. Pappy pulled out his syringe and covered Marks' mouth as he pushed the needle into his neck. Marks eyes went wide as he realized what was happening, and there was a moment when I thought he recognized me, but then his eyes rolled back in his head, and he was out like a light.

"Grab him and let's go," Pappy said.

I tried to lift him, but the man had put on weight from what his profile said. "Damn, this fucker's heavy."

"Let's go, Hud. We don't have all night."

I grunted as I tried to lift his dead weight, but it was useless. The man must have put on a hundred pounds. I flung his arm over my shoulder and lifted in a fireman's carry and my back about gave out. "Holy shit," I grunted. I could feel my face going red from the strain.

"Stop fucking around and let's move," Pappy jeered.

"You stop fucking around. Do you want to carry him?"

"I did my part. You're supposed to be the muscle."

"We didn't plan for a three hundred fifty-pound gorilla."

"You told me you could handle this alone," he mocked. "You said you did this shit all the time and it would be no problem."

"Shut the fuck up and help me before we get caught."

"Fine, give me his feet."

We shifted until we could carry the man down the stairs. Pappy went down first and Marks' body bumped along the stairs because his body bowed in the center. I didn't give a shit. The man wouldn't be living past tonight. A cat screeched and Pappy jumped, losing his footing and tumbling down the stairs. When he dropped Marks, I tried to keep myself upright, but I was tumbling down the stairs right after him. I landed on top of Marks and then rolled off so I laid on my back.

"That fucking hurt," Pappy groaned. "You didn't say anything about a fucking cat."

"There was nothing in his file about a cat."

"I thought you were doing recon? You didn't see a cat wandering around?"

"Fuck, stop busting my balls. I didn't know about the damn cat."

"You're never gonna live this down."

"If you ever mention this again, I'll slit your throat."

The front door creaked open and I immediately pulled my gun, ready to shoot whoever was stupid enough to enter. When Kate's head popped up, I lowered my gun and blew out a harsh breath.

"What the hell are you doing? You were supposed to stay in the truck."

She looked at us, a heap of limbs intertwined on the floor and raised an eyebrow. "I thought this was a quick in and out?"

"Cat," Hunter grumbled. Kate gave a funny expression and her lips scrunched up in question.

"I have to admit, this isn't what I was expecting. I somehow thought you would be more professional than this."

I rolled my eyes and got to my feet, holding out a hand for Hunter. He stood and pressed a hand against his back and groaned.

"I think I tweaked my back."

"Can we get on with this? I didn't want to be here in the first place," Kate said with a huff.

"Kate, back the truck into the driveway. We'll bring him around back."

Kate exited quickly and Hunter and I picked up Marks' body and dragged him out the back door. I went back in and quickly wiped away any evidence that we had been there and locked up behind me. When we got Marks loaded in the back of the truck, we all got in and headed back to the safe house.

"We'll take him downstairs. There's a room we can use. Has a drain and everything," Hunter said flippantly.

"A drain? What are you planning to do to him?" Kate asked.

"Whatever we have to in order to get the answers we need," I said, staring her down and watching her eyes widen in horror.

"You can't just kill him. He's a person."

"He's trying to kill us," I barked back. "You need to ask yourself whose life you value more—yours or his."

She looked over at Marks, who was still passed out from the drug and then back at me with tears in her eyes. "Isn't there anything left of Hudson inside you?"

That took me back. I thought she knew that Hudson didn't exist anymore. Now, I could see how much it really affected her to see who I really was. But that was the whole point, wasn't it? Cole had asked me to walk away, and I had, but this would ensure that she saw the man I had become and wanted nothing to do with me after this was over.

"Hudson died when I pulled the trigger on those three men."

She turned from me and took the stairs up to her room. Turning to Hunter, he shook his head at me. "You're fucking it up with her."

"She doesn't want me. She wants the version of me that doesn't exist any more."

"She didn't fall for the guy you were. She never even knew him, which means there must be something about you that she likes. You're just too stupid to see that."

"Someone's out there trying to kill us. Do you want to find out who it is or do you want to play Dr. Phil?"

"You're a grumpy bastard, you know that?"

"I'm about to be real fucking happy. Let's get this asshole downstairs."

We hauled Marks downstairs and strapped his ass to a chair. It was going to be a while before he was awake and I was finding it difficult to hold out for much longer. I had a lot of anger to take out on this man, but I also needed to hold it together so I could find out what the hell was going on. I was a killer and I enjoyed fucking with their minds before I killed them, but I didn't enjoy causing pain the way some killers did. It wasn't some sick enjoyment I got out of torture. I liked to instill fear in my targets, let them know that they would suffer the way their victims suffered.

As I waited for Marks to wake up, I ran over in my mind what had happened at Kate's house. How close she had come to taking a bullet or getting stabbed by that knife. I thought of her anger at having taken someone's life and I let it wash over me. This asshole deserved everything I had to give him. Kate didn't deserve to live in fear or have her world torn apart. She shouldn't have had to take a life when it's something she hates so vehemently. I was pissed at myself for that, but I directed my rage at the man who was starting to rouse in front of me. Normally, I would go for torture right away when trying to get information, but I had a strong desire to take out my anger on him with my fists.

When his eyes focused around the room and he saw me sitting at a table, the fear in his eyes almost made me laugh. He knew who I was and he was fucking scared. He should be. By the time I was through with him, he would rue the day he ever fucked with me or anyone close to me.

"McGuire." His voice shook as he took in my enraged state.

"Marks. Are you still collecting on soldier's deaths?" I asked as I pulled a knife and started sharpening it against a stone I had on the table next to me. My body language was relaxed, but he wasn't dumb enough to assume he would be getting out of this.

"I don't know what you're talking about."

"Don't you? Your accounts say otherwise. Only now that your friends are out of the picture, you're collecting their shares, or most of them anyway. You want to tell me where the rest of the money is going or do I have to make you tell me?"

He looked at the knife and visibly swallowed. "I'm not telling you jack shit. You're not going to let me go no matter what I say."

"That's true, but how you go is up to you. I can make it very painful or I can make it..not quite as painful. I'm not going to lie. Either way, I'm going to fuck you up, but how long it lasts is up to you."

"You're a murderer. I wouldn't trust a fucking word out of your mouth."

I chuckled and got up, pulling on a pair of latex gloves and strolled over to him. "See, that's where we differ. I'm a murderer, but I stand by what I did. Your men were fucking filth and they disgraced the uniform they wore so proudly. You profit from the deaths of the men you command." I leaned in close to him and whispered in his ear. "You have no honor and no right to wear that uniform and I'm going to make sure there's no way you can be buried in it."

I stood back and smirked at him. "Who's collecting the rest of the money, Marks?"

He shook his head slightly, his pale face showing a slight sheen of sweat. "You won't stop him. He'll do anything to get your attention. He wants revenge and he won't stop until he gets it."

I slid the knife along his face, slicing a thin line from his temple, down through his cheek, and into his lip. To his credit, he didn't make a noise, but his body shook with fear. "I want a name."

"You can't outrun him. He's been planning this for too long."

"I'm not going to outrun him. I'm going to end him. The name," I demanded, but he still wouldn't give it. I quickly grabbed his head, wrapping my arm around his head, locking him in place. I thrust the knife into his eye as he screamed in pain, twisting until I dug it out of his eye socket. Blood oozed down his face and his heavy pants filled the air as he gasped for control. I wiped the blood from my knife onto his shirt and stepped around him to look into his one eye.

"The name."

His whole body shook as adrenaline coursed through his body. I knew I didn't have long before he passed out from the pain, but that didn't matter. I could do this all night until he told me what I needed to know.

"Jensen," he croaked out.

I shook my head in disbelief. "No. I killed him."

His head started to lull to the side and I smacked his face to bring him back to the conversation.

"They just wanted you to think he died. He almost didn't make it, but he survived," his words slurred. "He's been in rehab for years, plotting to kill you. He's known who you are for years and has been tracking you."

"Why now? Why not any other time over the past few years? If he's really been tracking me, he could have had me taken out at any time."

He lifted his head to look at me as best he could. "Because of the girl. He finally found something that would break you. He wants you to suffer and your lady friend is the perfect target."

Chills raced down my spine at his words. This was so much worse than I had imagined because my actions over ten years ago were coming back to haunt me in a way I could never have seen coming. I had purposely kept my distance from everyone to avoid situations like this, but it hadn't mattered. The moment I started stalking Kate was the moment I sealed her fate.

In my anger, I flipped the knife so I gripped it tightly by the hilt in my fist and rammed it straight into his throat as I yelled in frustration. His eye went wide as the blade pierced him and he made a gurgling sound before his eye dimmed and his head flopped backward. There was nothing more I wanted at this moment than to find Jensen and put him in the ground, but if what Marks was saying was true, he would have contingency plans in place. I needed to find out who was working with him and make sure that I wiped out anyone who could possibly go after Kate.

I woodenly made my way back up to where Pappy was waiting in the kitchen. He was working on his laptop, but slammed it closed when I entered the room. He took in the blood on my clothes and shook his head. "Tell me you at least got something out of him."

"It's Jensen."

"Jensen?" He said in shock. "You killed that fucker."

"Apparently, he didn't die." I shook my head in disbelief. "I could have sworn he was dead. A shot like that should have killed him."

"Where's he been all this time?"

"Rehab. Plotting revenge." I walked over to the window and stared out at the dark night. "He's after Kate. All this time, I thought someone was just going after her to get to me. Jensen wants to hurt me. He doesn't want to just draw me out. He wants to make me suffer for screwing everything up for him. Kate's not just collateral damage. She's the fucking target."

13

KATE

My heart stuttered in my chest. Did I just hear Garrick right? I was the target? I didn't understand how that was possible. I was no one. I didn't have anything to do with Garrick before a few months ago.

"Fuck," I heard Hunter muttered as I stood back where they couldn't see me. "We need to call Sebastian. We can't take the chance that anything happens to her."

"I know. Fuck, I should have never followed her. I should have kept away from her the moment she ran from me at the safe house."

"You couldn't know this would happen, man."

"I damn well knew this could happen. I made a lot of enemies after I became Knight, but the fucked up part is that not one of them is coming after me. This all has to do with my past, and it's gonna get Kate killed."

"We won't let that happen. We just need to make a plan and get ahead of this. Kate will be safe with you."

"I'm the last fucking person she needs in her life."

"You're exactly who she needs in her life. You think I don't see the way you look at her? This isn't just some obsession. You're fucking in love with her. I knew it the day you asked me to install cameras at her house. You want to protect her and there's not a single person you've given a shit about in years."

"That doesn't mean I should be in her life."

Wait. Did that mean that he loved me? That wasn't exactly a confession, but I had the feeling it might be the closest I would get.

"That's exactly what it means. Who better to protect the woman you love than you? I know you won't let anything happen to her because it would kill you. I'm not saying you can do it on your own, because we have no fucking clue how much reach this guy has now, but when it comes to her, there's no one better for her than you. Besides, it'll be easier to keep an eye on both of you if you're together."

I watched as Garrick walked over to a chair and took a seat, hanging his head as he rested his elbows on his knees. "She doesn't want me around," he said quietly. "I'm fucking tainted in her eyes. I'm a killer, and nothing I do will ever make that better, but I will keep her safe. I swear to God, there's not a chance in hell I'll ever let anything I've done touch her again. She deserves so much better than that."

"Then let's get this shit done. We call Sebastian and find out where the fuck Jensen is and who his contacts are. Then we take it from there."

I snuck away as they continued talking about what they were planning and went back to my room. The doors for the rooms had old key locks, but Hunter hadn't given me a key when we arrived. I assumed that when they converted the building, they just didn't lock the doors to the rooms. I went into the bathroom and decided to take a shower. After what I just heard, I felt like I needed to scrub the filth from my body.

It all swirled in my mind as I stood under the hot spray. Me being the target because of something that happened in Garrick's past. Garrick almost admitting that he loved me. His vow to protect me no matter what. There was one thing that resounded through all of this and that was that no matter what terrible things Garrick had done, I couldn't help but admit that I was in love with him, too. I saw the man he once was and knew that deep down, Hudson was still a part of Garrick. Hudson was a man of honor and Garrick was an avenger of the defenseless. Together, they made the man I loved and wanted to spend my life with, if he would allow it. I wanted him, and all the reasons I gave him for wanting him out of my life no longer mattered when I heard I was the target.

Suddenly, I just wanted one more night with him, to feel his arms around me and feel cherished by him. That was what he did for me and it was something I had never felt before. I had dated other men and slept with them, but I never had a connection with anyone else before. Every date was pleasant and the sex was satisfying, but I realized that if I gave up Garrick, that's all I would ever have. I didn't want to settle for pleasant and satisfying. I wanted earth-shattering, mind-blowing electrical charges to my body. When this was over, if Garrick could only give me small pieces of himself, I would accept that because I would rather have that much of him than nothing at all.

I turned to get out of the shower and hunt him down to tell him exactly what I thought, but he was already there. Leaning against the counter like that first morning after he came to stay with me, Garrick watched me as I opened the door. Only this time, I didn't shut off the water. I opened the door wider and held my hand out to him. His eyes darkened as they trailed over my body and when I widened my stance, I knew I had him. He pulled his t-shirt over his head and shucked his pants in a few swift moves. His muscles flexed as he walked toward me and pushed me up against the shower wall. He had smears of red across his skin, blood from his interrogation of Marks.

I grabbed the washcloth from the bar and soaped it up. I didn't want him to have this blood on him. I wanted him to be clean, the way I knew he once was. I ran the cloth over his body, taking extra care to clean every drop of blood from his skin. His eyes burned into me as he watched my every move.

"You heard us," his low voice rumbled.

I nodded. "I did." I looked up into his eyes as my hand stilled on his chest. "Was Hunter right? Do you love me?"

His eyes searched mine before he gave an almost imperceptible nod. "I know I've fucked up everything in your life, but I'm going to make it right."

"Don't walk away when this is done." His brows furrowed as he considered my words. "I know what I said, that I needed my life back, but the truth is, without you, my life is very empty. I'll take whatever you can give me. If you can only come to me between jobs, then I'll take it. I know we won't have a conventional relationship and I know at times it'll be hard, but I would rather have those stolen moments with you than not have you at all."

"Why would you want that with me? I'm a killer," he said harshly.

"You are, but you're my killer. It's true that I don't agree with your profession, but maybe that doesn't matter so much anymore."

"Why? You didn't want me anywhere near you and now you'll take anything. I don't understand what changed."

I looked up at him, wanting him to understand the internal battle I had been fighting with myself. "I used to think I was just someone you were obsessed with. I didn't want to lay it all on the line for someone who could never love me. I wasn't even sure what my feelings were for you. But when I heard you talk with Hunter, I realized that I've been in love with you for a while. I just didn't want to admit it. I don't know how things are going to turn out after all this, but I know I don't want to go back to living the way I was without you. Every time you left, I felt so alone, but I had hope that you would return."

"If you really want me, I'll always return to you. I'll do whatever it takes to come back to you."

He crushed his lips to mine and pulled me roughly against him. His tongue slid against mine with a possessiveness that was all Garrick. His hands slipped over my body and touched me in ways that lit me on fire. I knew right then that I had made the right choice. There was nothing I wouldn't give to have more of him, to feel enraptured by him. He broke the kiss and pulled back, cradling my head in his hands.

"Before we take this any further, I need to know if what I do is going to ruin us. It's one thing to know what I do, but if you really saw what I do, you might change your mind. I need to know first. I want you to see Marks."

"What? I don't need to see," I said, taking a step back.

"I need you to see. I'll always try to keep you from seeing what I do, but we're in the middle of a shit storm. Chances are you'll see me do something and I need to know you can handle it. I couldn't handle it if you asked me to walk away again. I think it might kill me."

I could see in his eyes how important this was to him. He needed me to be sure that I could handle the killer inside him, and part of me questioned that, also. I took a deep breath and nodded.

"Okay. If you really think I need to see, then let's go."

He shut off the water and pulled a towel off the bar, wrapping it around my body. I quickly dressed and found a pair of sweatpants in a dresser. Handing them to Garrick, we went back downstairs and he led me to the basement to the room he had Marks in.

"Is he alive?" I asked as we stood outside the door.

"No, and it's not pretty."

"Okay." I took a deep breath as he opened the door and prepared for the worst. I was a little shocked by what I saw, but I wasn't sure why. I knew what he did and we had brought this man here to get information. I had just never witnessed something so gruesome before. There was a bloody eyeball on the ground and the man sitting in the chair was covered in blood with a knife sticking out of his neck. I could see why they needed the drain. They had to wash away the blood from the room, and there was a lot of it. Since I was a doctor, this was something I could deal with and not lose my lunch over.

"Who was this man exactly?"

"He was the commanding officer for my unit. My superiors answered to him. He was a part of the profiting scheme my superiors were running. I didn't know it until Reed Security checked into him. If I had, I would have taken him out with the others."

"Did you get what you needed out of him?"

"Yes. He said that one of the men I killed isn't dead." He looked at me and a look of pure hatred crossed his face. "He wants revenge on me for what I did to him. He was in rehab for years and I'm sure I messed with his income. He wants you."

"Yeah. I heard that part."

"We have to be careful. Until we know exactly who he sent for you, we have to assume that everyone is a threat."

"Even Hunter? I mean, he's been helping you all along."

"No. Pappy would never turn on me, but I don't trust the men he works with."

"They're good men. They'll help us if you let them."

"I don't know them. For all I know, they want me out of the way and would hand me over just to get rid of me."

"Except that you already said this guy wants me. Getting you won't satisfy him if that's true."

"Not everyone thinks the way you do."

I walked out of the room, deciding that I had seen enough. After Garrick followed me out and closed the door, I stopped him in the hall before we could go upstairs. "If you don't trust anyone else, trust me. I would never ask you to trust Sebastian if I thought there was the slightest chance that one of them would turn on you. Please. Do this for me."

"I do trust you. If this is what you want me to do, then I'll do it."

"Thank you."

We went back upstairs and Garrick stopped me outside my door. "Now you've seen what I'm capable of, and that's not the worst I've ever done. So, before we go inside that room, I need you to decide if you can accept what I do. If you need time, I'll leave and you can come to me when you decide. But I won't step foot inside your bedroom again until I know you want me there forever."

I grinned up at him mischievously. "Not even at night to watch over me like a creeper?"

He chuckled and gave me a swift kiss. "Not even then, but I make no promises for the future."

"I don't need to think about it." His face sobered as he waited for my answer. "You know how I feel about your job and that hasn't changed, and it won't just go away, but I also can't walk away from you. I need you in my life and I'll take you any way I can get you."

"Be really fucking sure about that because I'll kill anyone who tries to stand in my way from having you."

I was a little ashamed that it turned me on to hear him talk like that. Hearing how far he would go to protect me and keep me made me want to throw all my values out the window. For him, I would set my morals aside to keep him.

"I've never been more sure of anything in my life. Take me to bed."

His dark eyes smoldered and in a flash, I was hauled up in his arms and carried into the bedroom. I could feel the heat simmering within and I needed him to take me and show me how much he wanted me. I expected him to throw me down and have his way with me, but instead, he lowered me to the bed and climbed over me, covering my body with his. I could feel his erection through his sweatpants, pushing against my core. I ran my hands over his taut back muscles, feeling him flex as he rocked over me.

His mouth latched onto my lips and made slow love to mine. His tongue slipped in and out, sliding against mine gently. It was the complete opposite of everything Garrick was and made it that much sweeter. I threw my head back into the pillows as he rocked harder against me. I could feel my panties soaking with every thrust against me. It didn't even feel like there was any fabric between us. I was so close to coming just from him dry-humping my body.

I felt butterfly kisses across my cheeks and then his hot tongue caressing the shell of my ear. "I love you, Kate." He pushed against my center again. "I'll never stop loving you or wanting you." His hand grazed my breast, pushing at the fabric of my shirt until he could pull at my nipple. "You're mine and I'm never letting you go."

I wrapped my arms around his neck as he latched onto my nipple. His hot tongue circled the bud, nipping and sucking at it until my body clenched, and I squeezed my legs around his.

"Garrick," I cried as I rode the waves of my orgasm. He didn't let up. He continued to push harder and faster against me until I felt I might black out from pleasure. My hands slid down his back and underneath his sweats until I could grip his firm ass, pulling him against me and holding him there. "I love you, Garrick."

He spread kisses across my cheeks and down my neck until my heart slowed to a normal rhythm. "You're so beautiful when you come, but I'm not done yet."

In one swift move, he had my pants off me and was thrusting inside me. He hadn't even bothered to pull his pants off all the way. My heart raced as he pushed me higher and higher, whispering sweet words that I never would have expected from him. He rolled us over, so I straddled him, and his hands immediately reached for my breasts.

"Ride me, Kate. I want your pussy gripping my cock."

I did as he asked, loving the way he looked up at me like I was a queen. Sweat trickled down my neck as I moved faster and faster, wanting to push him over the edge until he spilled himself inside me. I lifted my hair off my neck and my eyes shot to his as he groaned. His eyes were glued to my chest and I smiled when I realized that Garrick was a breast man. He sat up and sucked my nipples into his mouth and I closed my eyes, memorizing the feel of his tongue on me.

He gripped my hips as he laid back down and started pumping up into me. His hips slammed against me over and over, spreading me wider with every thrust. When his fingers found my clit, I pulsed around him, clenching hard.

"That's it. Squeeze me, Kate. Fuck, that's amazing."

He grunted and then stilled as he pushed himself into me one last time, sitting up and pulling my body against his as he jerked inside me. We stayed that way for what felt like hours until we could both breathe again, his face pushed against my chest. He pressed soft kisses to my breasts and then pulled me down into his arms where he ran his hand over my back leisurely. I had never felt more loved than I did in that moment.

When I woke in the morning, Garrick was already awake and stroking my skin softly as he stared out the window. I knew this moment wouldn't last forever. He had work to do to ensure we would be safe from the man who was determined to kill us. Even after this mess was finished, we still wouldn't have many mornings like this. I had work to get back to and Garrick would go back to his job. I didn't want to think about that now, though. I wanted to enjoy the moment and think about the rest later.

"Did you sleep well?" he asked.

"Better than I have in a long time."

"Me too. I always sleep better when I'm with you."

We laid in silence for a while and I closed my eyes, relishing in the feel of his rough hands caressing my back.

"I've been thinking, when this is over, I think I want to see about working at Reed Security."

I sat up on one elbow and looked down at him. "Is that even possible?"

He blew out a breath as he ran a hand over his face. "Yes, but it won't be easy. I've made a lot of enemies and I'm a wanted man. It won't be as simple as taking a job there. I'm not even sure what Sebastian would have me do, but Pappy insists I would have a job waiting for me."

"Is that something you really want to do?"

He looked over at me and his eyes seemed to soften for the first time since I'd met him. There was none of the harshness that he usually hid behind. "It would give me a chance at a real life again. I don't know exactly what it would look like and I'm not sure what I would have to do to get it, but I want to try for it. I don't want to be dropping in a few times a month to see you. I want more."

My heart melted at his words. The fact that he was willing to try for me was more than I could ever hope for.

"Whatever happens, I'll take you however I can get you. If it works out, that's great, but if it doesn't, I'll still be here waiting for you."

14

KNIGHT

"The happy couple finally emerges," Pappy said as Kate and I entered the kitchen later that morning. I flipped him the bird and walked over to the cabinet for coffee mugs. Pappy had already made coffee, so I poured for Kate and myself and walked over to her, giving her a kiss. I was rewarded with a huge smile, followed by a blush when she realized Pappy was grinning at us.

"Took long enough for the two of you to get your shit together," he grumbled.

"Where's your woman?" I asked, looking around the room as if she would emerge any second. "Oh, that's right. You don't have one, so shut the fuck up."

"I figured that one of us had to hold out. I always thought it would be you. I never thought Hudson McGuire would settle down."

"Hudson McGuire isn't around anymore."

"That's even worse. An assassin that's a family man?" He shook his head, but was smiling. It reminded me that I needed to have a talk with Pappy before we took this thing any further. I needed to make sure I had a reason to give Kate hope.

"Kate, why don't you go take a hot shower while I make us some breakfast?"

It was a dismissal, and she knew it, but she didn't argue. She gave me a sexy smile that made me wish I could go back upstairs with her, so I headed for the stairs. When Kate was upstairs, I turned to Pappy and saw his demeanor shift from jovial to serious.

"So, what's going on? You just threw all your reasons for staying away out the window."

"When this is over, I want to try to go straight for Kate."

He scoffed, but grinned at me. "Took you long enough."

"Does that job offer with Sebastian still stand?"

"I don't speak for him. He made that offer a while ago and I would assume he would still have a position for you, but you'd have to meet with him."

"I don't have a problem with that, but I don't know how he plans to employ me. There are some things that can be worked around. I can get a new identity and I can fly under the radar, but I can't change my fingerprints. Aside from burning them off, there's not much I can do about it."

"That's something we'd have to work out with Sebastian. I'm sure he wouldn't have considered employing you if he didn't have something up his sleeve."

He studied me and I could tell he really wanted to ask me something.

"Just spit it out."

"You said you want to try to go straight for Kate. What happens if it doesn't work out the way you want it to?"

"You think I would walk away?"

"Look, you've done it before to her. I just don't want to see her get hurt. Just be sure this is really what you want because if it's not, you're gonna break her heart, and then I'm gonna break your neck."

"I appreciate you looking out for her, but there's no way I'm walking away from her again."

"Good. I'm gonna hold you to that."

"There's one more thing I need from you."

"Name it."

I glanced toward the stairs to make sure Kate wasn't lurking and then back to him. "If this thing goes south, you know I'll do anything to protect Kate."

"Yeah, I know that."

"I want the same from you." He nodded, but he didn't understand what I was saying. "If this doesn't go our way, I want you to promise me that you'll get her out and keep her safe. No matter what happens. I'll do whatever I can to make sure you make a safe exit, but you leave me behind and get her the hell out."

"I promise, but this is going to go our way. We'll take this bastard down and the two of you are going to ride off into the sunset on a white horse."

"Let's just focus on finishing the job before we plan out a whole fairytale ending."

I walked over to the fridge and pulled out the stuff to make breakfast. Kate came down right as I was finishing up and we got to work planning our next move.

"We need to send a message that we're not going to be fucked with. Jensen thinks he has me by the balls."

"What do you have in mind?"

"We still have Marks' body downstairs. I think we use it for recon and to send the message we're coming for him."

"How does using his body help with recon?" Kate asked.

"Right now, we know he doesn't have eyes on us twenty-four/seven because we wouldn't have gotten to Marks if he did. We need to know how often he's watching us and how many men he has on his property. We go in and watch for outside guards and then plant cameras where we can. Then, we leave Marks' body on his doorstep and wait for the chaos to begin. It should give us a good idea of what we're fighting."

"I want to call in Derek and Lola. They're my team and I trust them with my life. They can help us and I have a feeling we're going to need it."

"Do it. I'll take all the help we can get right now."

"Where will I be during all this?"

"Until we know how many eyes they have on us, you stick with me. I don't want to leave you behind and then find out they were trying to draw us out."

"We also need ears on the inside. We need to know who he's calling in for help," Pappy said.

"I can patch into the phone line, but his cell is going to be more complicated, and I'd never make it in there without him recognizing me."

"I have just the guy for you," Pappy grinned. "Rob, one of our techs, is great at this shit. We can send him in and he can clone Jensen's phone."

"Is he trained in the field?" I asked.

"He trains with us all the time. He's good."

"Alright, let's get them over here."

"What can I do to help?" Kate asked.

"Just do what we say, when we say it. I'll be able to do my job better if I don't have to worry about you as much."

Pappy went off to make a few phone calls and I took Kate upstairs to have my way with her. I wasn't sure how much time we would have left before shit hit the fan, and I wanted to spend every second I could with her.

"Derek, thanks for coming," Pappy said as Derek walked into the safe house. Lola and Rob were behind him, bringing in the rest of the gear.

"When the boss man tells you to do something, you do it. Even if it involves helping this asshole," Derek said, flipping his thumb in my direction.

I narrowed my eyes at him, hating that I had to rely on these people. I didn't have a choice, though. This was for Kate. If it was just me, I would have dealt with it on my own, not caring if I came out on top in the end. But now I had a chance at a real life with Kate and I was going to do anything to hold onto it.

"You do your job and I'll do mine, and we'll be fine," I snarled.

"Let's get one thing straight. I'm only here because of Kate. If Cap had ordered me here to help your sorry ass, I would have told him to fuck off."

"At least we're clear on that."

"Geez, you could cut the testosterone in here with a knife," Lola said as she set some bags down.

"I'd say that's what we have you for, but you probably have bigger balls than most of the men on the team," Pappy grinned.

"I can also shoot better than most of you, but I try not to rub that in."

Rob walked in with what looked like enough computer equipment for a small army. Pappy directed him to a room to set up in and Derek and Lola followed. For the first time in my life, I felt very out of place. These men worked together and actually liked each other. When I had worked with them a few months back, I didn't give a shit if they liked me or not because I wasn't sticking around when the job was done. Now though, I was relying on them to help me and was hoping to join their team when things were cleared up. I didn't have the slightest clue how that was going to happen. It was clear none of them liked me, and it wouldn't be easy for me to assimilate into their working environment. I was used to doing things my own way, but if I was to work with them on this job and in the future, I was going to have to learn to not only get along with them, but trust that they would work with me.

"Alright, Knight, how about you fill everyone in," Pappy said. I had a feeling he felt the tension in the air the same as I did and was trying to give me the chance to prove that I wasn't just a killer.

"I've been watching Jensen's place the last few nights. If he suspects anything, he's not showing it. He goes out during the day and he's back every night by seven o'clock. He has one man who follows him around, but he doesn't seem to be a real threat at this point. Probably more of a personal assistant than anything. His house has the typical security system that any one of us could crack. I've been monitoring his landlines, but so far, he's been smart and hasn't been making any calls to anyone from his house. That's where you come in, Rob."

"You need me to access his cell phone?"

"Yeah. He's going to have some issues with his security system tomorrow. We'll scramble his cell service so he has to make the call from his landline and then we'll intercept the call. You'll be going in to make repairs, and while you're there, you'll need to lift his phone and clone it. You'll also be placing cameras around his house so we have eyes inside." I picked up some small cameras and showed them around the table. "These connect wirelessly to his system. Once we access his security system, we'll be able to see everything inside. As of tomorrow, we'll be in control of his security system."

"What about outside?" Lola asked.

"Tomorrow night, we'll be going around the perimeter and placing cameras that will also connect to the security system. Once they're all in place, we'll be leaving a present at his gate."

"And what would this present be?" Derek asked.

"The body of his commanding officer, Marks."

Derek, Lola, and Rob looked completely shocked. They weren't filled in all the way as to what had gone down the past few days.

"You killed another officer?" Derek said in shock. "Where does it fucking stop, Knight?"

"He was in on it with Jensen. I just didn't know it at the time. I took him and made him talk. Now we know that Jensen is alive and he's behind all this."

That answer didn't seem to appease Derek, but I didn't give a shit. This was Kate's life we were talking about, and I would kill as many people as necessary to ensure her safety.

"We all know our jobs. Let's get ready for tomorrow," Hunter said, looking around the table at the serious faces. They nodded and everyone got up and went to work.

"CAMERAS ARE IN PLACE AND ARE CONNECTING TO THE WI-FI NOW," LOLA said over the mic.

"I'm starting to get feed on my end. I should have eyes on the whole property in just a few minutes," Rob said. He was in the van down the street, making sure everything was up and running the way we needed. He had gone in earlier today under the illusion that something was wrong with the security system and patched us in. He'd also cloned his cell and we'd been monitoring it. We'd been able to watch Jensen for most of the day and so far, he hadn't made any calls on his cell that were related to us.

"Alright, let's string up Marks and I'll make the call."

I watched as Pappy and Derek hauled Marks out of the second van and strung him up on the wrought iron fence. When Pappy gave me the signal, I dialed Jensen's number and waited for him to pick up.

"This is Jensen."

"I left a present for you on your fence."

"Who is this?"

"I would think you would know. You've been following me for years now."

"McGuire. What the hell do you want?"

"You want me, you come after me. I'll be waiting, but you leave everyone else out of it. This is between you and me."

"You stole years of my life from me. Do you know how much physical therapy I had to go through? I lost my job and the military took my pension. Now, I'm going to take anything that's important to you, including that pretty doctor of yours."

"Stay away from her," I growled into the phone.

"When I take her, I'm going to take my time with her. There won't be an unmarred surface on her sweet, little body. You won't even recognize her when I send her back to you," he laughed into the phone.

"If you thought what you went through last time was painful, just wait until I get my hands on you. I'm gonna gut you and splay your insides all over and leave you to rot."

"Then come get me," he taunted as he hung up the phone. Pappy placed a hand on my shoulder to calm me as the anger burned under the surface.

"You let him get to you," Pappy said. I wasn't sure when he had gotten there. I was so caught up in my rage that I hadn't even noticed that Derek and Lola were there also. "You have to get that shit under control or you can't protect her."

"I don't like this," Derek said. "Something's off with this guy. This is all too easy. He's been planning this for years, but we just walked onto his property and were able to hack into his security system? This screams disaster."

"I agree," Lola said, "I think we need to watch and wait. He wants you to go after him right now while you're mad, so I say we go back to the safe house and wait it out."

I nodded in agreement. "I think that's best. If I go after him now, I'm gonna fuck everything up."

"Then let's get back and see how this all plays out." Pappy nodded to Rob, who took off, driving us all back to the other van where Derek and Lola jumped out to drive it back to the safe house.

"He's scrambling," Derek muttered as we watched the footage from Jensen's house. "This doesn't make sense at all. Why would a man who's been planning his revenge for years be this unprepared? He had to realize that you would go after him."

"I wish I knew. Jensen was always the planner in the group, but it's been years since I dealt with him. He looks almost manic in the video," I pointed at the screen where Jensen was briskly walking around and barking orders at people. According to what we were hearing, they were totally unprepared for us getting our hands on Marks.

"He's acting like he wasn't prepared for you to strike back," Lola said, chewing on a beef stick. "Are you sure this guy hasn't lost a few screws over the years?"

"I'm not sure. I didn't even know he was alive. I have no idea what he was dealing with in therapy. Those records were all hidden."

"Let's take shifts getting some shut-eye," Hunter said. "We need to stay prepared in case this is all a trick. Who knows what the hell this guy is thinking. I'll take the first shift with Lola and Derek. We'll wake you and Rob in three hours and I'll take a second shift before I sleep."

"I can take a shift for one of you," I said. "There's no way I can sleep right now anyway. There's something gnawing at the back of my mind and I need to figure it out."

Derek shook his head at me. "You need to go to Kate. She's probably wondering why we're back and haven't told her what the hell is going on."

I couldn't argue with that, so I nodded my thanks and headed up to see her. As Derek thought, Kate was sitting up in the chair in the corner of the room and staring out into the dark night. When I opened the door, she turned to me with a smile.

"How'd it go?"

"Good. Too good." I sighed and sat down on the edge of the bed. Kate walked over and sat next to me, linking her hand with mine. "Something's not right with this and everyone feels it. We just have to watch and see how this all plays out."

"Is there anything I can do?"

"Help me escape for a while."

She stood and pulled her shirt over her head and I swallowed hard at the sight of her beautiful body, then got lost in her for the next hour.

I woke in the middle of the night to something, but I didn't know what. It was a feeling I got whenever I felt like I was being hunted. I sat up and looked around the dark room, but I didn't see anything out of place. Glancing next to me, I saw Kate lying naked on her belly. The sheet was pulled down and draped around her waist, exposing the gentle curves of her body.

The feeling of being targeted came back and my eyes wandered around the room again. I stood and looked out the window, not sure what I was looking for, but when I saw a light in the distance, I was brought back to a night years ago where I was sitting around a camp-fire in the desert with my brothers-in-arms and Jensen.

"*She actually sent me a Dear John letter. Can you believe that shit? I just proposed to her the last time I was on leave and I bought her a huge fucking diamond. Now she's back with her old boyfriend and I'm out thousands of dollars,*" Johnson said in disgust.

"*Good riddance,*" I said, throwing more wood on the fire. "*Be happy you got out now before it cost you more than just the price of the ring. Just think, you could have ended up in divorce court and she could have taken you for more.*"

Jensen, our superior who always wanted to act like one of the guys, chimed in. "Take them both out now. You can't let that shit stand."

"Take them out? She broke up with me, not killed someone."

"She stole from you. In life, you're either the winner or the loser. Losers walk away with their heads hung low. Winners take what they want."

"And what would you suggest that I do?" Johnson asked.

"If it was me, I'd make them think I was totally oblivious to what they had done to me. I'd let them think that they'd won. Then, when they least expect it, I'd strike back hard. Take them for everything they have and teach them a lesson. It's no fun to just win. You have to totally decimate them."

Johnson laughed nervously. "That's kind of fucked up, Jensen."

MAKE THEM THINK THEY'D WON.

Strike back hard.

Shit. That's what Jensen was doing. It was all a fucking trick. He was making us think we had the upper hand, but he was pretending all along.

"Kate. Wake up." I shook her shoulder and picked up my discarded shirt on the floor, flinging it to her when she sat up, rubbing the sleep from her eyes. "Put that on quick. We have to get out of here."

I found my pants and pulled them on when I heard a whizzing noise and the glass shattered at the window. Time stopped when I saw the grenade land in the corner, my head swiveled to Kate in slow motion and I leapt over to Kate, tackling her off the bed and covering her body with mine in the corner just as the night exploded around us. Small bits of shrapnel bit into my back, but I shook it off, standing quickly and pulling Kate up with me. She had managed to get my shirt on before the grenade came at us, so I pulled her behind me, toward the giant hole in the wall. Picking her up, I carried her through the wreckage and into the hallway.

My heart was hammering hard in my chest as I tried to figure out how the hell to get out of this and keep us safe. Once we were clear of the wreckage, I set Kate down, grabbed her hand, and ran toward the staircase at the end of the hall. Another explosion rocked the building in the room we just passed and the wall exploded outward, sending bits of drywall and the door sailing toward us. I pulled us harder down the hall, but the staircase was at the other end of the building.

"Faster, Kate," I yelled. "We have to make it to the stairwell!"

We flew down the hall as one room after another exploded behind us. I was hunched over as I ran, trying to shield my face from the blasts and kept Kate tucked into me as best I could. A particularly close explosion sent us flying into the wall and I wrapped my arms around her, trying to protect her from any shrapnel. She hit the wall hard and slumped to the ground.

"Kate!" I yelled at her, trying to rouse her, but she was out. Blood dripped from her head and a sharp gash cut across the side of her forehead. I tore at the bottom of her shirt and pressed the fabric to her wound, hoping to staunch the blood flow. I quickly looked around and saw more explosions happening further down the hall. Not able to wait for her to wake up, I hauled her up into my arms and took off down the hall, racing for the stairwell. I had to hope that they didn't know exactly where we were and were just taking shots all over the building. I had to get us out of here before the whole building suffered too much damage and collapsed.

"Garrick," Kate mumbled. I stopped running and set her down so she could get her bearings. "What happened?"

"You hit the wall. Look at me." She did and I checked her eyes as best I could in the light, not seeing any signs of concussion.

"I think I'm okay. Let's get out of here."

"Are you okay to walk?"

She nodded and winced a little, but got to her feet and linked her hand with mine. "I'm okay. Let's go."

"We're going to have to run. Tell me if you can't keep up." She nodded again and I took off down the hall at a slower pace so she could keep up. We finally got to the stairwell and I pulled her down the stairs, rounding each corner so fast that I almost fell once or twice. One more flight and we would be on the same floor as the rest of the crew. Turning the corner, my eyes widened as I saw the staircase had been blown out. I couldn't stop. I was going too fast. My feet slid out from under me and my hand shot out just in time to catch the railing. Kate screamed as she went over the edge. I gripped her hand as tight as I could, straining between holding onto the railing and keeping hold of her hand.

She screamed and wiggled as she tried to keep a grip on my hand. I could feel her slipping as she struggled to hold on.

"Kate. I need you to calm down and reach up with your other hand," I shouted. "You have to grab onto my arm and hold on tight."

"Okay." Her voice shook as she tried to calm herself. A few seconds later, I felt her swinging slightly, trying to get her other arm up to grip onto mine. My arm twisted and strained and I felt my hand slipping from the railing.

"Kate, move faster. I'm losing my grip."

My arm shook as my muscles pulled tighter. A few more minutes and we would both be at the bottom of whatever laid below us. Kate had a grip with both hands on my arm, but I was losing my grip too fast.

"Kate, I need you to wrap your body around mine and hold onto my neck. I need my other arm to help pull us up. You gotta do it fast or I'm going to drop us."

I felt her arms wrap around my waist and then her legs. My body was sweating and I could feel her slipping. "Wrap your arms around my neck, honey." Her breathing was harsh and I could tell she was trying to hold onto her sanity. I wrapped my free arm around her waist to hold her tight as she tried to climb up my body. "You're doing great, Kate. Just focus on moving up to my neck."

When her arms were tight around my neck, she looked up into my eyes and I looked back for a moment, hoping this wasn't the last time I saw her beautiful face. I strained my other arm up over my head and floundered for a minute as I tried to find a way to contort my body to grab onto the railing. Finally getting a grip, I used my upper body strength to pull us up until Kate could climb up to the stairs.

"Okay, Kate, I need you to grab onto the railing and pull yourself up."

"No, I could end up making you lose your grip," she said in a panic.

"Kate, I can't hold on too much longer, honey. I need you to do this for me. Grab onto the railing and pull yourself up. Don't worry about me. Just get yourself back up on the stairs."

She grabbed the railing and started pulling herself up, dragging her body against mine. When she made it to the top, her hand latched onto my wrist, the other holding onto the railing further up. I didn't know if it was enough to catch me if I slipped, but I couldn't wait anymore. My body was tired and I could feel myself slipping more and more each second. I swung my leg up until it rested on the stair and then hauled myself up the rest of the way, scrambling to pull Kate and myself back up to the landing. Lying on my back on the landing, I stared up at the stairs above us, breathing hard as my body shook from the adrenaline.

Forcing myself up, I knew we couldn't stay here. I didn't have a weapon on me and I needed to get Kate to safety. If they were launching grenades at us, it wouldn't be long before they entered the building and started shooting.

"Come on. We need to find another way to get to the others." I pulled Kate up by the hand and noticed she was shaking pretty hard and she was starting to space out. Cupping her cheeks in my hands, I forced her to look into my eyes. "Kate, I'm going to get you through this, but I need you to stick with me, okay? Just do what I say and I promise you, we'll get out of here."

She nodded as tears filled her eyes, but she sucked them back. "Okay. I can do this."

"Alright, honey. Let's get out of here."

We climbed back up one floor and pushed through the door. Light smoke filled the hallway, leaving a filmy haze, but we didn't have a choice. The only other place to go was the next floor up and that was where the grenades had blown through the building. Looking around for any signs the ceiling was going to cave in, I led us down the hallway until I saw the exit sign that took us down a perpendicular hallway. It was a longer route, and one I could have taken when we were one floor up, but I was trying to get us down to the others.

Once we were on the other side of the building, we started running for the other set of stairs. I could hear gunfire in the distance and every minute or two, the building shook from another explosion. Kate was squeezing my hand tightly with every shock, but I kept pulling her with me. There was no time to stop and reassure her. When we reached the stairwell, I cautiously opened the door and looked down the center of the spiral staircase. I didn't see any signs of damage yet, so I proceeded with caution. When we made it to the third floor where Reed Security had its base of operations set up, I opened the door to chaos.

Derek was barking orders into a mic as flames licked the walls on the far side of the floor. I had no idea where Rob, Lola, and Pappy were. When Derek saw us, relief flooded his face and he announced our arrival before tossing a gun my way.

"Never thought I'd be happy to see your face," he said grudgingly.

"Same here. It's a hell of a mess upstairs. What do we have?"

"Lola and Pappy are up top, taking out anything that moves. Rob is in the garage loading the SUVs so we can get the hell out of here. Jensen's got a small army with him, so we're going to have to take out as many as we can before we attempt to leave."

"We can't wait too long. The building's gonna come down around us. The stairwell on the north side is rubble now."

Pappy came flying through the door, followed by Lola seconds later. "Down!" he shouted just as a devastating explosion shook the building. I threw Kate to the floor and covered her body, thankful when nothing fell down around us. I quickly looked up to see the other side of the building was now missing.

"I told you something wasn't right," Derek yelled.

"That's why I said we had to keep an eye on shit," Pappy countered.

"Right, because I should have expected a fucking rocket launcher."

"Time to beat feet. We took out everyone we could, but we can't wait any longer. Jensen's lost too many men and he's losing his fucking mind out there," Lola said urgently.

"So, that's what the rocket was about," I quipped.

"Rob's getting the SUVs loaded. Lola and I will head out with Rob. Pappy, you and Knight make sure Kate gets to safety. We'll try to clear a path for you."

"Copy that," Pappy saluted and then started pulling us toward the stairwell. Flames were licking at the walls all around us and the heat was getting difficult to bear. Kate was coughing beside me as the smoke thickened.

"McGuire!" Jensen shouted from the other side of the building. I had no clue how he got up here, but I knew I had to end this while I could. As long as he was alive, he was a threat to Kate.

"Get Kate out of here," I told Pappy.

"Don't do this, man. We need to get out of here. The whole fucking building is going."

"I'll be right behind you. I need to end this."

Pappy nodded and took Kate by the arm, but she started shaking her head. "No. I'm not going anywhere without you."

"Kate. I need to stop him and I can't do that if I'm worried about you. Please."

She nodded slightly and then flung herself into my arms. "Please come back to me," she whispered in my ear. I pulled back and grinned at her.

"I'm not that easy to kill, honey."

I pushed her into Pappy's arms and turned to face Jensen, who was running toward me with fury written all over his face. I raised my gun, but before I could get a shot off, the ceiling caved in and I just barely had time to cover my head before debris was raining down all around me. Coughing and choking on dust, I shoved boards out of my way as I dug my way out of the fallen ceiling. To the right of me was a large beam that had just barely missed me. I would have been dead instantly. I could only hope that Jensen met that fate, but when I finally got out of the wreckage, I saw Jensen making his way out also.

I looked around, but my gun was gone, lost somewhere in the rubble below. Deciding this was my best shot, I charged over the ruins and tackled Jensen to the ground before he could point his gun at me. I got in two good punches before he lifted his knee and flung me off him. My ribs protested as I crashed into some fallen concrete, but I quickly twisted away from his foot that was headed for my face and got back to my feet. As he started to raise his gun, I spun around and kicked it out of his hand, sending it flying across the ground.

Fists flew and blood spilled to the point that it was hard to tell who was winning the fight. The fire was growing around us, making it difficult to breathe and anticipate Jensen's next move. I needed to end this fast and get the hell out before I burned alive in this building. When he kicked me in the chest and sent me flying backward, I quickly snatched the gun that was laying just within reach and jumped to my feet, whirling around and firing the gun just as pain shot through my chest.

Jensens' look of shock lasted only a moment as he fell to the floor, sporting a bullet hole in the center of his forehead. My breaths came in short bursts as I looked down at the man who had been trying to kill Kate and was a little upset I hadn't had the time to make him suffer. When he started to waver in my vision, I knew I needed to get out of there before I couldn't breathe through the smoke to get out. Coughing, I covered my face with my arm, trying to keep from taking a large gulp of smoke. When I pulled it back, I saw red covering my skin.

"Garrick!" Kate's voice echoed through my head and I glanced around, sure I was hearing things. She was at the door to the stairwell, tears flowing down her face as she screamed at me. I couldn't figure out what she was saying, but the look of horror on her face was confusing the hell out of me. My body started shaking uncontrollably, and suddenly, my legs just didn't want to hold me. I looked down to see a knife protruding from my chest with blood trickling down my bare stomach. I fell to the ground as my knees buckled and stared up at the ceiling as I realized that the reason I couldn't breathe wasn't the smoke, but that my lungs had been nicked by the blade.

Rolling my head to the side, I saw Pappy making his way over to me as he yelled at Kate to stay back. The building groaned around us and I knew they didn't have long to get out. I didn't want to say goodbye to Kate, but I wouldn't let her die in this building with me. When Pappy reached my side, he stared down at my chest and then back up at me.

"Just hold on, Hud. I'm going to get you out of here."

He put his arms under me, but the pain was too intense and I knew he wouldn't be able to get me out of here on his own.

"Go," I croaked out.

"What? I'll get you out of here. I just need to—"

"You promised," I choked out. "You fucking promised."

He stopped moving and looked back into my pleading eyes. He

shook his head slightly and his mouth hung open like he wanted to disagree, but he saw the determination on my face. He picked up the gun I had dropped and placed it in my hand.

"Don't ask me to do it."

"Keep...her...safe," I gasped and then started choking as blood filled my mouth. "Go," I said more urgently. He hesitated only a moment before spinning around and running back to Kate. I watched as he pulled on her as she screamed and struggled with him. A calm settled over me. She was going to get out and go on with life, and that was all that mattered to me right now. The heat from the flames licked closer to my skin and I knew it wouldn't be long now until I either passed out from the pain or the fire consumed me.

15

KATE

"No! What are you doing? Go back. We have to get him out of there," I yelled at Hunter as he dragged me down the stairs.

"He'll be fine. We have to get out of here."

"Are you crazy? The ceiling just collapsed in there. He could still be alive. We have to go get him."

He spun around and grabbed me by the arms, shaking me to calm my hysteria. "We can't fucking go back. He wanted me to get you out and that's what I'm fucking doing."

"I don't give a damn what he wanted. You're his friend. Go back and get him!"

"I'm just doing what he asked of me."

"You're a spineless bastard. You know he would never leave you behind," I yelled at him. He cursed and yanked on my arm, dragging me back up the stairs. When we reached the doorway, I pushed past Hunter, only to stop dead in my tracks when I saw a large knife being shoved deep into Garrick's chest. My breathing came to a halt as I watched Jensen fall to the ground and Garrick standing unsteadily on his feet.

"Garrick!" I yelled as my heart broke in two. The placement of the knife was lethal if he didn't get help soon. I could see it from here. I tried to go to him, but Hunter held me back and we watched as Garrick fell to the ground.

"Stay here. I'm serious, Kate. You stay here or I'm not going over there."

I nodded and watched as he ran over to Garrick, who was watching me with glazed eyes. I could see them shining in the distance and prayed that Hunter would be able to get him out. Moments slipped into minutes and then Hunter was standing and running back to me as Garrick stared at me. What was he doing?

"What are you doing? Do you need my help?"

"We're leaving."

"No!" I shook my head wildly. "I'm not leaving him."

"We have to. I can't get him out by myself and he made me promise to get you out of here."

"I'm not fucking leaving him," I shouted, but he didn't care. He hauled me up over his shoulder and started running down the stairs as I screamed for Garrick. Concrete started collapsing around us and we just barely made it out before the doorway collapsed in a pile of dust. I was hysterical, punching and yelling at Hunter as he continued to haul me further away from the fire—from Garrick.

"You can't do this to me! He's supposed to be with me!"

Hunter stopped outside the door and spun around, then took off running again as I continued to yell at him. A car door was opened and I was flung inside. I scrambled to sit up and looked out the back window at the burning building behind us. I was flung into the back side of the front seat as we tore off down the road.

I looked up front to see Derek driving and Rob sitting in the front seat. Lola was sitting next to me, staring out the window at the wreckage. "Lola, please, we have to go back. We can't leave him," I pleaded, but she just looked at me sadly.

"There's no way he could survive that. Going back would be suicide."

"Derek, turn the car around. I'll go myself if no one else will," I said frantically.

Hunter grabbed me by the arms and shook me as he yelled at me. "We can't go back for him. He's hurt too bad and the trip would have killed him. He wanted me to keep you safe and that's what I'm fucking doing! You saw the knife. There's no way he could survive that if he was jostled around. This was what he wanted!"

I looked into Hunter's eyes and saw the pain radiating from them. He didn't want this any more than I did and it was killing him to have left his friend behind. I knew he was right. Logically, I knew that Hunter would have done anything to save Garrick if he could have, but my heart didn't understand. The tears started pouring down my face with hiccuping sobs that threatened to take over my whole body.

"He can't be gone. He can't...I was supposed to be with him." My heart was breaking. It had been just hours before that we finally made our way back to one another. He had promised me he would end this and we would be together. "He was going to change things for us," I cried. I pounded my fists against Hunter's chest as the pain ripped through me. He wrapped his arms around me as I cried into his chest. I could feel Hunter's body shaking as he held me tight. I had no idea how long we drove or where we were headed. At some point, my cries died down and all I was left with was a numbness spreading through my whole body.

When we pulled up to a motel hours later, Hunter carried me into the room and set me down on the bed. I was grateful, sure that my legs would collapse beneath me if I tried to stand. He knelt in front of me as I stared down at the dingy carpet and took my hand in his.

"Hey, why don't you take a shower, then you can sleep?"

I didn't have the slightest desire to sleep. All I wanted was to go back in time and make Garrick leave that burning building with us. He would still be alive right now and he would be the one taking care of me instead of Hunter. I pushed Hunter back slightly and stood.

"You never should have left him," I muttered as I made my way into the bathroom and slammed the door. My chest was heaving as the tears built again, and I was sure I was going to lose it. I quickly turned on the shower and threw the T-shirt to the floor. I took off my filthy panties and stepped under the steaming water. As the dirt flowed down the drain, it felt like Garrick was being washed away. It was silly, but that dirt represented the last moments I had with Garrick, and now I wouldn't even have that.

I slid down the shower wall and sat on the floor, letting the water pelt down on me. I stared at the shower floor until the water ran clear and then closed my eyes, thinking about my last hours with Garrick. He was always so strong that I couldn't imagine him being taken out that way, and nobody actually saw him die in that building. There was every possibility that he got out. Plus, it didn't feel like he was gone. If he really was dead, I would know it, just like I always knew when he was watching me. I couldn't give up on him yet. Until someone showed me proof that he was gone, I was going to assume he was still alive and doing everything possible to get back to me.

I stood and finished washing, then shut off the water and wrapped a towel around my body. I refused to cry one more tear. Opening the bathroom door, I stepped out into the room where Derek, Rob, Lola, and Hunter all stood uncomfortably.

"Here. I got you some clothes," Lola said, handing me a bag.

"Thank you. I'll just get dressed."

I went back to the bathroom and quickly dressed, towel-drying my hair as I walked back into the room.

"So, what happens now?" I asked.

"We need to get back to Reed Security," Derek said. "We think that with Jensen gone, you should be safe, but we'll lay low for a few days to be sure."

"I think we should wait around here. We don't know for sure that Garrick didn't make it out and he could be looking for us."

Hunter sent an uneasy glance to the others and then stepped toward me. I knew what was coming. He was going to try and comfort me or talk me into his reality.

"Don't even think about it," I said before he could give me a lecture. "I know he was badly injured, but this is Garrick Knight we're talking about. He would have found a way to make it out on his own and you know it."

"I was with him, Kate. His injuries were bad. When I tried to move him, he was in too much pain. There's no way he could have made it out on his own."

"Then show me his body," I said defiantly. "Until you do, I'm going to choose to believe that he still had a chance to make it out."

"Kate, the building was collapsing around us. Our exit was blocked as soon as we made it outside. Where would he have gone?"

"I don't know," I said in frustration, "But this is Garrick and he's strong. He wouldn't have just laid down and let the fire take him. He would have fought with everything he had to get back to me."

Derek sat down in the chair by the desk and ran a hand over his face. He looked exhausted. All of them did. "Look, we can't stay around here. We need to make sure you're safe first. That's what Garrick wanted. If he's alive like you say, then he would find a way to get help. He wouldn't come looking for us because he would know that we would take you back to Reed Security. He'll go looking for you there. So, let's get there so that if he is alive, you're there waiting for him."

I couldn't tell if Derek was being sincere or just trying to appease me, but his face was kind and what he was saying made sense. I nodded and sat down on the bed, feeling suddenly exhausted.

"Why don't you let me clean up that cut on your forehead and then you can get some sleep?" Hunter asked.

"Yeah, I think that's a good idea."

"Rob, I want you to stay in the room with Hunter and Kate. Lola and I will take first watch."

"I'll jump in the shower while you clean Kate up," Rob said, standing and walking to the bathroom. Derek and Lola left the room and Hunter knelt in front of me with his medical bag. He must have kept them in the SUVs for emergencies. He got to work cleaning me up and I only winced slightly at the pain. When he was all done, he put some gauze over the cut and taped it in place.

"It's not too bad. We'll just keep it clean. You know the drill." He started cleaning up, but then stopped and looked up at me. "Kate, you know I would have done anything to save him. I never would have left him if I thought there was a chance I could save him."

"I guess we'll just have to wait and see," I said shortly. I didn't like that he was giving up so easily on Garrick. I knew in my heart that he was still alive. There was no way he would leave me. He spent months stalking me and I could always feel when he was around, and I felt empty when he was gone. I didn't feel that emptiness yet, and until I did, I wouldn't accept that he was dead.

"Kate, I know you want to believe he's still alive, but you need to prepare yourself for the fact that he didn't make it out. It would have been nearly impossible for anyone to survive that fire."

"But he's not just anyone." I stood and paced the room, my anger growing every minute that Hunter tried to convince me that Garrick was dead. "I can't believe that you not only left him behind but that you're giving up on him so easily. He's a fighter by nature. There's no way something like a knife would stop him."

"Alright, Kate. We won't give up yet," he said as if he was resigned to play along.

"Think whatever you want, Hunter. I don't care if you believe me or not. I'm telling you, he's not gone yet. I always know when he's around and I'm telling you that I don't feel the emptiness around me. He's still out there fighting for his life, and you're walking away. But Derek's right. He knows how to take care of himself, and when he gets better, he'll be looking for me at Reed Security."

Hunter nodded and took a step back as Rob exited the bathroom, clean and dressed in clean clothes. They must have gotten clothes for everyone.

"Shower's all yours."

"Thanks."

Hunter stalked off to the bathroom and I slipped under the covers. I needed to get some sleep so that when we got back to Reed Security, I could be prepared for Garrick.

"THE FIRE DEPARTMENT SAID THE BUILDING IS A TOTAL LOSS. IT'S GOING TO take some time for them to dig through the wreckage and look for... bodies," Sebastian said hesitantly as we all sat in the conference room back at Reed Security. "Until we can identify Jensen's body, I want you to stay with Derek's team at our safe house," Sebastian said, looking at me.

"Garrick is going to come looking for me. You have to let him know where I am."

Sebastian looked questioningly at Hunter who just shook his head. "Uh, Kate…"

"I know. None of you think he survived, but I'm telling you, he's still alive. I know it."

"Kate, I've seen the wreckage. There's no way anyone got out of there alive."

I was tired of repeating myself to these guys. They didn't know Garrick the way I did, and while I freaked out after I saw the building going up in flames, when I had a chance to stop and really think about it, I knew he was still alive and that he would come for me.

"What about my clinic?"

"Cole got another doctor filling in for you. From what the staff says, he's fitting in well and doing a good job."

"What did you tell the staff about me?"

"Family emergency," Sebastian supplied. "You don't know how long you'll be gone because it's an ongoing health issue with your mother."

"Well, at least I don't have to worry about that."

"In the meantime, Hunter will take you home so you can pack a bag. As soon as we hear more from the fire investigator, we'll let you know."

"Thank you, Sebastian."

I stood and followed Hunter to the door and down to the SUV. He took me home to pack a bag, and while I was there, I saw a few of Garrick's t-shirts that he had left behind. I grabbed them and shoved them in my bag, knowing they would help me feel closer to him until he came back to me.

The ride to the safe house was awkward at best. No one believed me that Garrick was alive and they kept shooting me worried glances, like I was going off the deep end. When we arrived, Hunter showed me to my room and I hid in there the rest of the night. For the next week, I only came out for meals, spending the rest of my days watching out the window for any sign of Garrick. I knew he would be coming once he found out where I was. It was silly to think that he would show up this soon. With the injury to his chest, he would most likely be recovering in a hospital for the better part of a week, but I still watched every day.

By the end of the second week, I still hadn't seen any sign of Garrick and I was starting to get a little nervous. Maybe he wasn't doing as well as I hoped. It was possible that he suffered complications from his injuries. I wanted to go to him and look at him myself, but nobody knew where he was. Deciding that I'd had enough waiting around, I went in search of Hunter. He was sitting at the kitchen table working on a laptop.

"Hunter, I need to talk to you."

He closed his laptop and gave me his full attention. "What's up?"

"I need you to do me a favor and look for Garrick."

"Kate..." He shook his head and looked away.

"I know what you think, but I'm asking you to look for him for me. I know he's out there somewhere and he could be suffering complications from his injuries. I just need to know how he is."

He stood and started pacing the kitchen, rubbing his hand along the back of his neck. "You need to stop this, Kate. This is crazy. I know you want to believe he's alive and out there trying to get back to you, but he's not," he yelled. "I want him back as much as you, but I can't take any more of this shit! He died in that building and you need to face the facts."

"I can still feel him. He isn't gone," I insisted.

"You can feel him?" he said incredulously. "Do you know how insane that sounds? You're a medical professional. Look at this from a medical standpoint. He was stabbed in the chest and coughing up blood, which means his lungs were compromised. He was in a building that was on fire and he wouldn't have been able to breathe very well as it was. It was obvious he was in a lot of pain, so moving around on his own would have been next to impossible. The building collapsed as we were getting out, so what are the chances that he miraculously got up on his own under those conditions and made a run to a different exit and made it out?"

I was silent as my eyes welled with unshed tears. Deep down, I knew that it was next to impossible, but how could he not be out there? I still felt him. As a doctor, a feeling meant absolutely nothing. I dealt with things I could explain medically, things that could be easily quantified. A feeling didn't mean anything to someone like me, but it was still there and I felt it as sure as I knew that I had gone to school and gotten my medical degree. But maybe Hunter was right. Maybe I was setting myself up for a horrible heartbreak, but until they gave me proof that he was gone, I wouldn't back down.

Hunter stepped toward me as I let the tears slowly slip down my face. He ran his hands up and down my arms in a soothing manner. "I know how hard this is, and trust me, there's not a second of the day that I'm not kicking myself for letting him stay behind or not being able to save him," he said with a slight croak. "He was like a brother to me and I wish more than anything that I could have him back. But wishing that he was still out there isn't going to make this any easier."

I stepped back from him and bit back the tears. "I won't give up yet. No matter what you say, I won't believe it until we put him in the ground."

I turned on my heel and walked away. If I stayed, he would just try to tell me how wrong I was and I didn't need to hear that right now.

"GARRICK! DON'T GO BACK IN THERE. STAY WITH ME," I BEGGED HIM AS HE tried to go back into the fire to finish Jensen.

"I have to do this, Kate. We'll never be safe if I don't kill him."

"Please, if you love me, you won't go back in there," I cried. He wrapped a hand around the back of my neck and pulled me in close to him.

"I love you and that's why I have to do this. I want it all with you and we won't get that if I walk away now. I'm going to finish this and then we're going to grow old together. I promise."

"Don't make promises you can't keep."

"I never do. Go with Hunter. I promise I'll find you when this is all over."

He kissed me hard and then turned back to Jensen. Hunter dragged me down the staircase, but when I heard something crash, I knew we had to go back.

"Wait! Hunter, he needs our help. We have to go back."

"No," Hunter said fiercely. "I promised him I'd get you out and that's

181

what I'm going to do."

I yanked my arm out of his grasp and ran back up the stairs. *"I won't leave him,"* I shouted. *I ran back through the door just as a knife was plunged into Garrick's chest. I watched in horror as he collapsed to the ground. The fire was spreading quickly and I knew I had to get to him fast if I had a chance of getting him out. Hunter sprinted past me and jumped over rubble to get to Garrick. Tripping and stumbling my way over, I shakily placed a hand on Garrick's chest, feeling the uneven rhythm. He didn't have long.*

"Hang on. We'll get you out of here," I urged him.

"No." He took my hand in his as his eyes glazed over. His breathing took on a ragged tone and blood trickled down his face. *"Please leave me. I promise I'll find you. Go with Hunter, and I'll find you again one day. It won't be right away, but I promise I'll come for you."*

"Please don't ask that of me. I can't walk away," I cried.

"I need you to do this, but I'll see you again. It won't be for a while, but I will come for you. Just keep believing in me."

I could tell it was getting harder for him to speak now and I had to go before it was too late to get out. Leaning over him, I kissed him one last time, my tears mingling with his, and I stood and walked away. The fire spread around me, but I was calm, knowing he would always be there to protect me. I glanced back, but he was gone. Hunter pulled me down the stairs, and this time, we made it outside just as the building collapsed.

I TOOK DEEP BREATHS, TRYING TO CALM MY RACING HEART. SWEAT POURED from my face and chills took over my body as I came down from the nightmare. Or was it Garrick trying to tell me that he was alive? I ran to the window and looked outside, sure that I could feel his gaze on me at this very moment, but I couldn't see anything. It was irrational, but I needed to talk to Hunter right now and tell him about my dream. Maybe that would convince him that he needed to look for Garrick. It had been four weeks since the fire. Surely, he would be able to find out something about him. I ran downstairs and stopped in my tracks when I saw Sebastian standing in the living room of the safe house. The only reason he would come is if he had news.

"What is it?" I asked as I ran into the room. Sebastian looked over at me with a pained expression.

"Kate, maybe you should sit down."

"No, just tell me. Did you find Garrick?"

"We did."

I sighed in relief and smiled at him, but it faded as Sebastian hung his head.

"The coroner was able to identify a few of the bodies. One belonged to Jensen. There was another body found near his. Dental records confirm that the remains belong to Hudson McGuire. They matched the dental records the military has. We would have gotten this news sooner, but the military wanted to be sure it was him, so they did their own autopsy of the body."

My mouth was suddenly very dry and I couldn't find the words to say. I looked to Hunter, but he looked just as devastated as I felt. I started shaking my head rapidly from side to side as my eyes blurred. I didn't even feel them sliding down my face. There was just a burning pain in my chest that made me feel like my whole body was on fire.

"No. He made it out of there," I shouted. "He didn't die in that fire."

"He had the gun still. The autopsy showed that he put a bullet in his head before the fire got to him. He didn't suffer," Sebastian said.

It was like I was back there the night that it happened. I could see him being stabbed and I could see him staring at me as Hunter pulled me away. Why had I left him? I should have tried harder. I should have fought for him. I leaned against the wall to hold myself up as the pain washed over me. I had done this to him. If I hadn't pushed him away, if I hadn't been so stubborn, things might have turned out differently. He might have fought harder for me. I wiped my tears as cold crept into my body and drained all feelings of life from me. I slowly raised my eyes and looked at Sebastian.

"I want to go home now." That was the only place I knew I would feel close to Garrick.

"Kate, maybe you should take a few days and—"

"No." I swallowed hard and fought back the nausea. "There's no point in staying. You said yourself that Jensen is dead. I can go home now."

Hunter walked over to me and tried to pull me into his arms, but I didn't want his comfort. This was all his fault. I took a few steps toward Sebastian.

"Don't come near me. You're worse than he ever was. He may have killed people for a living, but they were evil people. He died because you wouldn't save him. I hate you," I whispered. I turned and walked out the door, hoping like hell that Sebastian would take me home. I would walk if I had to because there was no way I could stand to be with Hunter for another minute.

"ARE YOU GOING TO HIS FUNERAL?" COLE ASKED AS HE SAT IN MY kitchen.

"Of course I am. Why wouldn't I?"

"I just thought it might be too hard for you."

"Somebody has to be there for him."

"Hunter will be there, along with all the people at Reed Security. They may not have worked with him, but he meant something to Hunter, and they all want to support him."

"Hunter. Right. He was such a good friend that he left Garrick for dead."

Cole sighed and ran a hand over his face. "You have to stop blaming Hunter for his decision. Garrick would have done anything to protect you, including telling Hunter to leave him behind. Hunter probably would have stayed if it weren't for his promise to Garrick."

"So this is my fault?"

"No, I'm saying that Hunter had a choice to make and he chose to respect his friend's wishes. You can't blame him for that."

"We aren't going to see eye to eye on this, so why don't we just change the subject?"

"Fine. Are you planning the funeral?"

"No. Sebastian asked if he could do it. He said the military wouldn't give him a funeral and he wanted to pay his respects to Garrick for his service."

Cole nodded in understanding. "That's very generous of him considering all Knight did."

"What do you mean *all he did*?"

"Well, he held Maggie at knifepoint and destroyed the Reed Security building. I would say Sebastian is being very generous."

I couldn't really argue with that. He had a point. Still, it felt wrong that all these people were going to Garrick's funeral, pretending like they actually gave a shit about him.

"Alex and I can pick you up tomorrow morning. We can all go together. I know this is hard for you."

"I appreciate that, especially since you didn't like him."

"I didn't like his life choices, but I know he loved you."

I felt so lost and the ache in my chest grew more painful every day. I didn't know what I was going to do from here. I had a clinic to run, but no desire to go back to work. For the first time in my life, I didn't want to put my career above everything else. I just wanted to curl up in a ball and hide from the world for a while.

"Kate." Cole was looking at me, his face full of concern.

"Huh?"

"I've been talking to you. Did you hear me?"

"Sorry, I got a little lost in my thoughts. If you don't mind, I think I'm going to take a nap now. Thanks for stopping by."

I didn't wait for him to leave. I headed up to my room and crawled under the covers, not wanting tomorrow to come, because when it did, I knew I would have to say goodbye to Garrick forever.

"Have you ever been to a military funeral? I suggest you go sometime. Look at the widow as she's handed the flag that her husband earned with his life. You can watch his kids staring at the casket, not understanding why their father isn't coming home."

Sebastian had arranged for a flag to be placed over Garrick's casket in honor of his service in the military. The men and women from Reed Security were all dressed in their military dress uniforms and standing at attention. There were other men in military uniforms, but I had no idea who they were. A bugle played Taps and I closed my eyes as I let the sound wash over me. With every melancholy note, my chest tightened more and more. I imagined all the men and women who had earned flags over the years by giving their lives in service of their country. When I opened my eyes as the song came to an end, I saw Hunter and Sebastian step forward and begin to fold the flag. Cole had told me they planned to give me Garrick's flag. He had no other family and Hunter insisted I should have it. It felt tainted somehow because he died fighting the man who had made him who he was in the end.

My heart pounded wildly in my chest as Hunter walked toward me with the folded flag. Spots filled my vision and I felt like I might pass out. I couldn't do this. I couldn't take that flag and admit that he was gone. I swallowed hard to keep my sobs from breaking free and Cole gripped my hand hard.

"Just breathe," he whispered in my ear.

When Hunter stopped in front of me, I looked up into his tear-filled eyes and felt my own fill. His voice was low and rough as he said his own version of the flag presentation. "On behalf of all of us who had the honor of serving with him, please accept this flag as a symbol of our appreciation for your loved one's honorable and faithful service." A tear slipped down his cheek and I wanted to be angry with him and tell him he had no right to cry over Garrick. I wanted to yell at him for letting him die, but this was about honoring Garrick, and now wasn't the time for my anger.

When I placed my hands on the flag, something inside me broke and that was it for me. Sobs wracked my body and I would have fallen to the ground if Cole wasn't holding me up. The pain in my chest was so intense that I felt like my chest was literally being ripped open. I couldn't look as they lowered the casket into the ground. No matter how hard I tried, I couldn't stop the tears as they flowed down my face. I saw Garrick lying in bed with me. I felt his eyes on me from the coffee shop. I heard him whispering that he loved me, but that was all I had now. Dreams of what we could have had and memories of the few months we had together. It was such a short time, but one that was filled with so much passion and desire that I didn't think I would ever be the same again.

16

KATE

THE SUN SHONE brightly in my room, so I pulled the covers over my head and hid from the day. It was a week after Garrick's funeral and I had barely left my bed, unable to face anything other than basic necessities. I went to the bathroom when I absolutely had to and I forced myself to eat when my body couldn't go without any more. I didn't have much of an appetite, so I usually forced down a spoon of peanut butter or something equally dissatisfying. Occasionally, I would hear pounding at my door, but I couldn't be brought out of my depression enough to care. Most of the time, I stared at the wall thinking about absolutely nothing. I wasn't even sure what day it was. I counted mornings, or what I could remember, but most days I was too tired to think about much.

When the pounding came again this morning, I ignored it like I usually did. I didn't give a shit who was there or what they wanted. I didn't want to talk to anyone and there wasn't much I cared about at this point. When I heard the footsteps on the stairs, I closed my eyes and sighed, knowing that whoever was there was going to try and force me to rejoin the rest of the world.

When the bed dipped behind me, I felt a delicate arm drape over my stomach. I smelled her perfume and almost lost it. The one person that had the power to make me break down was here. They brought out the big guns when they sent her over.

"I can't," I whispered. "Not yet."

"I know, sweetie. I'm just going to lie here with you," Alex's soft voice filled the air. She knew more than anyone what it was like to feel so lost and need some time to figure stuff out. She had suffered more than anyone I knew and if she could come back from her pain and live a normal life with my cousin, I knew that I would be okay, too. Someday.

"When does it stop hurting?"

"I don't know. I was so young when my parents died. It was different to deal with that as a kid. For me, it ended when Cole saved me. When I finally accepted him back into my life. He was the one who healed me and put me back together."

"I don't have anyone to heal me. He's gone," I said brokenly.

"I know. Which means that you have to do it for yourself, but only you can decide when you're ready."

"Today's not the day."

"Then we'll try again tomorrow and the next day until you are ready."

I nodded and closed my eyes. I was so glad that she wasn't trying to force me out of my cocoon. When I woke later, Alex was gone, but there was a delicious smell coming from my kitchen. I hadn't wanted food all week, but this was making my stomach growl. I climbed out of bed and shuffled downstairs in my three-day-old pajama pants and a T-shirt that was really starting to smell. My hair was a ratty mess and I could feel the oil building on my scalp, causing me to itch like crazy.

When I got to the kitchen, Alex winced at the sight of me. "You look like you need this," she said, handing me a cup of coffee.

"It's late," I said, looking at the clock. "If I drink this, I'll be up all night."

"You've been sleeping for a week straight. It might not hurt for you to be up for a while."

I took the cup and drank a few sips, but I needed some food in my stomach before I tackled coffee. "What did you make?"

"Jambalaya."

"Mmm. I haven't had that in a long time."

"I found a recipe online about a year ago and I fell in love. Don't tell Cole I made it for you, though. He thinks I make this only for him," she smiled.

"I won't say a word."

I sat down and ate a whole bowl, more than I had eaten in a week, and suddenly felt very sleepy. I rested my head in my hand and allowed my eyes to drift closed as I looked out at the night sky. I was nodding off when I felt him. My eyes snapped open and I jerked upright in my chair. I stood suddenly, pushing the chair backward as I ran to the window and looked outside. It was impossible to see in the dark, but I knew he was out there. He had to be. I always felt him when he was around. Flinging the door open, I ran outside into the darkness as Alex yelled for me from the house.

"Garrick!" I looked everywhere, sure he was hiding behind a tree or on the side of the house. I raced around the yard, looking every-where I could, but he didn't come out. Why wasn't he coming out? "Garrick, please," I whispered. "Come back to me."

When he didn't step out of the shadows, I broke down and fell to the ground in a heap of tears. I was so sure he had come back for me. Why did this keep happening? Why did he torture me like this? If he wasn't really here, why did I still have to feel him?

"Kate?" I looked up to see Hunter standing next to me. He looked at me sadly and squatted down next to me. "Are you okay?"

"I thought he was here."

"Kate, you went to his funeral. You know he's gone." There was no heat behind his words, only sadness.

"I know," I said with a sniffle, "But I felt him again. It was like before when he was stalking me. I always knew when he was around."

Hunter looked around into the night and then back to me. "I'm sorry. I wish I could make this easier for you."

I shrugged as I wiped the tears from my face. "What are you doing here?"

"Alex called. She said you had been sitting out here for about an hour and she was starting to get worried. She couldn't get ahold of Cole, so I came over."

"You didn't have to. I'll be fine," I said as I stood and brushed the dirt from my clothes.

"How are you doing other than that?"

"Numb," I said after a minute. "I just feel numb. I wish that I was angry or sad, but I just feel empty."

He nodded and shoved his hands in his pockets. "Kate, it's been over a month since he died. I think it's time to try to get back to work, or at least some kind of routine for yourself. Garrick wouldn't want you wasting away over him."

"Maybe tomorrow," I said as I walked back to the house.

FOR THE PAST MONTH, I HAD BEEN FORCING MYSELF TO GET UP EVERY morning and at least take a shower. Alex or Cole stopped by every day to check on me or visit with me. I hadn't seen Hunter since the night I ran out of the house looking for Garrick, but I knew he worried about me. He called several times a week to check on me, but most of the time I refused to answer. I had come to accept that he did what he had to do for Garrick, but it still hurt to see Hunter when he wasn't the one I wanted around.

I had already had my shower for the day, but that was exhausting enough for me. Deciding that I really didn't want to face the day, I crawled back into bed and pulled the covers over my head. At least I was clean, even if I was lying in smelly sheets.

"Kate?" Cole's voice called from downstairs. Groaning I pulled the covers tighter over my head and hoped he would go away. "Kate, do you want to tell me why your lights aren't working?" he said as he walked into my bedroom.

I flung the covers off and glared at Cole. "What?"

"Your lights aren't working. Did you blow a fuse?"

"Like I even know what that means. Go away." I pulled the covers back over my head, but he was there in a flash, dragging them back down.

"No, you're not going to lie in bed all day again. This has to stop."

"Really? How long did you stay in bed after you got back from your last deployment?"

"Do you really want to throw that in my face?" he snarled. "I'm just trying to help you the way others helped me. I'm not going to let you drown in grief. You need to start living again."

"I don't want to."

"Too fucking bad. This has gone on long enough. Maybe start with paying your fucking bills. How long has it been since you paid the electric bill?"

I shrugged and he growled in frustration as he ran a hand over his face. "You have a clinic to run and you're leaving it up to someone else. Now, if you want to keep that other doctor on so that you can go back part-time, I'm fine with that, but you need to start doing something."

I wished that I felt something when he said that, but I was still so empty. I wasn't ready to break down and no light bulb came on in my head, telling me he was right. I just didn't feel anything. I didn't want to do anything. Taking a shower was hard enough to accomplish for one day. He held out his hand to me and I grudgingly took it.

"Come on," he said, pulling me up. "We're going to go do just one thing today. What sounds good?"

"Nothing."

"There has to be something that sounds appealing. What about going to get your hair done? I'm sure Alex would take you."

"Cole, I really don't give a shit about my hair. I don't want to do anything and I don't care about how the clinic is doing."

"What do you think Garrick would say if he saw you right now? Do you think he would want a woman who gave up on life because of him? He would be ashamed of you right now."

His words cracked something inside me and the dam that was holding back my emotions broke. I had been doing so well at pretending I was numb to everything, but suddenly I felt everything all at once. Fat tears rolled down my cheeks as I collapsed in a heap on the floor. My head pounded the more I cried and the deep ache inside intensified.

"I don't want to do this anymore," I cried. "I want him back so bad."

"I know," Cole said as he sat down beside me and pulled me into his arms, running his hand soothingly over my back. "I know this sucks and it's hard, but you'll get past this, Kate. You're a lot stronger than you know."

"I used to be," I sniffled. I lifted my gaze to meet Cole's and shook my head. "I don't know who I am anymore without him. That seems so stupid because I only knew him for a short time, but it was so intense."

"No one can tell you how to feel, Kate. Sometimes love just happens like that. With Alex, I knew within weeks that she was mine. I was so drawn to her and I wanted nothing more than to be the one she turned to. When she didn't remember me anymore, I was devastated. I thought we were done for good and it was nearly impossible to walk away from her. I really thought I might fall back into the depression I was in when I got back from war."

"Why didn't you?"

"I guess I just kept thinking that if we ever had a chance of making it back to one another, I needed to be the man she deserved. I couldn't fold in on myself again."

"But you had someone to go back to," I griped.

"True, but that doesn't mean that you won't ever meet someone who makes you feel ten times what you did for Garrick. I know you don't want that now, but if you close yourself off to the world, you won't have a shot at ever being the woman you were again."

"I don't think I'll ever be that woman again."

"Maybe not. I'm definitely not the same man I was before I went off to war, but those experiences make us who we are. This will definitely change who you are, but only you can decide if it makes you stronger or not. It's okay to be sad, Kate. Just don't let it consume you."

I nodded and sniffed back my tears, wiping my nose on the sleeve of my shirt. I was such a mess. "I think I need some help, Cole. I don't think I can do this alone."

"Alex and I are here whenever you need us. Just tell us what you need."

"That's the problem. I don't know what I need."

"Then we'll figure it out together," he said as he wrapped his arm around me and pulled me in for a hug.

———————

"Have a good night," Kathy said as she left for the night. I gave a small smile and waved her out the clinic door. I had been back to work for two months now and only a few weeks full-time. I had decided to keep Dr. Carson on staff because he had brought in a lot of business in my absence. I had been thinking of adding him on as a partner and expanding the clinic, but I wanted to be sure before I approached him about it.

This was my first night staying after clinic hours. In the past few weeks that I had been back full time, I had left every day with the other staff, but tonight I was feeling a little more like my old self and decided to stay behind and look at my budget and what I could do for the clinic. I hadn't had extra income since I had stopped working for Reed Security on the side. I wasn't sure if I would go back to that again or not. I wasn't sure I could handle the reminder of where I had met Garrick.

It was well after nine o'clock when I finally turned off the lights and headed for the clinic door. As I stepped outside, a strange chill crept over me and I found myself looking around for danger, but I didn't see any. I started for my car at a quick pace, wanting to get to the safety and comfort of my home. I had been a little more jumpy when I went out since I had been the target of a killer. My keys fumbled in my hand and fell to the ground in my haste to get away. I swore and bent over, sure that at any moment, someone was going to attack me from behind. I glanced over my shoulder several times as I found the keys and quickly stood and flung open the car door.

As soon as I got inside, I felt him. I spun around in my seat and looked in the back seat, but no one was there. I locked the doors and looked around in the darkness, but there was still nothing. This had been happening to me almost every day since I started back at the clinic. It was like his ghost was following me around, except it wasn't comforting like it once was because I knew he wasn't actually there watching out for me. There was nothing a ghost could do for me if I was attacked, and he wouldn't be slipping into my bedroom later that night to bring me comfort.

I drove home and barely made it inside as my heart thudded out of control. My hands shook uncontrollably as I slammed the door closed, flipped the lock, and slowly stepped away from the door. I turned on the lights and looked in every room of the house, sure that I was going to find something, but there was nothing. I was losing it. He wasn't here anymore. He was dead and in the ground. If I kept imagining he was there, I was going to go crazy. Maybe I already was.

I went to my bathroom and got into the steaming shower, doing the one thing I allowed every day. I sat on the floor of the shower and let my tears go for just a few minutes as I grieved for Garrick. I couldn't do this around Cole or Alex. They thought I was doing so much better, and in some ways I was, but it was mostly because I was forcing myself to appear normal. I didn't feel normal or whole. I didn't feel like I was healing in any way, and the presence of Garrick's ghost, or whatever the hell it was, was making getting over him all the more difficult.

I crawled into bed, exhausted from the day and my attempts at appearing fine and closed my eyes. Every night, I dreamed of Garrick and the night he died, and every night, I woke up screaming his name. Tonight was no different, except when I woke up this time, he was sitting in the chair in the corner of my room staring at me. I shot across my bed to the nightstand and turned on the light, but when I turned back, he was gone. Had I imagined it? Was my mind playing tricks on me again? It was like when I imagined that he was around, but he never was. How the hell was I supposed to keep going when I couldn't even make it through the night without thinking about him?

I laid back down and stared at the ceiling until the sun rose. There was no way I was falling back asleep after that. When I got up in the morning and made myself a cup of coffee, I frowned when I looked at the date on my phone. It had been exactly six months today since Garrick died in the fire. Calling Dr. Carson, I asked him to rearrange my patients for me because I was taking a sick day. He knew some of what had happened and he had been very understanding so far. I was happy I didn't have to explain everything to him.

I hadn't been back to Garrick's grave since the funeral because I didn't think I could handle it, but I decided today would be the day. Maybe it would bring me closure, or at the very least, a little comfort to feel close to him again. When I arrived at the cemetery, I quickly found his grave and stared at the headstone. Logically, I knew that he wasn't here, and coming to visit him and talk to him was ridiculous. If I really wanted to say something to him, all I had to do was say it.

I sat down on the grass and pulled some of the weeds that were coming up around his headstone. "Hey, Garrick. I want you to know that this is one of the weirdest things I've ever done. I don't know if you can hear me or not, and I'm not sure I believe that you can, but I wanted to come see you anyway, just in case. It's been six months now and…I miss you so much." My throat started to constrict, but I pulled it back so I didn't have a meltdown in the middle of the cemetery.

"I keep thinking I'll wake up from some horrible dream and you'll be here. I just can't believe you're really gone. I had it in my mind that you were indestructible." A few tears slid down my face and I quickly wiped them away. "Which is just crazy because we all bleed and we all die eventually. I just didn't think I would have such little time with you."

I picked at the grass by my feet and stared at his headstone. My chest ached so much, and I wanted to break down in tears and cry just being here. "This just isn't fair," I whispered. "I wanted more time with you. Why didn't you leave the building with me? We could have found another way. You didn't have to die in there."

My tears suddenly dried up and I no longer felt sadness, but anger. "You chose to stay behind when you should have chosen me. You should have walked away. The building was on fire and you knew that it was dangerous to stay, but that's who you are, right? You were so sure you could defeat him that you chose to stay behind and end him. Well, congratulations. You killed him, but you also managed to get yourself killed and leave me all alone." I stood and kicked at his head-stone. "You fucking idiot! You left me!"

I started crying uncontrollably and then felt strong arms wrap around me. For a moment, I was sure it was Garrick, but then I turned and saw Hunter's sad eyes looking down at me. "He left me," I cried as I pounded at his chest. "He knew better than to stay in that building, and he chose killing Jensen over being with me."

Hunter squeezed me tight to his body and ran a hand up and down my back. "I know. I'm sorry he's not here, but he did it for you. He needed to know you were safe."

"I would have been safe with him next to me. All he had to do was walk out of that building and we would have found a way. Why couldn't he do that for me?"

"Kate, he did what he thought he had to. We can't change it."

"I know," I whispered brokenly. "I can still feel him. He's always there and it's so hard to deal with. Everywhere I go, I can feel him watching me just like he used to."

Hunter sighed and pulled back to look at me. "Kate, I've been watching you. He asked me to keep you safe and I've been worried about you. Ever since you went back to work, I've been following you to make sure you're okay. I'm sorry if that was overstepping, but I knew he would want me to look after you."

I took a step back and wiped my eyes. "So, all this time, I wasn't feeling him?"

"No. I'm sorry, Kate. I just wanted to make sure you were okay."

I nodded slightly and gave a slight smile. "It just felt so real. All this time, I thought he was still here looking after me. I was just imagining it all."

"Kate—"

"No. This is good. I really needed to know that it was just you." I looked back at the grave and then back to Hunter. "He really is gone," I said shakily. "I need to accept that and stop imagining he's here. It's time for me to move on with my life, and I can't do that if I'm always thinking about him."

"You don't have to stop thinking about him."

"Yes, I do. If I don't, I'll be stuck in this hell where I never move forward with my life." I huffed out a laugh and shook my head. "You know, I never thought he would give up his job for me, and it turns out

I was right. He died doing his job and that's what I should have expected."

"He was doing it for you," Hunter repeated. "He was trying to create a life with you."

"You keep saying that, but he didn't give up his job for me. He gave up his life to do his job, and I have to remember that. Now, it's time for me to move on with my life." I started to walk away, but then I turned back to Hunter. "I'm sorry for blaming you. I know you did everything you could and you were just doing what he asked. There's no excuse for the things I said to you. Goodbye, Hunter."

I turned and walked away, knowing now that I would have never filled the desire that Garrick craved from his job. I was a distraction, but apparently not enough of one to make him choose me.

———

It had been a year since Garrick died and I was determined to start living my life again. For the past six months, I had been consumed by work, determined to lose myself in the clinic so I didn't think about Garrick. I hadn't seen most of my friends since I first met Garrick, so when Samantha called and asked me out for drinks, I accepted without a second thought.

I dressed in a tight, black dress, wanting to feel sexy for the first time in a year. When I looked over myself in the mirror, I wanted to be happy that I was going out and that I looked good, but as I stared in the mirror, all I saw was a woman trying to move on without her man. Shaking the thoughts from my head, I grabbed my purse and headed out.

When I got to The Pub, I swallowed down my nerves and entered the bar with as much confidence as I could. When I saw Samantha, my nerves melted away and I practically ran to her for a hug. I hadn't realized how much I missed her. She didn't know about Garrick or what had happened, so I almost broke down in tears when she came to me and hugged me. I wiped the few stray tears that fell and laughed off her concerned look.

"Are you okay?"

"Of course. It's just been so long and I missed you."

"Well, you shouldn't work so much then."

I didn't tell her that I spent a few months wallowing in pity at home. Then I would have to tell her the whole story and I just couldn't do that. We sat and chatted for a while as we drank down Cosmos. She filled me in on all that had happened over the past year and showed me the brilliant diamond ring that now adorned her left ring finger.

"Oh my gosh! That's beautiful."

"I know. I can't wait for you to meet Jeff. He's just amazing."

I put on my best happy face and listened to her gush over her fiancé for the better part of an hour. It was getting harder and harder to keep the smile on my face as the hour drew to a close. I was on my third Cosmo and feeling no pain, so at least there was that. I had just ordered another drink when I felt him. Hunter was here to keep an eye out for me. He had continued to follow me whenever I went out after that day at the cemetery. He took his loyalty to Garrick very seriously. Well, if he was here to watch out for me, I didn't have to worry about how drunk I got tonight, and I definitely planned to let go.

Samantha's eyes widened when he came up behind me and slid his hand around my waist, something he had never taken the liberty of doing before and I definitely didn't like it. I wasn't his and I didn't want him to think he could claim me as his just because I had been with his friend. I stiffened at his touch and when his lips came down and grazed my neck, I jerked away.

"You've stopped looking for me."

The blood drained from my face and I could feel my heart thumping wildly in my throat. Samantha was staring at me with a raised eyebrow and I desperately wanted to ask what the man looked like that was holding me, but my throat was so dry that I couldn't have spoken if I tried. I swallowed hard and turned just enough to get a look at the face that was so close to mine.

All the noise from the bar faded and everything around me swirled in a dizzying, spotty pattern. The dark eyes that I had fallen so hard for stared back at me with a hunger I used to crave. I blinked slowly, trying to snap myself out of whatever nightmare this was and come back to some normal kind of reality. It was no use. My whole body started shaking uncontrollably and my breathing became erratic. I knew I should calm the fuck down, but I couldn't. All I could think was that I was on the verge of seriously losing my shit.

"Breathe." I couldn't hear him, but I read the words on the lips that knew my body so well. The lips that I had dreamed about for the past year and had prayed many nights would come back to me.

"Garrick." My eyes fluttered closed and I started to slip off the bar stool. Blackness took over as I fell into the arms of the man I loved.

17

KNIGHT

I WATCHED her from across the street like I always did, lurking in the shadows of the alley. This was her first time being out with friends and she looked absolutely stunning. She had done her hair and was wearing a tight dress that showed off what little curves she had left. I missed the feel of her body against mine and I had watched over the past year as she deteriorated into someone I didn't recognize. That was my fault and I absolutely hated it, but if I wanted her back, I had to follow the rules Sebastian had set forth.

When she walked into the bar tonight, she looked unsure of herself and didn't start to let go until she had a few drinks in her. By that point, I wasn't entirely sure that she was looking out for herself. I didn't want to approach her in front of others, but at this point, I didn't see another option. She was putting herself in danger by drinking so much.

"Garrick," she said, right before her eyes rolled back in her head and she collapsed into my arms. Looking at her friend, I grinned and lifted her up bridal style.

"I have that effect on women. I'll make sure she gets home safe, Samantha."

"Wait. How do you know me? You look familiar."

I grinned at her and shook my head. "I only know you through Kate. Trust me, I'd remember a beautiful woman like you."

Her eyes softened and I knew I had her. I carried Kate out of the bar and to my car, which was waiting down the block. After I got her safely tucked in the car, I pulled out my phone and dialed a number I hadn't used in a year.

"Hello?" Pappy's voice said like he was pissed off for being interrupted.

"Pappy, it's been a long time, man."

There was silence on the other end of the line and for the second time tonight, I had totally shocked someone.

"Who the fuck is this?"

"Hud."

"Fuck you. Hud's dead."

He hung up and I sighed, calling him back.

"What do you want, asshole?"

"Just meet me at Kate's house and I'll explain everything."

I hung up before he had a chance to respond. I knew he would show up there. He had been a good friend and watched out for her like I asked. There was no way he wouldn't show up at the mention of Kate. I pulled into her driveway a few minutes later and carried her inside, laying her gently on the couch. I had been in this house so many times over the past year, watching her sleep and being tormented by nightmares. Sometimes I even laid down in bed with her, but I never allowed myself to touch her. It would break me to feel her skin and not pull her in close to me. So, instead, I watched her from her chair or just wandered around her house so I could feel close to her. Now she would know the truth and I just prayed she was willing to forgive me.

I heard the screeching of tires as Pappy pulled in the driveway and I hurried to the door so he didn't break it down to get to Kate. When I flung the door open, his anger turned to complete astonishment. I grinned at him, hoping to break the tension. I didn't expect the fist that flew at my face and knocked me on my ass. It took me a minute to figure out what the hell was happening. Pappy was on top of me, pummeling the shit out of my face and when I finally snapped out of it, I started fighting back. I managed to get behind him and put him in a chokehold. His hands were fighting to break the hold, but I had him locked in.

"Are you ready to listen and stop beating the shit out of me?"

He tapped out, and after a moment, I released him, letting him get his bearings as he turned on me with a sneer.

"You want to tell me where the fuck you've been for the past year?"

"I'll explain everything when Kate wakes up," I said, jerking my thumb in her direction on the couch.

"What the hell happened?" he asked, rushing to her side with concern. I narrowed my eyes, wondering if Pappy felt more for her than friendly concern.

"She passed out when she saw me."

He pressed his fingers to her neck for her pulse and sighed in relief when she appeared fine.

"When did that happen?"

"She was at a bar with her friend, Samantha."

"And you thought that was the best place to make your magical comeback?" he sneered.

"She was drinking too much. Why weren't you there watching her like you were supposed to?"

"Why wasn't I there? I've been keeping an eye on her for the past year. Where the hell have you been?"

"I couldn't come back yet. I wasn't allowed to."

"By who?"

"Sebastian."

He stiffened and his face darkened. "He knew? All this time, he fucking knew?"

A groan from the couch had us turning to see Kate starting to sit up, holding her head. "Oh my God. What the hell happened?"

She winced as she swung her legs over the edge of the couch and then her eyes widened when she saw first me and then Hunter. Shaking her head, she closed her eyes and then opened them again.

"I thought it was a bad dream," she mumbled.

"Not a dream, honey." I walked over to her and knelt down in front of her, taking her hands in mine. "How are you feeling?"

She smiled at me and when she closed her eyes, tears slid down her cheeks. She flung her arms around me and cried into the crick of my neck. I swallowed hard and tightened my hold on her. I had needed this for the past year, and now that I had her back, I couldn't imagine ever letting her go again. When she pulled back, she wiped the tears from her eyes.

"How are you here?"

"It's a long story and I promise to tell you everything. I just want to know that you're okay first."

"I'm fine. I just don't understand any of this." She looked to Pappy, back to me, and then back to Pappy again. When she stood suddenly, I almost fell backward on my ass to get out of her way. "You knew?" she asked Pappy accusingly, not giving him time to answer as she continued. "All this time, you've been pretending to care about me, to make sure that I was okay and you knew he was alive!"

"Whoa, whoa, whoa," he said, holding out his hands. "I just fucking found out about this. I got a phone call and I came right over. When I saw him, I was just as shocked as you."

"Okay, how about we all just settle down and I'll explain everything."

Kate sat down and Pappy walked over to sit next to her. I ran a hand over the back of my neck, trying to figure out how the hell to explain all this. "I don't even know where to fucking start."

"How about you start with how you made it out of that building," Pappy said.

I nodded and took a seat across from them. "Derek had called Sebastian earlier that night to tell him he didn't feel right about what was happening. Sebastian was on his way when we were first attacked. He showed up with Chance's team and they were there when the fire spread. We didn't have communication with them, but they made it inside and found me. It must have been right after you left," I said, turning to Pappy. "I don't remember much about how they got me out. I just remember waking up days later in a private hospital. I was in pretty bad shape and I didn't get released for almost another week."

"Why didn't you come find me?" Kate asked with tears in her eyes.

"I couldn't. Sebastian took one of Jensen's men and tossed him in the fire where I was. He gave the guy a stab wound and everything to match mine. Everything burned and he knew it would. He had Becky switch my dental records with the guy he used to replace me. It took a while because the military wanted to do their own investigation to make sure I was dead. They wanted the case wrapped up tight before they officially declared me dead."

"So why didn't you come back after you were pronounced dead?" Pappy asked me.

"Because I had two lives. It's fine for the military to declare me dead, but I had a whole other life as an assassin. Sebastian set things in motion for me to be killed on a job, which I officially was, but it took time and a lot of planning to make sure it was done right. Then, we had to wait and make sure that word spread of my demise. I couldn't just show back up in your life, Kate. Everyone would have known I wasn't really dead, and then it would have all been for nothing."

"You could have told me," Pappy said. "I work at Reed Security. Do you honestly think you can't fucking trust me? Even after everything I did for you?"

"It's not that simple, Pappy. Nobody knew but the people that had to. Do you honestly think you could have kept this secret from Kate? I asked you to look after her for me. I couldn't let you know I was alive and risk you telling her. All it would have taken was one person to think something was off and all my efforts would go up in smoke."

"So why now?" Kate asked. "Why are you suddenly back?"

"Sebastian was able to get me a new life. He's been working for months to make sure I have everything I need to start over. I couldn't see you until it was all taken care of. He finished up last month."

"Last month, and you're just now coming to see us," Kate shook her head in disgust.

"It's not like I could just walk back into your life, Kate. I've been gone for a year. I wasn't sure how you would take me being back."

She stood and shoved me back a step. "So you just walk into a bar and wrap your arm around me to let me know you're back? Do you know what that felt like for me? Do you know how badly this past year has fucked me up?"

She stormed out of the room before I could respond and left me alone with Pappy. Sighing, I took a seat and scrubbed a hand down my face. "That didn't go as I planned."

"How did you plan it? Because that's one fucked up way to walk back into her life. Do you have any fucking clue what she's been through?"

"Yes. I've been watching. I was always watching."

"You were watching, but you weren't there to see her so depressed she couldn't get out of bed. You didn't see her standing by your grave on the six-month anniversary of your death and watch as she broke down because she could still feel you. Christ, all that time, she was right. She said she could still feel you with her. You were there the whole fucking time."

"Pappy, I didn't have a choice. If I wanted a life with her, that's the way it had to be."

"But you made that decision without her. She thought you were stabbed to death and burned in a fire. She fucking blamed me for months because I didn't drag your ass out of there. Because I listened to you. I fucking blamed myself," he yelled. "All this time, I thought I had let her down because I let you die in that fire. I kept trying to figure out what I could have done differently so that you could have lived." He flexed his fists open and closed and shook his head as the tension rolled off him.

"Pappy, I know this is fucked up—"

"Fucked up? This is so far beyond fucked up. I buried you! We all wore our dress uniforms and gave you our version of a military funeral because the military sure as shit wouldn't give you one. I gave Kate a fucking flag!"

"Sebastian took care of all that. I didn't have any say in it. He basically told me that if I wanted a life with Kate, I had to follow his rules to a T. He did it. He gave me my life back. I can have the life I wanted with her. He gave me a job at Reed Security."

"Looks like everything turned out just fucking peachy for you."

"Don't give me that shit. It's been fucking hell to be away from her for all this time. To know that I had to have you watch over her for me because I couldn't do it. I saw what I did to her. I saw how she became a fucking toothpick because she wouldn't eat. I sat in her room at night and heard every single nightmare she had and I couldn't do a fucking thing about it. I couldn't hold her and tell her it would all be alright. I couldn't kiss her or tell her I loved her. I watched as you struggled to get her to see reason. I fucking saw it all," I yelled. "I wish it could have been different, but that's the way it had to be and I'm fucking sorry!"

Pappy paced the room for a few minutes as he tried to gather his thoughts. I could tell he was on the verge of pummeling me again, but he was trying to control his urges. Finally, he turned for the door and pulled it open, stalling as he stepped through the door. "I'm glad you're not fucking dead, but this is going to take me some time."

He walked out and left me alone in the living room. Fuck, none of this had gone the way I hoped. I had imagined a teary-eyed Kate running back into my arms, so glad that I was back, but she couldn't stand the sight of me. Not even my only friend wanted anything to do with me right now. I couldn't leave Kate alone no matter how much it was the right thing to do. Now that I was back in her life, there was no way I was walking away.

I headed upstairs and knocked lightly on her bedroom door.

"So now you knock? I don't think you've ever knocked a day in your life. You usually just enter whenever you want."

I walked in and sat down on the edge of the bed. She was sitting back against the headboard with her knees pulled up to her chest. "Kate, I wanted to tell you so badly, but I couldn't. I needed to make this work for us."

"There is no us. You destroyed us," she said robotically.

"That's not true. I didn't stay away from you for a whole fucking year just so you could push me away."

She glared at me with daggers that I felt deep in my soul. "Do you know that I cried over you for months? I couldn't do anything because I was so torn up over you. But then I went out to your grave and I realized something. You chose to go back into that building. You chose Jensen over me. We could have run together and figured something out, but you didn't choose to stay with me. You say that you did this all for me, but I don't believe you. I think you'll always choose what you want over me."

206

"I didn't want that life for you. I've lived a life on the run for years and you don't deserve that. You have no idea what it's like to be all alone. To not be able to make friends because you know you'll put them in danger. There was no fucking way I was going to do that to you. So, I ended it, and yeah, I almost fucking died for it. But when I saw Pappy trying to pull you away from me, I didn't regret a single fucking thing because I knew you were finally safe. That's all that has ever mattered to me."

"Well, you got your wish. I'm safe and now you've lost me."

"I'm not going anywhere. Sebastian did all this for me so I could have a new life with you. He gave me a job. I won't spit in his face because you're pissed at me."

"Do whatever you want. I don't give a shit anymore. Just leave me alone."

I got up from the bed and stared down at her. "You may be pissed at me and I understand that. I won't ask you to forgive me all in one day, but remember something." I lifted my shirt, showing her the scar from where I was stabbed. "I did almost die in that building. I didn't make any of that up. I didn't leave you willingly, but I'd do it all again if it meant that you lived and I might have a chance at a normal life with you."

I turned and walked out the bedroom door, but I heard her start crying before I even hit the stairs. I paused, my heart breaking as I heard her strangled cries. I hated that I did that to her. I never intended to hurt her so much, but what was done was done, and there was nothing I could do to change it.

"I SEE YOU MADE YOURSELF AT HOME," PAPPY SAID AS HE ENTERED THE house I had stayed in before all this shit went down. I was standing at the window, looking through my binoculars at Kate. She had been up all night and now she was getting ready for work. I wanted to go talk to her, but now wasn't the time. She didn't want to see me right now, and I couldn't blame her for that.

"Didn't have any place else to stay."

"Where have you been all this time?"

"Safe house."

"Really? We've used all the Reed Security safe houses over the past year. I never saw you at any of them. Pretty sure we wouldn't be in this mess right now if I had."

"It wasn't a Reed Security safe house. OPS put me up in one of theirs. I was under strict orders to stay the fuck away from everyone."

"Then how did you know how Kate was doing?"

I smirked at him. "I never was very good at following orders. I always made sure I was back at the safe house before anyone knew I was gone. I couldn't just walk away from her."

I looked back at Kate's house and sighed, wondering how the hell I was going to get through to her. She had to realize eventually that I did this for us. "So, are you still pissed at me?"

"Let's just say I'm still trying to wrap my head around the fact that you were never really dead. So, when do you start working?"

"I'm supposed to meet with Sebastian today to figure out exactly how this is going to work."

"What a mind fuck." Pappy shook his head and walked over to the window to look out with me. "She'll forgive you eventually. You just have to give her time to adjust. It's not going to happen overnight either."

"I knew this would be hard on her, but I saw it going differently in my head. I thought she would see me and run into my arms or something."

"This isn't a movie, Hud. Whether it was on purpose or not, you fucked with people's lives, and that's going to take time to get over."

"I know," I said quietly.

"So, man with the answers, do you want to fill me in on what the hell happened that night? How the hell did Jensen hit back so quick?"

"He played us all along," I scoffed. "I woke up that night remembering this time back in my military days with him. It was so insignificant, but he basically told one of the guys that you lead your enemy into a state of security. Make them think they've won and then you hit back hard. I knew then that we'd been played. I had just woken up Kate when the first grenade hit."

"We all knew something was off, but we never saw that attack coming."

"That's because Marks was in on the whole thing. Becky found out later that Marks was dying. He had Multiple Sclerosis. He was hiding the symptoms well, but it was only a matter of time before the disease took over."

"So, he chose torture?"

"I made his death too quick. It didn't even take long to get the information out of him. I should have known it was too easy, but I was so focused on Kate that I couldn't see anything else."

"We played perfectly into their hands."

I nodded as I stared out the window at Kate getting in her car. "They didn't win, though, and I have to remember that. No matter what, that shit allowed me to get my life back." I ran a hand down my face, trying to wipe the memories of that night from my mind. "I'd better head into the office. Fuck. I never thought I'd be saying anything like that again."

"I'll go with you. I'd sure love to hear what Cap has to say about all this."

We pulled up to the Reed Security building ten minutes later and Pappy went through all the security measures since I didn't yet have clearance. Sebastian had done a good job keeping the building secure. When I had broke in last year, it had been a lot harder than I had anticipated. Now, he had upgraded and the place was like Fort Knox.

Walking into the lobby of Reed Security, I was well aware of the stares that I received by everyone. They all thought I was dead and here I was walking around. Pappy led me to Sebastian's office and knocked before swinging the door open.

"Did you lose something, Cap?" Pappy said as he stepped aside to let me enter. Sebastian raised an eyebrow and waved us in.

"So, you finally decided to make an appearance. How'd it go?" he asked me.

"Not as well as I hoped."

"I imagine it didn't. How's Kate?"

"She pretty much hates me and doesn't want to see me."

"Well, we knew this wasn't going to be the easiest thing to pull off. You good, Pappy?"

"Just fucking peachy. It's not every day that your friend comes back from the dead."

"So, still pissy over the whole thing," Sebastian quipped. "Get the fuck over it. I'm relying on you to get Knight on board with the way we do things around here."

Sebastian opened his desk drawer and pulled out an envelope and tossed it to me. "All your documents are in there."

I opened the envelope and pulled out my new driver's license, social security number, and all the other shit that went with changing your identity. "Hudson Knight?" I said, raising an eyebrow. "Don't you think people will catch on to that?"

"There were only a handful of people that knew the two identities were one and the same. One of them's dead and the rest aren't going to say jack shit. Unless, of course, you're worried about Kate ratting you out."

I shook my head at him. "Why Knight?"

"Because we all know you as Knight and it's too fucking confusing to change."

"I guess that's as good a reason as any. So, what am I going to be doing here?"

"For now? Training. Until the guys trust you, you won't be in the field. Pappy can show you the training center and what programs we currently have. You can tailor it however you want."

"That's it? Just like that?"

"What do you mean?"

"You just want me to tailor a new training program without me running it past you?"

"If you fuck up, I'll know."

"Cap, there's something I don't understand," Pappy said. "You've given him a new identity, but you can't change his fingerprints. What the hell do you do if he gets taken in and fingerprinted?"

"Easy." Sebastian looked at me with a serious expression. "Don't get fucking caught. My buddy, Sean knows who you are. He can only run interference so far. It's better for all of us if you don't go out in the field too often. I don't want anyone to have to lie for you. We're all taking a risk by having you here with us."

"So why are you doing this for me?"

"Kate's been good to us and Pappy is a member of this team. We take care of our own."

"Still, you're putting a lot on the line for me."

"Yeah, we are. And don't think I've forgotten that you've destroyed two of our buildings. I'd say that you owe me big time, and I always collect."

"Glad we're on the same page."

"Pappy, show him around now. I've got shit to do."

Pappy shook his head and headed for the door.

"I appreciate what you've done for me," I said to Sebastian.

He nodded and I followed Pappy to the training center that would be my new place of employment. Somehow, I would find a way to pay Sebastian back for everything. He had really stuck his neck out on the line for me and I never let a debt go unpaid.

I WAITED UNTIL I SAW HER LIGHTS GO OUT AND THEN I WAITED A GOOD half hour before I made my way over to her house. I slipped in easily enough and looked around. An empty bottle of wine sat on the counter and some dishes were in the sink. I made my way up to her room and watched her from the doorway. She was staring out the window as she laid on her side.

"I'm surprised you waited so long," she muttered.

"I gave you one night. I'm not waiting any longer."

I shrugged my leather jacket off and walked over, slipping into bed behind her. I wrapped an arm around her and pulled her against me, even though she grunted in protest.

"I don't want you here."

"I don't give a shit. I didn't survive a knife and fucking fire just to have you push me away."

She rolled over and shoved at me. "You left me for a whole year.

You let me think you were dead! I cried for months over you. I was devastated. And it was all for a liar and murderer."

"I don't do that anymore."

"Lie or kill?"

"I haven't killed anyone since Jensen. When I told you that Sebastian did this for us, it was with the understanding that I left my old life behind, and I've honored that. He risked a lot to help us."

"No, he risked a lot to help you. I wasn't even factored into it."

Anger overtook me and I rolled on top of her, caging her body in with mine. "Are you fucking kidding me? You were the only factor in all of this. He did what he did because I told Pappy that I wanted to try for a normal life with you. He took the opportunity that presented itself because he knew killing me off was the only way for us to get the life we wanted."

"He should have told me."

"And then you wouldn't have acted the way you did and it would have all been for nothing. Think what you want, Kate, but this was all for you and I'd fucking do it all again to know that I could spend the rest of my life with you."

I crushed my lips down on hers and thrust my tongue into her mouth. She pushed against my chest, but I didn't let her have her way. She had her night to process everything, but I'd been waiting a whole year for this moment and I was taking it. She stopped fighting me and dug her fingers into my back as she pulled me closer. I ripped her shirt over her head and took her breast in my mouth, sucking the bud until it was rigid. She moaned as I ground myself hard against her.

She screamed my name over and over as I pressed my erection harder and harder into her core. She needed this as much as I did. I had watched her for a year and there hadn't been anyone. Even if there had, there was nothing that would ever come close to the electricity we felt when we were together.

I couldn't wait anymore. I tugged at her pants until she was bare for me. Her hands fumbled with my belt and pulled at the zipper. She shoved my pants down and spread her legs wide for me, her pussy glistening with desire. I kissed her deeply as I thrust hard inside her.

"Fuck!" I yelled as I bottomed out inside her. Her pussy was

clenching around me so tight that I didn't think I would last more than
a minute inside her. Her fingers dug trails into my back as I pumped
deeper and harder inside her. The bed was jerking against the wall and
the lamp on the nightstand was rattling as the bed hit the table.

"Garrick, don't stop." Her legs wrapped around my waist and she
drew me tight against her body, leaving hardly any room for me to
move. I lowered myself on top of her body and ground my hips into
her with every move. I took her nipple in my mouth and bit down,
sending her over the edge until my cock felt like it would fall off from
lack of circulation.

My cock jerked over and over as I spilled my cum inside her. My
breathing was ragged and blackness was creeping in from the intensity
of my orgasm. I rolled off her and pulled her into my chest, not giving
her the opportunity to pull away from me. Slowly, my body relaxed
into a sleepy state that I hadn't found since I woke up in that hospital
alone. I felt her tugging away from me, so I tightened my grip and
pulled her further onto my chest for the night. After a few minutes, she
stopped fighting me and rested her hand over my heart and we drifted
off into a peaceful sleep.

18

KATE

I DON'T KNOW what the hell I was thinking last night. Sleeping with Garrick so soon after he reappeared in my life was the stupidest thing I could have done. How was I supposed to protect my heart when I gave in so easily to his demands? I laid in bed and watched him sleep. In all the time we had been together, I had never seen him sleep so peacefully before. He was always the first one up and he never seemed to sleep well at night. It made me wonder how much of an effect his job had on him. Had his decisions in life affected him so much that they plagued his dreams?

Looking at him now, I could see that he looked more tired than I had ever seen him. He had circles under his eyes that hadn't been there before and he didn't seem quite as muscular as he was a year ago. I ran my hand over his chest and paused on the scar where he had been stabbed. My eyes pricked with tears as I remembered seeing him stumble to the ground at the safe house. He had been so weak, and after I visited him at his grave, I had finally accepted that Hunter was right. There was no way he could have gotten him out on his own. His injuries would have been so severe that the jostling would have most likely shifted the knife and caused more damage.

Sebastian must have had at least two guys carry Garrick out of that building. That was the only way I could see moving him and him surviving. It would have been very painful and I hoped to God he had passed out before they moved him.

I continued to look over his body, telling myself this wasn't really him. Everything was pretty much the same except for one very obvious difference. His tattoo on his wrist was gone. There was faint scarring where the tattoo had been, but other than that, it was as if it was never there. For some reason, it made me sad that another piece of Garrick was gone. I had come to love those little things about him and now I would never see it again.

Sitting up in bed, I pulled myself together and grabbed a robe from my closet. I couldn't stay in bed with Garrick and pretend that everything would be fine now. It had been painful enough to lose him once and I wasn't sure if I could trust him again with my heart, or maybe I just didn't want to take the chance that he might break it again. I went downstairs and started the coffee, staring off into the backyard as it brewed. I didn't normally sit and enjoy my morning coffee. I always found ways to keep myself busy so that I didn't think about Garrick. Now that he was here, I found myself sitting down at the kitchen table and enjoying my first cup.

I kept glancing at the stairs, waiting for Garrick to walk down and when he didn't, I decided to make breakfast. Except there was nothing in my fridge to make. I threw on some clothes and was surprised when he still didn't wake. I ran to the store and bought groceries. I wasn't sure why I bought so much, especially considering that I didn't want him to stick around, but I found myself loading my cart with things he would like. I hadn't bought this much food in the last year.

When I got home, I unloaded everything and chastised myself for acting like he was actually going to stick around. He hadn't made any promises to me and other than saying he wanted me back, I had no idea what that actually meant for us.

"I'm such an idiot," I mumbled to myself.

"Don't talk about my woman that way." I looked up to see Garrick standing at the bottom of the stairs in his jeans. He didn't have his belt on and his jeans hung low on his frame, showing off the deep v that was cut from his abs. He was leaner than before, but he still had that sexy, dangerous look to him. His eyes trailed over the length of my body, pausing on my breasts and my crotch. I felt tingles shiver through me and I had to keep myself from squeezing my legs together.

I turned around and busied myself with getting stuff together for breakfast. I needed a distraction so I didn't jump him and fall back into bed with him. He came up behind me and wrapped his arms around my waist, pulling me into him and kissing the side of my neck. My eyes slid closed as his tongue left wet trails from my ear down my shoulder.

"You taste so good. You shouldn't have gotten out of bed this morning. I still have plans for you."

My eyes snapped open and I turned around in his arms, pushing against his chest as much as I could. "Last night was a mistake. I think you should leave."

His eyes turned deadly as they narrowed in on me. He stepped back into my space and crowded me against the counter. "Let's get one thing straight. You don't get to tell me to leave anymore. I gave you time to work shit out, but we've been apart too long and it's not going to happen again."

"You mean until you decide that something's more important," I quipped.

"So, that's what this is about." He nodded and stepped back to the counter on the opposite side, leaning against it with his arms crossed over his chest. "You think I'm going to leave again."

"Aren't you? I mean, you're working for Sebastian now. You could go out on a job and not come back."

He nodded, "That's true, but I could also leave you a hundred other ways. I could get in an accident or I could get sick. Are you telling me that you'd rather not take the chance?"

I felt so vulnerable around him. He had a way of making me see things his way even if I didn't want to. What I really wanted was some space to figure out where my head was. "Look, this is all just happening too fast. I haven't even had time to process that you're alive. I don't know how to feel about all of this."

"It's simple, Kate. I'm here and I want you. I don't ever plan on letting you go again. If something happens to me, it's not going to be because I want to leave you. I didn't make that choice last time and I won't in the future." He walked over to me and ran his hand along my face and to the back of my neck. "I love you," he whispered as he leaned in to kiss my lips. "I shouldn't have survived that night, but I did, and there's no way I'd waste another chance with you. I want to marry you and have kids with you. I want to be around to see them grow up and have their own lives. There's no way I'll do anything to jeopardize this second chance. I'm yours for the rest of my life."

I melted into a puddle at his words. I couldn't fight him on this anymore. I wanted him more than ever, and even though I was still upset that I had been in the dark for a year about his death, I couldn't deny that my feelings for him were just as strong as ever. I had been lost for the last year without him, but now that he was back I felt my body come to life again. It was in the way he touched me and let me know that I would only ever be his and he would only be mine. I felt it deep in my soul that I was meant to be with him.

"I love you, Garrick. Just promise me that you won't ever do something like that to me again. I couldn't stand to go through that again."

"I promise. You'll never go through anything like that again."

"Wait. You said that you want to marry me, but I don't even know who you are anymore. Which man am I marrying? Are you Hudson McGuire or Garrick Knight?"

"I'm both, Kate. I'll always be both men no matter what my name is. I'll be Hudson when you need a good man to love you and cherish you, but I'll be Knight when you need someone to protect you. Either way, I'll always be the man that loves you."

"What do I call you?"

"Hudson Knight."

I stared up into the loving eyes of my man and smiled. "It's fitting. It represents both the man you were and the man you've become."

"So, does that mean you've forgiven me?"

"Yeah."

"Good. Then start planning a wedding because there's not a fucking chance that I'm going to let you slip away again."

I HAD COME TO TERMS WITH GARRICK BEING BACK IN MY LIFE AND WHAT he had to do to accomplish that. Things were better than back to normal because he was at home with me every night and we woke up each morning in each other's arms. When I thought about the number of mornings I had woken up over the past year and wished that he was here with me, I was ashamed of my reaction when he came back into my life.

Before we could truly move on, though, there was something I needed to do. Garrick was at work, so I used the opportunity to ask Sebastian to meet up with me for coffee. He agreed, but I could tell that he wasn't looking forward to the meeting. I needed answers, though, and I couldn't move on until I knew everything.

"Kate," Sebastian said, drawing me out of my thoughts. He sat down opposite me and turned his coffee mug over to signal to the waitress that he wanted coffee. She came and filled it, asking us if there was anything else she could get us, but we weren't here for a meal. "So, what did you want to meet me about?"

"I need answers. I want you to tell me how you got Garrick out of that building and I need to know what happened after that."

"First, you need to stop calling him that. His name is Hudson and if you don't call him that, it could cause problems." His eyes were friendly, but held a warning.

"Okay. Hudson."

"We were on our way up to the main floor, but it was difficult getting there. Some of the stairs were blown out and the elevator wasn't an option. We had to go in the back way. We saw Hunter dragging you off and we could see you shouting for Hudson. I sent Chance over to search for him and when we found him, he was in pretty rough shape. There was no way we could get him out of there in the condition he was in without causing a lot of damage. Gabe was able to get a door that wasn't burning yet and we used it as a backboard. Jackson grabbed one of Jensen's men that was about the same height and weight as Hudson. We traded one body for another."

"But you couldn't have known that Garrick would have survived. You took a gamble with all your lives by staying inside the building so long."

He nodded. "Kate, Hudson may not have been a part of the Reed Security family then, but he was like a brother to Hunter and he was in love with you. You've been a part of our family since you first started helping us. There was no way we would pass up an opportunity to make things right for you and Hudson. I'm sorry we had to do it the way we did and that we let you believe he was dead, but we did what we had to so he could have a life with you."

"I get that now. It was a little hard to accept at first, but I've come to terms with it. So, what happened after you got him out?"

"He was out of it for days. Honestly, we didn't think he was going to survive. The surgeon said that if he woke up, he had a fighting chance. When he didn't wake up right away after surgery, we really thought that was it. But he pulled through and then we set him up at a safe house with OPS to recover. It was a slow recovery for him and he wasn't too happy that we made those decisions for him, but when we explained what we were trying to do for him, he came around to our way of thinking."

"So, he stayed away for the whole year?"

"No. We had to send him out on a job and we sent Chance's team with him. We made it look like another team took him out and we made sure that everyone necessary knew that Garrick Knight was dead."

I nodded, satisfied with his answers, but there was one thing I still needed to know, but I didn't know if it would get Hudson in trouble.

"Kate, whatever it is, just ask."

"Was Hudson always at the safe house otherwise?"

Sebastian's eyes glittered in amusement. "Not for more than a day at a time. He thought he was sneaking out on us, but we always had someone watching him. He would leave the safe house and come back to check on you. No matter how much we told him not to, he just couldn't stay away from you. As long as he never let you know he was alive, I let him get away with it. I know I wouldn't have been able to stay away from Maggie if I were in his position."

"So, you weren't upset with him?"

"Nah. You can't deny a man the love of a good woman. If he

couldn't have you, he could at least be close to you and know you were okay."

"There's just one more thing and then I promise I won't bother you again."

"Anything."

I looked at him as fiercely as I could, hoping that I could get my point across. "I'm going to be marrying Hudson." A smile spread across his face, but I wasn't done. "I don't ever want to be kept in the dark again about him. If he's out on a job for you and something goes wrong, you'd better keep me informed. I won't ever go through what I went through this past year again. Do you understand me?"

"Clearly. I promise that will never happen again." I smiled, feeling a weight being lifted from my shoulders. It finally felt like all the pieces were falling into place. "Now, I have a question for you. Are you going to come back and work for us?"

"I think I can do that. I'm taking on a partner at the clinic and that should free up some of my time."

"Good. It'll be about the same as before, but we could always use an in-house doctor. Hunter is really only there as a team medic. He does our physicals now, but I have a feeling he doesn't want that to be a part of his job forever."

"How about I go over things with Hunter and then I work up a schedule that works for me? I'll send it over to you and you can give me notes on changes."

"That's perfect. It'll be good to have you back, Kate."

I knew he was referring to more than just being back to work at Reed Security and I felt the same way. It was like my life was finally back on track and I had rejoined the world. I had Hudson, I had my clinic, and we were finally going to start living our life.

19

KNIGHT

"THE NEW RECRUITS are here to run the course, Knight. Let me know how they do."

Sebastian stood in the training center with his arms crossed over his chest. The new recruits were standing behind him looking completely smug and I was ready to kick their asses and wipe those looks off their faces. I had made the training more advanced than it had been in the past and I pushed the requirements for joining Reed Security past what they had been before. I wanted to ensure that every team member had the skills to perform at the level I expected. All the guys that currently worked here had passed with flying colors, but then I had asked for input from all of them in areas that they felt needed improvement. They all took to the training with a professional attitude that gave me a new level of respect for all of them.

Over the past few months, I had found my rhythm at work and eventually earned their trust. I wanted to make this work more than ever, not just because of Kate, but because I wanted the camaraderie I had once shared with Pappy and all my brothers when we were serving. I hadn't killed anyone in over a year and I no longer felt the itch to take someone's life. Until today, that is.

I was in the middle of working with the new recruits and they were running the weapons training course. Most of them weren't doing half bad, but one of the guys, the cockiest of them all, was all over the place. I blew the whistle, needing to get this asshole under control before he hurt someone. I walked onto the course and everyone had holstered their weapons except this jackass. He spun around and discharged his weapon before I could try to take cover. The bullet pierced my side, causing me to jolt back from the impact.

I looked down to see blood seeping through my side, almost exactly where I had been shot when I was on my first mission with Reed Security. I breathed deeply through my nose, trying to get control of my anger, but I was failing miserably.

Pappy, who was on the training course in case of an injury, came running over to me with his medical kit. "What the fuck was that, Benson?" he shouted at the recruit.

"I didn't mean...I just...he shouldn't have been on the course," Benson stuttered.

"I blew the fucking whistle," I yelled. I didn't realize I had my weapon in my hand and raised until Pappy stepped in front of me and pushed on my arm to lower my weapon.

"Let's not kill the new recruits just yet," he said as he took my gun from me.

"He fucking shot me."

"Yeah, I can see that. How about we get you cleaned up?"

"Get that fucker off the course now before I grab another weapon and take him out," I growled.

"Benson, go see Sebastian. You're discharged," Pappy barked.

"But I didn't finish the training," Benson argued.

"If you don't get off this fucking course right now, I'll make sure you never finish anything again for as long as you live, you stupid fuck," I yelled at him. He took a step back at the vehemence in my voice. I hadn't gotten this pissed since I had gone straight. One stupid fucker was bringing back all that rage that had me wanting to go kill someone. Benson stumbled from the course and then ran for the door that would lead him to the elevator that would take him to the main level of Reed Security.

"Hud, calm the fuck down. Your rage is making you bleed out," Pappy said, shaking his head.

He pulled me over to a chair and lifted my shirt, checking the wound from the front and sighing when he found an exit wound. "Well, I think you'll be fine. 'You're going to be laid up for a while, but I don't think it hit anything major. I'll take you down to the med room and we'll check to be sure."

He stood up and turned to the recruits. "Due to the idiocy of your fellow recruit, training is done for the day. We'll pick up tomorrow, with a different instructor. If any of you want a chance at being on the team, I suggest you don't do anything as fucking stupid as Benson did. Dismissed."

The recruits hurried from the room and Pappy dragged me down to the med room.

"You know I have to do it, man."

"Don't you fucking dare," I growled at him.

"Sorry, Hud. If I don't do this, I'm going to have one pissed-off woman on my ass, and I already had to deal with her for a year where she pretty much hated me."

"I swear to God, if you do this, we're no longer friends."

"I'll take my chances," he grinned.

Fuck. I was so screwed.

"HUDSON KNIGHT! DO YOU WANT TO TELL ME WHAT THE HELL YOU WERE thinking getting shot?" Kate yelled as she stormed into the med room.

"Honey—"

"Don't you honey me. You haven't even worked here a year and I already get a call that I need to get down here because you've been shot!"

"I didn't—"

"No! I don't want to hear any excuses. You're not even in the field. Who shot you? Tell me right now."

"Calm down, Kate," Sebastian's voice came from the doorway and I sighed in relief that I would now have some backup. Pappy was fucking useless, standing over in the corner laughing his ass off. "He's not hurt that bad. Pappy has instructions to call you if Hudson is ever injured because that's what you and I agreed to."

"So, he's fine?" she asked calmly, but I could hear the hitch in her voice. I looked closer and saw that she had tears in her eyes. She was fucking crying. Shit. I could kill Pappy and Sebastian for doing this to her.

"I'm fine, Kate. A recruit got a little trigger-happy, but he's already been dismissed."

"The bullet was a through and through. It was about the same place he was shot the first time you met him," Pappy finally spoke up. "He'll be fine. I already checked him out and there's no internal bleeding. I just called you so that you didn't kill me, and I thought you could take him home and make him take it easy."

"You're off for the next week," Sebastian said.

"Whoa, I don't need a whole week off." That sounded like fucking torture. What the hell was I going to do that whole time?

"You'll take off whatever time he tells you and you won't argue," Kate said as I saw tears slip down her face. I motioned for the guys to leave us and pulled Kate into my arms.

"I'm sorry they scared you, but I promise you I'll be fine. Pappy got it cleaned up right away and I'm doing pretty good now."

"Does it hurt?"

That was a fucking ridiculous question because I had been shot. Of course, it hurt, but I wasn't about to tell my already crying fiancé that. "Pappy gave me something for it. I'm fine."

"Okay," she nodded. "Let's get you home. I can take care of you there and make sure you don't overdo it. I'll call Dr. Carson and have him take over my patients for the next few days."

"You're too good to me, Kate. What would I ever do without you?"

That was the shit you said to your near hysterical fiancé to keep her from flipping the fuck out. I didn't want Kate to stay home and give up days at her clinic for me, but I wouldn't say jack shit after seeing her on the verge of tears.

"You'll never have to find out."

"SAY *FUCK IT* AND STAY HERE WITH ME," I WHINED AS KATE GOT READY FOR work on Wednesday.

"I can't. Dr. Carson can't take over in the clinic for me. If I call in, I have to reschedule all those appointments."

"Who gives a fuck? People get sick all the time."

"I give a fuck. Some of these people need to have medication checks and if I cancel on them, I might not be able to get them back in for weeks."

"Fine. Go take care of the poor, sick people while I lie here on my deathbed."

"Why is it that all men turn into babies when they're sick or injured?"

"I'm not being a baby. I just don't want to be alone," I pouted. "I'm bored out of my skull. There's nothing to do but watch TV. I don't have a single person to kill." She raised an eyebrow at me, but I just shrugged. "I'm just joking." She narrowed her eyes at me. "Sort of."

"You know, I think I liked it more when you were this dark and dangerous man who stalked me."

"I'm still that man. I'm just not used to sitting around on my ass. Believe it or not, before you came along, I was a badass who didn't get shot quite so often."

"So, you're blaming me?"

"No, I'm just pointing out that loving a woman is dangerous. Practically downright lethal."

"Well, it's a good thing that I'm marrying Hudson Knight then. He's pretty much indestructible."

"Kate, I know I've said this before," I said in all seriousness, "but I would do anything to make it back to you. I never really gave a damn about my life over the past few years, but then I met you and everything changed. You made me change the way I look at everything and there's nothing I won't do to be the man you deserve."

"You're already there. I don't need a white knight, Hudson. All I need is you, my dark Knight."

ALSO BY GIULIA LAGOMARSINO

Thank you for reading Knight and Kate's story, but don't worry! It's not over yet! Continue their journey in the next book, Irish!

Join my newsletter to get the most up-to-date information, along with new content in the Reed Security series.

https://giulialagomarsinoauthor.com/connect/

Join my Facebook reader group to find out more about my obsession with Dwayne Johnson!

https://www.facebook.com/groups/GiuliaLagomarsinobooks

Reading Order:

https://giulialagomarsinoauthor.com/reading-order/

To find the individual series, follow the links below:

For The Love Of A Good Woman series

Reed Security series

The Cortell Brothers

A Good Run Of Bad Luck

The Shifting Sands Beneath Us- Standalone

Owens Protective Services

Made in United States
Orlando, FL
05 September 2024

51170358R00140